# NEVER THE MOON

# CONTENTS

*For John, who shows me every day, what real love is.*

# PROLOGUE

*2017*

The years had not touched him, not to her. He didn't seem to see her though and had walked right past her. She put her head down, trying to quell its spin, and placed her hand on the knee of the boy next to her as a sign to get moving.

He looked at her questioningly. 'Nan? Would you like to leave?'

She nodded and they both rose slowly and he led her to the elevator. Standing at its door, waiting for it to arrive, she couldn't help but glance back. He was mouthing something to the concierge, but his gaze was locked on her and catching his eye, she felt her stomach flip. A sensation so overwhelming hit her and she dropped her gaze for a moment, but when she looked back, he was already looking the other way. No, he hadn't seen her, perhaps hadn't recognized her. She felt the melancholy she always did when she thought of him, but the sight of him there, right in front of her, a little more than a few steps away, shook her. So close, she could be in his arms in a matter of seconds. She stepped into the elevator and leaned on the rail, holding her hand to her aching heart.

'Are you okay, Nan?' Lucas raised his big brown eyes at her, and she just nodded. She couldn't speak, anything that left her mouth would betray her; she could already feel the tears beginning to well behind her eyelids.

She closed the door to her suite softly and leaned against it, her heart beginning to slow. Lucas had gone back to his own room and she felt very alone, but at least safe, as safe as she could feel with Jack. She heard him in the shower and a shiver ran down her spine. Had she gotten his suit ready before she left? She couldn't remember and didn't want to care right now. She wanted to remember him, her David, her strong, beautiful David, except he wasn't her David, not anymore, not for a very long time.

She wandered to the window and looked out to the purple sky, serene and mocking. The last specks of sunlight were still flickering between the buildings and she watched as the sun dipped behind a cloud.

There was no moon.

She felt the tears start to well again and she clenched her teeth. She couldn't, not now. She had to get ready.

But David. What would she say if she came face to face with him? He was in the same hotel. But it was a big hotel, she reasoned; they may never cross paths and they would be gone by tomorrow morning. She knew she wanted to see him again, just to savor his face, to feel his gaze on her once more, but she also knew that it would incur the wrath of Jack.

She would pay. She would pay dearly. She was paying right now …

# CHAPTER 1

*1983*

*Jennifer*

'Jennifer, are you ready?' Judy called through the bathroom door.

'Mother! I'm nearly done!'

'David is waiting, hurry up!' Her mother gave a frustrated smack on the door before going downstairs to make small talk with David while he waited. David, whoever that was.

Jennifer was sitting on the edge of the bathtub, finishing her make-up. She rolled her eyes at her mother's knock. She had no intention of hurrying up. She was irritated. She tilted her head to the side and ran a finger down her nose. *Straight, too straight,* she thought, and then surveyed her eyes. Deep set, jade green, and curved at the edges, 'just like a cat,' her mother always told her. Teasing her fringe, she wondered what people saw in her looks; she didn't think much of them herself and tonight, she hadn't made much of an effort. What was the point? Shrugging, she replaced the comb in the drawer and stared at herself in the mirror.

Jennifer sighed and then took a deep breath. 'Not for much longer.'

She was tired of being set up with eligible bachelors and just wanted to choose someone for herself, and in her own time. She was in love with Michael, but no one knew about them, so she had to go through with these charades to keep her mother happy. Michael was in love with her too and they planned to elope when she was eighteen, and that was only a few months away. For Jennifer, it couldn't get here soon enough.

Her mother wanted to get her out of this town; at least that was something they agreed on. Judy had moved with her daughters, Jennifer and her elder sister, Elle, to Tandaro when Jennifer was twelve, after their father had died, leaving his family penniless and in debt. She remembered her father well and missed him immensely. Tall, strong, so strong he would lift both sisters on either side of him and swing them around, while they laughed and squealed in dizziness. Judy would lovingly scold him and he would drop them to the floor gently and pick her up, carrying her over his shoulders.

She'd shriek and the girls would urge him on. He was always so much fun to be around and Jennifer felt at the time that Judy was a little jealous of their fun. She later came to learn that their relationship was a tumultuous one, and although they loved each other without doubt, they had their share of arguments. They were careful to keep it from the girls, although Elle, being older and more perceptive than Jennifer, had suspected as much.

Before the death of their father, they had lived a comfortable lifestyle on the outskirts of New York City. Being taught at the best schools and wanting for nothing, the move to Tandaro came as a shock. Apart from the absence of a father who was, among other things, a spendthrift and a gambler, as Elle and Jennifer learned later, their new environment was a blow.

Tandaro, with roads that seemed stretched like rubber bands, hills that went on forever, and waterfalls that poured out endless streams of froth, was certainly a lovely place to live, but with such a small area and population, it was so different from the hustle-and-bustle lifestyle that the family was used to.

Judy, never having worked, was faced with taking on menial jobs, such as sewing and ironing for other families, and at times, she had to travel a long way, often coming home and soaking her feet in a hot bath, prepared by one of her girls, who were pained to see their mother in such agony. The money she received for the work she did was not enough to support two growing children, so she took jobs in Syracuse, and neighboring towns, with travel times of two hours or more, cleaning for more affluent city dwellers. This was still not enough to keep the family in the style to which they had become accustomed, but both girls did whatever they could to help their mother. When they were old enough, they got part-time jobs to contribute to the family home, against the will of Judy, who urged them to study hard so they could be whoever they wanted to be, not someone who had no skills to boast of, like herself.

Most of their possessions were sold before the move and they had enough money to rent a little two-story cottage off Main Street. It was supposed to be a temporary move, until they got back on their feet, but they never seemed to get there. Her mother, still a young woman with beauty and vigor, couldn't bring herself to think about another man and focused her life on making a better one for her own children. She vowed she would get them out, somehow.

And Jennifer vowed to leave.

Except she would be leaving with Michael. She smiled when she thought of Michael. He was everything her mother despised, and she even thought this was perhaps the attraction. For her to be with someone like her own father, a wonderful, caring man, but who had let down his family in such a bad way, was detestable and she wanted to be with someone whom Judy wouldn't have chosen. Michael was exactly that.

Large, not just tall, but rippling with muscles, he scared people and Jennifer loved that about him; it made her feel safe, and it made him exciting. Michael had only completed eighth grade a few years before and was working as an apprentice at a garage. He would sometimes take a hot rod that had come in for a service and they would drive around doing burnouts and speeding past police stations. It was inevitable in this town that his boss would always find out and would reprimand him with meaningless words, but he was one of the best workers—one of two—and he knew he would not be fired. Michael was wild and she was his girl.

She quickly assessed the plan for after her 'official' date. Yes, Michael was aware of the pretences she had to go through and although he allowed it, he had his own revenge. It was usually by turning up at the allocated date spot and breaking Jennifer out of her jail of a date by punching the chosen suitor. Sometimes he would just waltz in and whisk Jennifer away and she would happily dance off with him, not giving the astonished young man a second glance. She got a little thrill from it, but she also felt a little bad for them when she thought about it later. It really wasn't their fault that Judy and their mothers made plans for them without their knowledge. Sometimes Michael even slashed a tire or two and Jennifer would protest. He would laugh and say that the guy deserved it 'for trying to push in on my woman'. She liked that; loved it when he called her 'his woman'. It made her feel like she belonged to someone.

Jennifer had friends, but had only clicked with one girl, who lived a block away from her. Angel was a kind and giving friend and she, unlike other girls her age, didn't have a jealous bone in her body. Whenever Jennifer made friends in school, she would find that they didn't stick around for long and at first, she wondered why; she was friendly enough, didn't think she was that boring, interested in the things that others talked about. When she began to get attention, and a lot of it, from male classmates, she understood. She resented these girls for their jealousy and tried hard to win their approval at first, but Angel was different. Attractive herself, olive-skinned with jet-black hair, she never begrudged Jennifer for how she looked. She was always there for Jennifer and they talked about things that were different from other girls, not just boys and make-up, but movies, especially old ones, history, and their own dreams of escaping this town. New York—that was their goal.

'The two of us together,' Angel would exclaim,

her eyes shining.

'And Michael,' corrected Jennifer.

'Yes.' The glow would dim in Angel's eyes. 'That's what I meant.'

Jennifer knew Angel didn't approve of Michael, even though her friend would never admit it to her, but she knew herself that Michael was a bad influence on her. She didn't need Angel to confirm it.

Jennifer had officially met Michael at the local diner even though they had been at school together, but as Michael left when he was quite young, they had never had reason to interact and Jennifer had never taken a second look at him at parties and town events. When he asked her out on a date, which he later told her he'd been psyching himself up to do for a while, she was taken with his physique and confidence, and had accepted immediately. They had been together for two months and she still hadn't introduced him to her mother and didn't have any intention of doing so yet. But she knew he was her ticket out of this place.

She would make it up to Judy and Elle when she got to New York. They would stay here, but not forever. When she got out, she would take them out of here too and they would forgive her for leaving. Elle had been working full time as a receptionist at a real estate agency in a nearby town and had given up her dream of being a journalist because she had to help support the home. Jennifer would help her achieve her dream—she didn't exactly know how, but she somehow knew she would. Her mother wouldn't be scrubbing floors for rich ladies and Jennifer would leave the florist, where she worked, while she figured out her future. Yes, she had a plan. Michael was her way out of Tandaro … and she did love him.

****

Now, floating down the stairs, Jennifer again felt that irritation and wished that her plan with Michael would materialize soon.

*I can't do this much longer*, she thought. The nights out with boys she wouldn't have looked at twice, the small talk, knowing it wouldn't be going any further, the wet palms reaching over the table to touch hers, the attempted kisses, which she shied away from, playing coy, all the while wishing Michael would hurry up and save her. It was wearing thin. She sighed again.

Then she saw him.

All thoughts of Michael vanished as she surveyed this stranger, who seemed to be in polite conversation with her mother. Dressed in a black shirt, carelessly open at the neck, and blue jeans that hugged his rear end, he was holding a bunch of yellow flowers that her mother was trying to relieve him of. He was lean and slightly unshaven—no, her mother wouldn't approve; she wondered why she was disappointed about that.

'Oh look, here she comes,' said Judy, looking up at Jennifer and wrenching the flowers from him.

David turned around to face her and she let a small sigh escape. He walked to her and introduced himself.

'Hi, Jennifer, it's good to meet you.' Husky, inviting.

# CHAPTER 2

*2017*

Walking through the big glass door, framed in gold, Jennifer felt like a fraud. She always did at these big galas. But this was her life. She had chosen this, to be here, to live this life. The silver silk skirt that draped past her feet swished around her ankles and her sleeveless matching blouse that rose to her throat gave her a regal air. She still turned heads, but she didn't care anymore; she never really did, even though she knew she would never have been here if it wasn't for the way she looked. She smiled wryly at that and wondered how much of her life she really regretted, fully knowing that she had had almost everything a woman could possibly want, almost

…

She felt Jack's hand on her back, pushing her forward, and just for a moment, she wanted to resist, just to see what he would do in front of all these people, but not feeling in an especially good mood, she knew the evening would just keep going downhill.

David was still in her head.

She surveyed the scene before her; things did not change much at all. Being fashionably late, the large room was already full. She regarded the grand ballroom and thought that she should be feeling like a princess. Chandeliers twinkled high above her and seemed to tinkle to the music that could be faintly heard in the background. Giant plant ensembles led the path to a dance floor, which curved out into mini trails that guided people to their tables. Straight-backed waiters wearing black and white walked by quickly, serving drinks and appetizers, and one approached them, giving a short bow before gesturing for them to follow. Jennifer smiled and nodded and felt the nudge at her back again. She sighed and moved forward. She wasn't looking forward to this; the incessant small talk with people who cared nothing for her, or she for them, for that matter.

At one of the main tables, they took their seats, Jack acting the perfect gentleman and holding out her chair for her. She smiled at him and sat down. Jack seated himself and then, turning his back to her, immediately began a conversation with an elderly, distinguished man sitting on the other side of him, who gave a small nod of acknowledgement to Jennifer. She nodded back to him; an associate of Jack's, she had met him on a number of occasions. She looked around the room. There were quite a few familiar faces and she smiled and nodded obligingly to them when a bustling figure caught her eye.

She could see Celia hurrying in her direction and managed to keep the smile on her face.

'Sweeeeeetheart!' Celia's high-pitched voice screeched at her. 'I just *have* to tell you about James, you know James, the older fellow with a nasty foot,' she began, taking the empty seat next to Jennifer and leaning into her.

*Yes, I remember James,* thought Jennifer, *he is in fact three months older than I am and twelve months older than you! Nasty foot!—Yes, I'd like to shove that somewhere!* 'Hello, Celia, er, I think that seat is reserved for someone else.'

'Oh, don't worry, darling, they can wait.' Celia waved her hand as though swatting an irritating fly. Celia was a woman of entitlement; born and bred rich and spoiled, she spent her spare time, of which there was a lot, hosting parties and spreading gossip.

'How are you, Celia? James, what about James?' They air-kissed both cheeks.

Celia droned on and Jennifer nodded politely and oohed and aahed at the right times. Celia was in the middle of a monologue about her husband Ralph's latest flavor of the month, when she felt her spine stiffen. She instinctively looked around the room and her heart caught.

David was seated three tables away and he was watching her. Her eyes widened in excitement and fear and her heart thumped hard beneath her silk top. She closed her eyes slowly and opened them again. He was still there, still gazing at her.

*Her* David! Looking as he always had, the same beautiful face she remembered so well that was imprinted in her memory.

'Sweetie, you okay?' Brought out of her reverie, she felt Celia's hands on her shoulders, shaking her slightly, and her face was leaning in close to her own— she looked concerned. Jennifer realized she must have turned as white as a ghost. 'Jack, darling.' Celia began to reach out to Jack, who was still occupied with his neighbor.

'No, no, I'm fine.' Jennifer was quickly brought back to reality. 'I think I'm just very tired.'

'Sweetie, you should see someone about that.'

'I'm fine, I just haven't had much sleep lately.' *Go away!* Jennifer shouted in her head. She couldn't think straight and Celia just would not stop babbling at her.

'Sweets, I can give you something for that.' Celia leaned over conspiratorially.

Jennifer tried to smile patiently and wondered how to get Celia to change the subject or even how she could get rid of her, but she didn't have to bother.

'Sweetie, I see James and Fiona, I must say hello and inquire about his foot.' Jennifer wanted to protest—that was not polite conversation—but she also wanted to free herself from the woman and gather her thoughts.

'Yes, you must, I will catch up in a little while.'

As Celia flitted away, calling out to James, Jennifer sighed and slowly raised her eyes again. David nodded to her and raised his glass and she smiled shakily in return. He then turned around to talk to his companion.

Jennifer looked at her. Dressed in emerald green, her hair rolled into a French bun, she inclined into David, placing her hand on his knee. Jennifer winced and felt a shooting in her belly and her body tensed. She remembered the feeling, he could always do that to her. Her mind started to go back, back in time, so long ago …

Jack was poking at her and whispering furiously. 'Jennifer, answer me! Where is my drink?'

'I haven't ordered drinks yet.'

'Seriously? What is wrong with you tonight?' He poked at her ribs harder.

'Really, Jack? The waiter was just here, why

didn't you ask for it yourself?' She regretted it the moment it was spoken; she forgot herself. 'Wait, there's one there,' she quickly said. He may not do anything in public, but for Jack, it could wait, and waiting was worse. She motioned for the waiter and turned back to Jack to confirm his drink of choice and felt her blood drain. He was staring at David, his brows knotted in confusion, which turned into a malicious snarl.

'Jack, what do you want?' she tried to say as calmly as possible, but she knew it was too late.

'What … the … fuck?' he said slowly through clenched teeth. 'I will fucking kill him.' He wasn't talking to her; he was already in a trance.

Panic began to rise in Jennifer. *No, I must handle this.*

'Jack,' she whispered, leaning over. 'What's the matter?' Jennifer's voice was one of innocence, but her throat was tight and she already knew there was going to be trouble.

'Are you serious?' Jack was still talking to himself and she felt her heart begin to race, but there wasn't anything she could do now.

'Jack, be quiet,' she whispered. 'People are starting to look at you.' Appealing to his vanity, she desperately needed to distract him. Jack craved acceptance and admiration and the ploy worked, but when he turned his attention to her, she drew back instinctively. His face was contorted and she felt his hate pierce through her. He wouldn't. Not here. She was not so sure now …

The gentleman on the other side of Jack tapped at him, watching Jennifer at the same time, which brought him back to his senses. He stiffened and changed his expression, before turning away to face his companion. She let out a sigh; she had been holding her breath, but at that moment, she felt his hand on her thigh. He was pinching hard, again and again, digging his fingernails into her skin, through her thin skirt. She felt tears start to well and gave her leg a quick tug but his hold was so tight, she couldn't free herself from his grip. She stood up quickly and excused herself from the table. Jack turned around and looked up at her, his eyebrows curled in suspicion.

Collecting her purse, Jennifer walked toward the ladies' room with her head held high. She felt the looks around her, she always did. They loved her and yet hated her. Some women admired her, some were envious, and men just ogled, but right now, she wasn't thinking about them. She wasn't thinking, she just wanted to get to the ladies' room as quickly as possible; she could feel a tear that had already escaped and was threatening to roll down her cheek. Her thigh was smarting and there would be a bruise tomorrow, but she was not worried about that now.

The ladies' room was empty and she quickly got herself into a cubicle and sat down. She put her head in her hands and wept.

*I hate him. I hate him!*

Then she thought of David. She loved David. After all this time, she knew her heart was still with him.

She heard the door of the ladies' room open and then, voices. She shoved the scrunched-up toilet paper against her mouth and began counting in her head. *10, 9, 8 …*

She could hear women talking, but she wasn't listening, at least not until she heard his name.

'I think David wants it to happen soon, tick tock, you know,' said a voice that sounded like green-dressed lady's would.

Was this *her* David they were talking about?

'Well, what's the problem?' another voice questioned, older, less refined.

Jennifer leaned forward to hear more and her purse clattered to the floor, alerting the women to her presence. She held her breath.

'Shhhh, someone's in here.' That was the older woman.

Jennifer picked up her purse and opened her

compact. She surveyed the damage to her make-up. *Not too bad,* she thought. She was a clean crier and her make-up was always the best. She was dusting her face when she heard the door again. They were leaving. She walked out of the cubicle and stared at her reflection in the mirror.

'Who are you?' she asked.

# CHAPTER 3

*1983*

'I'm Jennifer,' she said and stuck out her hand.

David looked unsure of what to do with the offering and took it with an amused smile, turned it over, raised it to his lips, and kissed it ever so softly. Jennifer felt a slight shiver run up her arms.

'Come on, you lovebirds, shouldn't you be on your way?' her mother cut in.

Jennifer narrowed her eyes at Judy and picked up her cardigan from the armchair.

'It was good to meet you, Mrs. Mason, maybe next time, I can meet your other daughter too.'

'Oh, please, Judy, it is! Yes, Elle is out tonight; poor Elle, working late again, that girl works so hard, poor thing.' She waved her hands about her face. 'Oh, enough with me, come on, get going.' She shooed them out the door and Jennifer felt David's hand on the small of her back, gently pressing her forward. She felt her stomach flutter and she quickly walked to his car, releasing herself from his touch.

She suddenly remembered Michael; he could be anywhere, watching, even now. She looked around furtively but couldn't see any sign of him. *Shit, Michael.*

David led her to the passenger side of an older model Ford Fairlane. He opened the door for her and she got in as daintily as she could, putting both her feet in together as her mother had always taught her to.

He jumped into the driver's seat and started the engine and Jennifer found herself tongue-tied. Her palms were already beginning to feel moist and she tucked her hands under her thighs. She was suddenly very self-conscious, which was unusual for her. Boys she had dated before never made her feel so nervous and she began to wonder if she had made enough of an effort with her choice of clothing, not to mention her make-up. She looked down at her legs, long and tapered, and wished she had worn a shorter skirt that emphasized their shape, instead of the bulky tartan one. The dowdy cardigan, a pale green, highlighted her eyes, *so at least that's something*, she thought.

Both didn't speak and Jennifer was trying to find something to say that would come out easy and refined, but her mind was blank and she knew if she tried, it would come out all wrong. So, she remained silent, and so did David. She wondered what he was thinking about and she tried to peer at him out of the corner of her eye. She couldn't see anything that mattered, but she felt his presence—a musky scent she couldn't identify filled her nostrils and she breathed in deeply. Then as he shoved a tape into the player, he brushed her arm and she felt her stomach flutter again.

*What is wrong with me!* Jennifer thought, frustrated with her reaction to him.

The night was cool, but the moon was high and Jennifer stretched forward to see it, more for something to do than out of curiosity or any attachment to it, but it seemed to glint at her mockingly and she sat back in her seat staring out of the window at the passing trees, swaying with the light breeze. It seemed that this night was made for romance and Jennifer scowled; this was not how it usually went. With the music of the Eagles filtering out of the tinny speakers, David drove for two blocks and pulled up to the curb. He turned off the ignition.

Jennifer looked at him questioningly. He leaned toward her and she jerked backwards, assuming he was going to kiss her. He smiled, a small smile that was trying not to laugh. Her hackles rose and she felt a shudder of annoyance.

Pouting, she folded her arms and looked out of the window away from him, her cheeks flushing. *Well, why the hell would he not want to kiss her?* She turned back to him, her eyes piercing through him in question.

David leaned back in his seat, the smile still on his lips. 'Look, we can split up now. I have stuff to do anyway and you clearly don't want to do this.'

Jennifer's mouth fell at the same time as her heart.

'Where can I drop you off?' he continued and looked lazily over the steering wheel. He was brushing her off, rejecting her!

'Look, David …' she started angrily.

He let out a quick laugh. 'Chill out, Jen …'

'Don't call me Jen!' Her ears were becoming hot.

'No, no … sorry, I mean …' He looked at her again; this time his brows knitted, his mouth twisted in confusion, and he leaned forward. 'It's just that, I know you don't want to do this. Your mother and my aunt want this to happen for some reason. I just figured we would get this evening done and then tell them it wasn't meant to be.'

Jennifer folded her arms tightly again and turned to face the windscreen. 'Well, David, you said you would take me out. Take me out!'

'Um, oh, okay, so, where do you want to go?'

David looked flustered and turned on the ignition.

It was her turn to smile. She looked at him and her tone softened. 'Wherever you want, I'm happy to go, but I have to warn you, I am starving.'

'Thank God, a woman who eats.' He seemed relieved that the tension was broken.

# Chapter 4

*2017*

She picked at her food, trying to avoid the direction of David. She was unable to raise her eyes to him, as badly as she wanted to. Jack had his eyes glued on her from the moment she stepped out of the ladies' room. He had been waiting outside the door for her to emerge and had grasped her elbow and whispered in her ear, 'You! You knew he was here, you lying bitch.' She hadn't seen him with this much hate in his eyes for a while now, and she was scared.

She jerked her arm from him and walked past without answering. There was no point arguing the point; it was too late. So, she sat at the table and made small talk with the young, impeccably dressed girl beside her, another familiar face, name unknown.

Jennifer noticed Jack downing his drinks very quickly and her fear began to escalate. She put her hand on his arm and with the glare he gave her she jerked it away and put it on her lap together with the other trembling one. She knew he was capable of killing her, he had come close before. There were still scars on her right breast, large splashes of yellowy white, which meant she was unable to wear anything too revealing, which suited her just fine. It suited Jack just as much. It didn't matter to her anyway as she preferred not to show too much of herself but looking at them every day made her feel like less of a woman, like a pathetic, weak animal. She would fight back, she always did, even knowing that it would make the punishment worse, but she still had to keep some self-respect for her own humanity. She hoped no one suspected and would have been mortified if anyone had an inkling.

Jack, the ladies' man, tall and strong and charming, more handsome than Paul Newman; Jack, the most eligible bachelor at one time, the owner of one of the biggest ranches in the industry. Jack, the wife-beater—no one would believe it.

One spring afternoon, some years ago, Jack had lost his temper in a fit of jealousy after a meeting when a young man had commented on his beautiful wife and had sent his regards to Jennifer. Barging through the front door, he had lunged at her without realizing that her friend Angel was over. She was in the kitchen, making them both coffee, ready for a catch-up with her best friend. Angel had heard the snarl and barrage of profanity and came running into the living room to find Jennifer crouched beneath Jack on the sofa, while he shook her shoulders violently. He knew if he held her shoulders, she would be pinned down and would find it hard to fight back, but she was trying.

That was the scariest part. His attacks were calculated and he didn't completely lose control, not always. He knew what he was doing. Yes, once it was over, he would claim to have lost control and would apologize profusely, but she knew better, and yet, she accepted his apologies and gifts and forgave him. She had to; there was no choice.

Angel had dropped the cup she was holding, screamed, and lunged at Jack. He looked up in surprise and was hurled over by the force of Angel. She jumped on top of him and punched his face repeatedly, while he just lay there, stunned, and Jennifer had to use all her strength to pry her friend off him. Jennifer dragged Angel into the bedroom with her and locked the door, leaning against it. Angel was heaving, her face white.

'What the fuck, what the fuck … Jenny, what the fuck was that?!'

Jennifer slumped to the floor and put her face in her hands. 'I'm sorry, I'm sorry, I'm so sorry.'

'What the hell are you sorry for?!' Angel paced and counted. '10, 9, 8, 7… Oh my God, Jen, what the hell!' She crouched down and pulled Jennifer into her arms. They stayed that way without speaking, rocking back and forth until the light began to fade.

'What now?' Angel leaned back on her haunches. 'I can't leave you with him. Come with me, Jenny. Stay with me, just till you figure out what to do; you know you're always welcome at my house.'

Jennifer regarded Angel's innocent, earnest face and then looked away. 'I can't.'

'This isn't the first time, is it, Jenny? I can tell. I'll stay here then, at least until it's safe.'

'It's never safe,' Jennifer said without emotion. 'But I can handle myself.'

'Come with me. Leave. Why are you here?'

'Angel, you have to go now.' Jennifer sighed. 'It will only get worse if you don't.'

'Are you out of your mind? No fucking way!'

Jennifer stood up and smoothed her clothes.

'You have to go now,' Jennifer repeated. 'Thank you, Angel, but you must leave now.'

She missed Angel, her best friend who had been around for as long as she could remember. They had grown up together, worked together at one point, and had been roommates for two years. They'd stay up late

on weekends, drinking coffee and talking; they could talk
and talk about any and everything. They knew each
other so well that when one of them was in a bad way,
the other instinctively knew it. They supported each
other through the bad and the worse, so it was surprising
that Angel was clueless as to what was going on with
Jennifer and Jack.

Angel had never been a fan of Jack from the
beginning but Jennifer knew her friend would have been
stunned to see first-hand the extent to which his temper
would go. After that day, more than six years ago,
Jennifer had not seen her, except at a wedding and at a
funeral, and even then, she avoided her. She refused her
calls and didn't open the door when Angel knocked and
banged at it. Quite soon after that incident, Jennifer and
Jack moved and she hadn't let Angel know where she
was. Angel had gotten in touch with Jacky, Jack and
Jennifer's son, who was not oblivious to his father's
activities, but was powerless to help. He had spoken to
Angel, warning that any insistent contact would put
Jennifer in more danger.

Angel had stopped trying, but she had kept in
touch with Jacky as long as was possible and kept track of
Jennifer's life as much as she could. She sent messages
and gifts but Jennifer didn't reply or reciprocate as she
didn't want to encourage her. For Angel to re-enter their

lives would mean danger for Jennifer and she was also worried for Angel. She was aware of what Jack was capable of and couldn't be sure of how far he could go, which had nothing to do with his violence. Jack was well connected and could make life miserable for just about anyone.

Angel, for her part, sensed Jennifer's feeling and stayed away. Jack was pleased that Angel was no longer around as facing her would cause him embarrassment and require some sort of explanation, although, previous to that particular altercation, he had quite liked the woman and she would have come in very handy in the last couple of years, when dealing with Jennifer's illness. Instead, he had to care for her himself, as she refused help of any kind, even from her mother.

****

Now, Jennifer contemplated Jack and something snapped. She picked up the bottle of wine from the table and poured herself a large serve. Jack narrowed his eyes, and she very deliberately pushed her glass to his, clinking them so firmly, she thought they would break. Jack raised his eyebrows in astonishment.

'Cheers, my darling husband,' she said softly and downed the drink in one long gulp. She almost gagged, but managed to keep it down, feeling it warm her stomach immediately.

'What are you doing?' A furious whisper between clenched teeth.

'Having a drink with my husband, that's what!' she replied, staring straight into his black eyes, and then smiled broadly at him.

'Perhaps you should go back to the suite,' he whispered, trying to grab hold of her arm, which she deftly dodged.

'I'm just fine, darling.' Then, very deliberately turning her back on him, she reached out for the bottle again.

She hesitated and then raised her hand and gestured to the waiter, who was there so quickly, she wondered if he was a genie.

'Vodka, rocks please.' She smiled sweetly at him.

The young lady next to her smiled at her and began to chat about the grand hall and how beautiful everything looked tonight—small talk again, but it was better than looking at Jack. She could feel the wine now burning her empty stomach and wondered whether she had been foolish, but at that moment, a glass of vodka was put in front of her. She looked up at the waiter.

'Thank you, but could you keep it coming?'

He nodded obligingly and moved away. Jennifer

emptied the glass in one swig and almost in an instant, there was another full one in front of her. She wondered if Jack had noticed but didn't risk looking his way.

Her head was becoming light and she was not caring so much anymore. She looked over to David's table, but he wasn't at it. She looked around in panic and saw him at the bar. He was in conversation with another man, but his eyes were penetrating through her. This time she was the one who raised her glass. She felt invigorated. She was still slightly scared, but she knew it was too late; she had thrown caution to the wind and she was going to bear the consequences of David's existence here tonight anyway. What was a little more? In any case, she was hoping he would go so far as to kill her soon. He would be killing two birds with one stone. She would be free from her misery with him as well as the pain she had to endure every day, and hopefully, he would be in jail!

*Wishful thinking,* she sighed. Then she smiled at David, that dazzling smile that he had loved so much.

David's eyes widened in shock and then his eyebrows furrowed. He knew this was dangerous for her, he knew there would be consequences. He shook his head slowly.

Jennifer didn't care anymore. She gulped what was left in her glass, picked up her purse, stood up, and strode over to where he was. She didn't look back to Jack; she kept her chin high and her eyes on David. He looked flustered and put down the drink he had just received. She reached him and she suddenly didn't know what to say.

'Take me away, quickly,' she blurted.

It was as if time had not passed. David clutched her hand and strode toward the exit. They didn't look back.

# CHAPTER 5

*1983*

The date with David was unexpectedly fun and exciting and Jennifer had not believed in love at first sight until then. He was open and at ease with her and she felt her spine tingle whenever he glanced in her direction, which was quite often. She wanted to gaze at him, to take everything in, but that would have just been plain awkward, so she sized him up through, at first, embarrassed conversation.

David also seemed shy, and Jennifer was pleased as she felt in control of the situation again and she also knew that it meant that he was attracted to her too. The mix of emotions she felt, alarmed and excited her. The restaurant, a small bar on the corner of Main Street, was filled with a mix of people from older men and women to others having date nights just like theirs. It was dim and old country songs played softly, trying to be heard over the din.

David and Jennifer sat at a table donned with a red-and-white checkered tablecloth that was adjacent to a window in an alcove. They picked at their burgers, Jennifer with shyness, and David with not much more zest, and both took furtive glances at each other. At one point David reached out for his glass and slyly brushed his hand against hers; it was as if she had just gotten a shock. She looked at him, surprised at his boldness.

And then they laughed.

It broke the tension and their conversation came easier; the rigidity of his posture slackened and Jennifer felt that she now knew what the word 'bliss' really meant. She gazed into his eyes; light gray and soft, they seemed to be in battle with the rest of his face which was chiseled and harder. His hair, almost black, fell in wisps around his ears and she resisted the urge to seize a lock of it and run it through her fingers.

She told him about her move from New York and her dream of living there again one day and he told her about his studies and his need to be back in Boston soon. Jennifer didn't like that part. It was as they were about to leave that she thought of Michael again. *Damn,* she had completely forgotten. How could she have forgotten?

She looked around but he was nowhere to be

seen. She was suddenly very conscious of the situation they were in, the situation she had put David in. She looked around and leaned back in her chair, trying to give herself enough distance from David so as not to provoke Michael further, should he see them. David noticed her change in demeanor and leaned toward her.

'Are you okay?' He put his hand on hers and she quickly pulled away, fearful that Michael could be out there, watching them.

David flinched and his eyebrows furrowed.

'I'm fine,' she said quickly, wondering if she could tell him about Michael. Was it too soon? They had already talked about so much, but yet knew each other so little. How would he react?

'We have to go home, I, um, forgot that I have to, er, get up early tomorrow.' She would be horrified if Michael did something rotten; she couldn't let anything happen to David.

David, quite clearly bothered by the sudden change in atmosphere, stood up suddenly.

'Yes, I'd better take you home.'

'David ...' she started to protest, wondering what she could say to explain it.

'Yes, well, I have an early morning too, let's go,' he said stiffly.

Jennifer sighed and stood up, just as Michael

ambled through the door.

'Hey, baby, let's go.' Michael arrived at their table and gave David a smirk.

'She's all yours.' David pushed his chair back, got up, and strode out of the restaurant. Michael and Jennifer stared blankly at his receding figure.

'That was easy,' said Michael, promptly sliding into David's seat and eating what was left of his fries. Jennifer looked at him and for the first time, felt distaste. What did she see in him?

'Wait here for a minute,' she said, hopping out of her seat.

'Hey, what gives? Where you going?' He grabbed her hand as she tried to rush past him.

'I'll be back, just wait here, he, um …' she stuttered and saw David's wallet sitting on the table. 'He forgot his wallet.' Jennifer breathed a sigh of relief, thankful for it. She picked it up and ran out of the door. She got to where they had parked his car and found him leaning on his bonnet and looking toward the sky. A cigarette dangled from his lips and his eyes were narrowed.

He glanced up as she neared and casually looked away again. She ran straight to him and kissed him right on his mouth, holding on to his arms tightly. She could feel they were tensed, but then she felt him soften as he enveloped her in his arms, kissing her back. She felt like she was in a dream; thoughts of all else faded and she fell limply into him. She broke away and looked into his questioning eyes.

'Take me away, now, quickly,' she pleaded with him.

He looked at her intently for a second, then moved her to the passenger's side and opened the door for her. He almost sprinted to the driver's side, got in, and they sped away. They didn't look backwards and had they done so, they would have seen Michael standing at the door of the bar with his mouth open and several of David's fries lying on the ground beside him.

They drove for a few minutes in silence. Back to her senses, Jennifer was unsure of herself again.

'So, you want to explain? What on earth was that about?'

Jennifer bit her lip. She had to tell him. She knew she was going to marry this man.

Getting rid of Michael had been a problem in the beginning. He wasn't as tough as he led everyone to believe and became whiny and clingy once she had decided to end it with him. It was harder than she had expected, but he eventually accepted it; he didn't have much of a choice.

And Jennifer was content, more than content;

she was in love and it was nothing she had felt before. That night, after their dinner, they had driven for an hour, talking and laughing, and she had related the story of Michael to David. She was sorry that she had to hurt him, but she couldn't let David leave that restaurant, not without her.

Sure that he felt the same, Jennifer was honest about her relationship with Michael. David, clearly as smitten as Jennifer, said he was relieved that she had come after him, he was on the verge of barging back in and clouting that rude fellow. They spent the rest of the evening walking in the park and holding hands under the moon. Jennifer didn't want the night to end, but eventually David drove her home, walked her to her door, and kissed her deeply at her doorstep. Then he regarded her face with a troubled look and for a split second, Jennifer wondered if she would ever see him again. She pushed the thought from her mind as David lifted her hand to his lips and kissed them, this time smiling at her as he did. She tousled his hair with her free hand and he leaned over and kissed her again.

'Bye, Jen.'

'Bye.' Jennifer lingered at the door, watching him walk to his car, and when he drove away, she walked in, his lips already imprinted on hers. She closed the door and leaned on it, now grazing her lips with her fingers.

She felt a thrill run up her spine.

'I am going to marry that man,' she said to nobody in particular, but got the fright of her life when she heard a chuckle from the living room. She had forgotten that Judy always waited for her to get home after her dates, and she hurried up to her room without a word.

They hadn't made further plans that night, but Jennifer spent the next morning moving from the living room window to the kitchen window, her heart in her mouth. When she saw David's car roll up at the curb, she squealed, and picking up her cardigan, ran out the front door.

'At least play a little hard to get,' yelled her sister behind her, but Jennifer didn't hear her or didn't care; all she thought was that he had come back and she got to spend the day with him again.

There was not a lot to do in Tandaro; it was a beautiful place with hamlets and streams and wooded paths where leaves covered the ground, but one could walk the whole place in a day. But as far as David and Jennifer were concerned, they were the only two people in the world, they could be in a mouse cage and it would be enough for them, as long as they were with each other.

They made love under the moon, and Jennifer

was relieved that Michael had been patient with her lack of sexual response toward him. She had wondered why she hadn't been so keen, but now she knew. She was in love and to compare this with what she had felt for Michael was ridiculous, even though she never really stopped to consider the comparison. David, for his part, was a tender and passionate lover and many an evening was spent in an old barn a mile away from Jennifer's home, a dilapidated structure that smelled of old hay and mold. They made love and talked of their dreams and then make love again and talked of their future.

'When I've finished my degree, I want to move to New York,' he said one evening, his arm around Jennifer, her head in the crook of his neck.

'I want to be there now,' she replied. 'But I want you to be there with me too.'

'We will be together …' He paused and Jennifer looked up at him. A troubled look crossed his face and disappeared just as quickly.

'But what?' Jennifer sat up and faced him, a shiver running down her spine.

'But nothing,' he said, pulling her to him. 'I can't support you without a job and while I'm studying, there won't be too much money …'

'Oh, David, don't talk about money. It's so … crass. And so not romantic.'

'But I will need to …'

Jennifer straightened her shoulders and frowned at him. 'You will need to what? Support me, like you said?' She laughed. 'Hell, no. I'm not going to be a homely wife. I want to work too. I want a job … honestly, I don't really know what I want to do …' She scratched her chin in thought. 'But it doesn't matter what for now. It's New York! I will be able to work anywhere if I'm there!'

'We still have to wait, Jen.'

'Why do you call me Jen?'

'Because it's your name?' He laughed.

'I'm not sure I like it.'

'Okay, Miss Mason …'

'Stop it.' She brushed his shoulder lightly and leaned into him, her lips grazing his neck. 'Well, I don't care what I do or what you do. Just as long as we are together.'

'Mmmm,' he murmured. 'That's what I want too.'

'And we can get a little place and we can sleep in every day, and go to work late, and …'

'And get fired.' He laughed.

'Just go with the dream,' she whispered. 'And sometimes we can just stay in bed all day and all night …'

'And then we would die of starvation,' he joked.

'I would happily die for you,' she said, and raised her head to peer into his eyes, which looked back at her with such tenderness, her heart caught and she felt a tear well. Why, she didn't know.

'And I would for you. You are my life now, Jennifer.'

'You can call me Jen. I don't like it when anyone else does, but I love the way it sounds when you do.'

He pulled her into his embrace and she clung to him, a premonition of loss engulfing her.

The days stretched to weeks and they knew the time was coming for David to have to leave, to go back home and then to Boston, back to his studies. She didn't want to think about that time, although he kept reminding her that their time was limited.

David had been spending time during his summer break with his Aunt Gladys while her husband's health was deteriorating and it was only a matter of time before he passed away. As a favor to his mother and also to his aunt, of whom he was very fond, he had come to stay in Tandaro for the summer. He helped around the house and took care of their finances and did whatever he could to help out to make the transition easier.

He was in his second year of university, studying psychology, but Jennifer didn't care whether he was studying to be a dustman, she knew she would grow old with this man. When he touched her, she shivered, and when he spoke to her, she felt like she was the only person in the world. And when they made love, she wanted the world to be as happy as she was.

They spent most of their days together and her family adored him, but they wondered how it was all going to work.

'What are you going to do when he goes back?' Elle asked.

'There are these things called letters, Elle,' she replied sarcastically.

'Have you discussed your future?' Angel, who was visiting, piped in.

'Of course. There is no future without him,' she retorted.

'Just be careful, Jennifer,' her mother put in.

'Don't ruin this, Ma,' she pleaded.

'Oh no.' Her mother looked horrified at the thought. 'David is … David is wonderful! Better than that young man you were seeing. What was his name? Mikey or something like that?'

Jennifer's eyes popped open. 'You knew about Michael?'

'This is a small town, my dear.' She chuckled. 'Besides, I'm your mother. I know more than you think.'

She snickered again and winked.

'Did he ask you to marry him?' Angel asked, her eyes shining.

Jennifer frowned. He hadn't. 'It's still too early for that. But we have decided we want to live in New York, once he finishes his degree …'

'And what will you do?' Judy, who was sitting beside her, got up and put her hands on her hips. 'You need to be independent, Jennifer. Don't rely on a man for anything,' she spat with some bitterness.

'Oh, Ma.' Jennifer rolled her eyes. 'Just because Dad …'

'No, you listen to me,' Judy said harshly and sat on the table in front of Jennifer. She took her hands. 'Promise me you will look after yourself. I love David. I think he is special. I think he will make you happy and I know he will look after you. But I didn't bring my girls up to be looked after. *You* will look after you.'

Jennifer blinked at her mother, her jaw slightly ajar. 'Yes, Ma. I know that and I will.'

Judy kissed her daughter's forehead and with a sigh, rose from the table. All eyes were on her as she left the room. At the door, she turned around. 'He's a dish too,' she said with a grin as she disappeared into the kitchen.

The three girls burst into a fit of giggles. As

straight-laced as Judy could be, sometimes they saw sparks of the girl that she once was.

'And where are you going to live?' Angel continued, almost as excited about Jennifer's future as she was, even though Angel knew the answer. 'And when will you get married?'

New York. That was the only place she wanted to be. At least that was decided. She left the second question hanging in the air. He hadn't proposed. Yes, Jennifer knew it was too soon, but she still wanted the reassurance that he would come back for her. It would make her loneliness when he was gone a little easier. Judy didn't own a telephone, so she wouldn't be able to speak to him while he was gone, but they had both promised to write.

They walked under the moon every evening and Jennifer clung to his hand while he held her close, so close she could smell the soap on his skin, mixed with the light splash of aftershave that lingered on his neck.

'What will I do when you've left?' she moaned on his last night, just the thought of it hurting her, almost physically.

'I will be thinking of you all the time,' he said, planting a kiss on her head.

'Sure you will,' she replied, pouting. 'How can I know that?'

He stopped and pointed to the moon, which was a full white circle in the dark leaden sky. 'Every evening, at six o clock, go outside, look at the moon and think of me. I will be looking at the same moon at the same time and I will be thinking of you,' David said. 'And the time will fly.'

'I will think of you all the time anyway,' Jennifer replied, not wanting to think of being under a single moon without him.

'But don't you see? We will be looking at the same moon. It will keep you connected to me.'

Jennifer looked up and had a strong sense of foreboding. The moon seemed to frown on her tonight and she looked away.

The day David left was one of the worst days of Jennifer's life. They clung to each other at the station and didn't let go until the doors of the train began to close. She gripped the glass, his hands mirroring hers, and she walked with the train as it slowly chugged off, gaining speed.

Jennifer was distraught. Angel had spent the first night consoling her and convincing her not to follow him to Boston, and she spent the next few days locked in her room, unwilling to talk to anyone, including her mother who tried to be kind, then tried to be stern, and then just gave up trying to get her to go on living her normal life.

'Sometimes I wish I had never brought him into this house,' she yelled at the door and gave it a thump. There was no answer.

Then one day, when Judy went up to check on her, she found her door open, Jennifer sitting on her bed, dressed for work. She knocked lightly and went in.

'You don't want me to call in sick for you?'

'No, Ma,' she replied. 'I'm sorry. I know I haven't helped out lately.'

'Don't worry about me. I'm managing just fine.'

'I've only missed a couple of shifts. I'll get more. I'll make it up to you.'

'Jennifer, I don't want your money. I want you to be happy. But I think it's time you got back to living.'

Jennifer smiled shakily. 'I do love you, Ma.' She leaned her head on her mother's shoulder and Judy patted her hand.

So Jennifer dragged herself out of her room and began her new life—the one where David was a million miles away.

The weeks turned to months and it got easier day by day. She wrote letters to him every day and she received them from him almost as often. Her days were spent at work and her evenings were spent reading and rereading his letters. He didn't mention the date of his return, but she knew that he would be having a semester break soon and held out hope for his arrival. She spent every evening talking to the moon, making plans, and counting the days. And yet the time dragged on.

And the moon remained.

****

Autumn was in full swing and the change in the weather, although beautifying the streets with the sprinkling of red and orange leaves, made Jennifer sad. The moon hid itself often and she missed David and kept holding on to the memories they had made when he was with her, but she continued to hold out hope and plan for when they would see each other again.

David would come for her and they would go to Boston together. There, she would work in a florist or anywhere, as long as he was with her, until she figured out what she wanted to do with her life. He would finish his degree and they would move to New York, her home, and they would be married straight away. She wanted three children and David had wanted four and they would live happily ever after. Ever after seemed like such a long time away.

Right now, all she wanted was to see his face again, to touch him, to hear his voice. The thought of seeing him again made her heart start and she wondered if it would stop altogether when the time finally arrived, she had built it up so much.

Jennifer's mother was concerned with her obsession and even attempted to set up dates for her again, so as to distract her, to which she blatantly refused. Michael had also tried to re-enter her life and as badly as she felt for him, she wanted no part of any other man. She kept herself busy with work and stayed at home watching old movies and reading David's letters, waiting for the day of his return. His letters were becoming infrequent, so she waited impatiently and treasured the ones she had. In the meantime, she continued to write loyally at least every three days. Every night at six, she would rush out and stare up at the moon.

'I miss you so much, it hurts,' she'd whisper, her neck stretched to the sky, almost expecting a response, but all that she could hear was the rustling of the trees in the quiet of the evening. 'Come back to me.' When there wasn't a moon, she was despondent and stood outside, looking at the sky, waiting for its emergence. Her mother chided her at times when she looked out the window and caught Jennifer in the rain, sometimes without an umbrella or a coat.

She remembered it was a Thursday, why she remembered that she could never tell, but Thursdays were forever etched into her mind as a day of doom. It was an evening at the end of November when Elle came into the living room and sat beside her on the sofa; Jennifer had come home from work and was watching *Gone with the Wind* for the ninety-ninth time and still wondered why Scarlett was so daft not to recognize Rhett's gift of love.

Elle and Jennifer were close, but not so much so that they confided in each other, so she looked up in surprise and a little suspicion when her sister took her hand.

'Jenny, so, um, how are you doing?' Elle said cautiously.

Jennifer instantly knew that something was not right. 'What is it?'

'I think we should go out this evening, you know, Darren wants you to come with us tonight.'

'Why?' Jennifer screwed up her face. Darren was Elle's fiancé and she liked him well enough, but they didn't really spend that much time together.

Elle sighed. 'Just come, Jen!'

Jennifer protested. 'I just want to stay home tonight … maybe another evening, and don't call me Jen.' She was comfortable on the sofa, tucked up in her oversized blanket, watching her movie. She had no intention of leaving her movie—or her letters.

Elle stood up and leaned over her. '*Jennifer!* He's not coming back!'

Jennifer looked at her sister quizzically. 'What? Who?'

'David! David is not coming back to you!' Elle quickly sat down again and grabbed her sister's hand, poised for whatever came next. Jennifer recoiled as if she had just been burned.

'What?' She didn't understand what her sister was saying.

'David is not coming back to you,' Elle said again, but this time, she said it softly, a quiver in her voice.

'Why would you say that? What's wrong with you?' Jennifer strained her neck backwards and looked at her sister, confusion on her face.

'He's going to be married to someone else.' Elle reached out to Jennifer's hand again. Jennifer looked at the fingers of her sister's entwined in her own, her knuckles white, and then looked back at Elle's scared face with venom. She tugged her hand back to her and tucked them both into her armpits.

'Why would you say that to me? What is wrong with you? Are you jealous? Is Darren not doing it for you anymore? You need to poison my life with your own misery?' Jennifer knew she was trying to hurt Elle, hurt the truth out of her. This could not be happening.

All the while Elle sat with her eyes focused on the brown living room rug, one foot tapping the other.

Jennifer continued her tirade. 'You need to get a life. I hate you for saying that. Where on earth would you hear that shit anyway? How the hell would you know what's going on in my life, or David's, for that matter? Get the hell away from me.' She looked over her sister's shoulder. 'Where's Mom? Mom!'

'She's not home yet, Jen, but I need you to listen, please.' Elle put her hands on her sister's shoulders and faced her. Jennifer wrenched herself away and jumped up off the couch.

Her head was spinning. Her mind was thinking a thousand thoughts and something else was niggling at her. She couldn't think of what it was. She stood there frozen, her body unwilling to move. Elle stood up, reached out to Jennifer and slowly sat her down. Jennifer let herself be seated and then stared at her sister in that puzzled way again. Elle remained quiet but kept her eyes on Jennifer's.

Jennifer's mind was still not clearing. She felt as though she had just drunk a gallon of vodka, but her mouth was parched. A few minutes passed and Elle shook her arms.

'Do you want something to eat, drink?' she

offered. Jennifer nodded slowly. 'Okay, I'm going to get you some water, is that okay?' Jennifer nodded again. Elle went to the kitchen and as she poured the water out of the tap she looked out of the window. She saw Jennifer running across the yard in her pajama pants and a skimpy tank top.

****

Jennifer didn't know where she was going. She just ran until she ran out of breath and stopped to lean on a tree, a wide-trunked willow that welcomed her tired self. She sat on the wet ground, breathing heavily. She looked up and saw that it was a moonless night; David was not with her. As she regained her breath, she thought about what to do next. She tried to put her thoughts together. What was it that was niggling at her brain? She couldn't put it together, but she knew there was truth in what Elle had told her—why, she couldn't say yet, but she knew. She began to sob.

On a night such as this, wet, with a chilly breeze that brought goosebumps to her arms, there wasn't anyone about; they were all in their own homes, probably watching old movies like she had been. Their worlds weren't turned upside down.

She clung to the tree, burying her head in its

grain, and wept. The ground beneath her was cold and Jennifer was suddenly aware that she was sitting on a sidewalk in barely more than her nightclothes. She would freeze. She didn't care. She wanted to die here. She leaned on the tree and closed her eyes.

# CHAPTER 6

New York City was everything that one would imagine. To Jennifer, it was life without David, but it had always been home.

Jennifer knew life had to go on, so after four days of mourning following the night that changed her world, she shook herself off and made a decision. She would not rely on a man to get her out of this town; she would do it herself.

Her sister told her of how she came upon the news that was to shatter her world. David's aunt was preparing to move to Boston to be with her own sister, David's mother, and had mentioned that she was attending the wedding of her nephew. When Jennifer heard this, her mind immediately went to David's brother.

'Then it's a mistake!' she declared. 'His brother must be getting married.' The look on Elle's face sobered her. 'It's his brother that's getting married, not David!'

she said, uncertainly now, and Elle slowly shook her head. And it was then that she realized that his brother was already married and living in North Dakota.

Angel was a constant fixture in the Mason household for those days and had to force Jennifer to eat and drink and even pushed her into the bathroom to shower. Her mother had been beside herself with worry and had threatened to stay home from work, so Angel had offered to remain for a while, aware of the financial distress that Judy's staying home would cause. Angel was still job hunting, 'So I'm free anyway,' she said with a forced laugh.

In times of lucidity, Jennifer had talked to Angel about her future. She didn't want one, but knew she had to do something. At first, she sought the truth. She scoured her brain for what had been bothering her. She pored through the letters from David and even engaged Angel in her search for it. Angel, unsure of what she was looking for, came upon it. Two of the final few letters had included the word 'commitment' and another word, 'obligation'. She had assumed at the time that it meant his study commitments, but now the word dripped with meaning. What was he talking about when he told her their plans would have to be delayed for a while?

There was also something else; David was supposed to have gone to Boston shortly after he reached

Maybury, back to college, but his letters had never alluded to his college life. Jennifer never pressed for information and had never thought it strange, and as long as he was professing his love for her and making plans for their future, she hadn't cared where he was. She checked the postmarks and all his letters had hailed from Maybury. It only now struck her as odd.

In the first few days after Elle had told her the news that was to break her world, Jennifer had only left the house to run down to the letterbox when the postman arrived. She did not trust anyone to check it for her. She was left disappointed and devastated and her nerves were left raw. She knew she had to do something. She was getting restless; she didn't want to face the world, but she knew she couldn't stay holed up forever.

New York City.

It was where she had planned to go eventually. Why not now? Now when she needed a change of pace, a change of scenery. She was too scared to leave the house as everywhere she ventured would remind her of David. A plan began to form in her mind: not a fully developed idea, but a start. She discussed it with Angel.

'I can get a job. I'll stay at a hotel until I find a small apartment. I have some money saved.' She could feel an excitement she thought she would never feel again. 'And I can walk up Fifth Avenue …'

'And we can stay up late and go out to shows on Broadway ...'

'You're gonna come with me?' Jennifer's eyes popped open in anticipation and Angel blushed, unaware that she had accidentally involved herself in Jennifer's plans, but they both began to think seriously about it.

They needed money first, a place to stay, jobs to live on ... the more they thought about it, the more disheartened they were about the prospect. It was such a big move, and by themselves ... They decided it was time to discuss it with Jennifer's mother. She would need to be okay with it; Jennifer couldn't leave her without anything and the income she brought in helped out immensely.

After bringing her into her bedroom, Judy listened to the excited girls spill out their idea, then she stood up and walked out. Jennifer's heart dropped. She didn't think her mother would be this disappointed. Angel looked at her and they both knew this was a crazy idea. They began to talk themselves out of it.

'It will be too hard, anyway.'

'There is so much crime there, I heard on the news the other day ...'

'We will be alone.'

'It's so expensive there ...'

'Mom needs me here anyway.'

'I will have to convince my parents too,' said Angel. 'And they won't be too happy.'

Jennifer fell back on her bed and looked at the stained ceiling. Now what? Back to the drawing board. But at least she had looked past a life with David, even if just for a moment.

The bedroom door opened and Judy walked back in with a small brown tin box. She sat on the edge of the bed and the girls looked at each other, not daring to say anything. She opened the box and pulled out a small white piece of paper, while the girls crept up to her.

'This is the number of Lydia, my oldest friend. She lives in the city and she'll set you up with a place. You may have to stay with her for a few days. I can organize that.'

Jennifer and Angel looked at each other again, their eyes wide, not daring to hope yet.

Judy dug into the box again and pulled out a wad of notes. 'This should tide you over until you both get jobs. I will write to cousin Anne, she will help you find work.' She turned to Angel. 'You leave your parents to me.' She placed the piece of paper and the cash on the bed and looked at Jennifer, her eyes creased and watery. 'This is your way out. You get out yourself, you don't need anyone to rescue you.' She placed a kiss on her forehead, and standing up, straightened her dress and her face. She began to walk toward the door and Jennifer leapt on her mother and squeezed her hard. Angel joined in and they jumped up and down with glee. For a split second Jennifer forgot David—for a split second.

****

Jennifer had still not received a letter from David before she left home and as much as she wanted one, she knew it may hamper their plans. The pace of their leaving was fast and it was less than a week since their discussion that they said goodbye to Tandaro.

The night before they left, with very few of their belongings—a trunk with clothes, make-up, and toiletries (they wore their thickest coats)—Jennifer gathered all of David's letters and sat herself down in the living room in front of the fireplace. Her mother was at work, Elle was out with Darren and she was grateful for a moment to herself. She took out the letters and read each one slowly, weeping as each of them, one by one, was placed slowly, deliberately in the fireplace. She felt that with each one, she was removing David little by little from her life, and as she placed the last one in, she closed her eyes.

She looked at the clock; there was still fifteen minutes. She walked out into the cold evening, hugging her coat close to her, and looked up and down the street. Not a sound could be heard, except for the soft swish of the night breeze, and walking to the mailbox, she checked it, merely out of habit. There was nothing in there, except for old leaflets that had remained in there for a while, and she felt that small stab of disappointment that she always did. She checked her watch and looked up at the moon. She began to shiver.

'Goodbye, David,' she said and slowly walked back into the house. She couldn't help but wonder if he was out there somewhere doing the same.

****

It was hard. Moving away from the world she had known, leaving everything familiar behind, was terrifying. Even though she was only three hours away from home, Jennifer was homesick for her mother and even Elle, all the time. Angel was her saving grace. They both got jobs more quickly than they thought and soon rented a small apartment above a pizza shop.

They were also a little scared. The hustle and bustle of the city was unlike anything they had experienced before, at least not on their own, and they found themselves holding close to each other when walking on the streets in the beginning. But New York

City was abuzz with life and walking the bustling streets with constant noise and movement always managed to perk up Jennifer's dreary mood.

Jennifer found a job at a nightclub called Jang. She served drinks and worked in the ticket booth, and Angel, though it took a little longer, found a job with the help of Judy's contact, in a café not far from Jang, so they walked to work together whenever their shifts matched.

Jang was a jazz club in a busy hub with a mixed clientele and Jennifer was always popular with customers, some of whom tipped her well. The dimly lit hall with corridors that lent themselves to rendezvous was always crowded, and the constant stream of people, young and old, that frequented the place for its music and atmosphere kept Jennifer on her toes. She was glad for it as it kept her mind from David and although she was propositioned numerous times in every shift, she declined with a laugh and a wink. She always had a smile on her face and made time to chat with the customers, quickly becoming one of the more popular waitresses.

Jennifer sent most of her wages home as she didn't need much to live on and as time went by, her earnings increased and she even managed to save some money. She enjoyed work, but still felt like she was existing. Not overly ambitious, she felt like she wanted more but she was still unsure of what she wanted to do with the rest of her life; nevertheless, she was impatient to get there and knew she had to take a day at a time.

She also knew that part of her yearning for more was the yearning for David. David was never far from her mind and although she tried to push back thoughts of him, they always resurfaced, leaving her frustrated and broken-hearted. Angel coming with her to New York City was the best thing that could have happened.

'I can't believe we're actually here,' Angel said one afternoon as they sat by the river eating pine nuts. It had become a tradition, the short break between the end of Angel's shift and the beginning of Jennifer's, spent walking by the water, indulging in the experience of living in this place.

'I know. I've wanted to come back since we left.' Jennifer put her hand to her forehead, shading her eyes from the sun as she surveyed the water. 'This used to be the place where my dad took us. I thought it would seem smaller, but it's as big and as crazy as I remember, maybe more.'

'I've never really been,' replied Angel. 'I'm just so glad we got work so easily.'

Jennifer nodded. 'But nothing that will last, I guess. Everything seems so far away right now.'

'I know what you mean,' Angel said, sighing. 'I don't mind the café but what I really want to do is work in the hotel.' Her eyes became large and took on a faraway look. 'I want to run a hotel.'

'That's always been your dream,' said Jennifer, laughing. 'I used to think that was a weird dream for a little girl.'

Angel pouted. 'When I was four, we were on a holiday in Chicago, the only one we ever went outside of Tandaro. We were at a hotel and it was the most beautiful place I'd ever seen. And the concierge was so nice and everyone treated us like royalty. I thought we were special, but then they were like that to everyone.'

Jennifer nodded and grinned, having heard this story several times already.

'And so,' Angel continued, 'I decided I wanted to be the person that made people happy.' She smiled widely and Jennifer pushed her playfully.

'You are so cheesy!'

'And I want to run the Hilton, and maybe even manage a chain of hotels, maybe even have one of my own.'

'With that enthusiasm, I think you will!'

'What about you?'

'I wish I had a dream,' said Jennifer ruefully, thinking of David. 'I don't know what I want to do, even now. There are so many choices too. All I know is whatever it is, I want it to get here soon.'

'We're still young,' said Angel philosophically. 'There's still plenty of time. And the café is paying the bills right now.'

'And we're here,' replied Jennifer, wishing David was here with her too, but quickly banishing the thought of him from her mind.

As if reading her mind, Angel put her hand on Jennifer's. 'It will get easier. At least, that's what I hear,' she said, giving Jennifer a lopsided grin.

But they were in New York City, and for now that had to do. They thought about how fortunate they were to even be here and hoped that they would survive and thrive and not have to go home to Tandaro with their tails between their legs. They vowed to see it out and made the most of their holidays and spare time, enjoying the nightlife when they were not working and lunching at food stalls and small cafés.

Some days they would walk past the big restaurants and stop to look at the menu in the windows. They would pick out the most expensive items, some of which they had never heard of, and tell themselves that they would dine there one day when they were successful. Sometimes, they would see something that looked so scrumptious that they would go to the grocery store, buy the ingredients, and cook it up themselves. Then they would stay up late watching movies into the night on a small black-and-white TV, donated by the previous resident of their apartment. Jennifer and Angel knew they had had a fairly smooth move to New York and also knew it could have been much rockier, so they appreciated their lives and enjoyed their time together, working hard and having fun.

But at night, Jennifer would fall asleep alone, crying into her pillow, knowing that David was sharing his bed with another woman.

She never once looked at the moon.

****

Jennifer was at Jang for about six months when one evening, her manager, Joe, asked her if she would like to be the face of Jang. Joe, a short, stocky man, was gruff and unpolished, but he had a heart of gold and took Jennifer into it. He told Jennifer that modeling for Jang would mean that her face would be splashed around New York and that may lead to many opportunities, such as other, bigger modeling jobs, and maybe even acting.

'With that face and that figure, you don't belong in this place,' he said to her. 'Even though you are good for business.' He laughed.

'I don't know, Joe,' she said thoughtfully.

'Just a test shoot then. You may not photograph well anyway,' he said with a wink and Jennifer punched at his arm.

She'd never considered modeling before; she knew she was attractive, her teenage years had shown her that, but she had never been interested in being ogled, she had had to put up with that for most of her life. It didn't interest her and she, at first, had refused. Joe then discussed how much he would pay her for the shoot and she thought about what the money would mean to her mother. She decided that this once was okay as it was only for Jang. As she worked there anyway, she was already the face of it, she reasoned.

It was a cold day, but the shoot was hot. That's what she always remembered about her first modeling gig—the heat. A little old lady named Francie, who she had never met before, did her make-up, while two men, one of whom worked at the club, went about setting up part of the club where the photos were to be taken. Then she was given a gold lamé dress that looked like a handkerchief and she wondered what to do with it. Once in the bathroom, she figured how to put it on and looked down at herself in horror. Her breasts were exploding out of it and she felt that she may as well have not been wearing anything at all. Her mother would be mortified; she herself was mortified. She was suddenly sweating, wishing she hadn't agreed to this, and wondered if it were too late to bug out. She clutched the sides of the mirror and took a deep breath.

'Think of the money. One time, just one time,' she told herself sternly.

Once out of the dressing room, she was pulled onto a bunch of furs that were heaped in a big pile in front of a giant lightbox. A fox fur was thrown around her shoulders and the clicking began. The photographer threw orders at her.

'Pout …'

'Clench your teeth …'

'You're angry with me, look at me, you want to kill me,' the photographer yelled.

Jennifer didn't want to kill anyone, she just wanted to get out of there as quickly as possible, so she obeyed every command, hoping it would just end, and finally, two hours later, it was over. Jennifer felt exhausted, more than she had ever felt in her life. Once the shoot had finished, she wiped the fancy make-up off her face and started her shift.

Her life in modeling had begun. Seeing the proofs, she was not convinced that she had what they wanted. Joe had given her a set to keep and she showed them to Angel. Although Jennifer was underwhelmed, Angel was ecstatic.

'You have to do this, Jenny, this is what you were meant for!' she exclaimed.

'I look like some weird sort of animal, what are you seeing?!' Jennifer peered closely at the pictures and couldn't find anything that looked remotely like the models she had seen in magazines and shopfronts. She did admit her legs looked great.

'You are kidding me! I know this is not your thing, "don't judge me on my looks," and all that.' Angel rolled her eyes. 'But it can make you a bit of money, until you know what you really want to do.'

'C'mon Ange, in any case, it's a one-off, just for the club.'

But even before Jennifer's posters were on the streets, more offers came in. She didn't want to do them, but she kept believing that each time would be her last and the money was coming in handy, making her feel less guilty for leaving her mother and sister. A number of agencies had approached her and tried to make her sign a contract for exclusivity, but Jennifer knew that this was not her dream, so she freelanced and took on jobs that were temporary. She kept her job at Jang and the place became more popular than ever. With her popularity and her modeling came more money, most of which she sent home. Within the next year, she had even made enough to send her sister to college. But she remained in her apartment with Angel, who was now seeing a very nice young man, Neville.

Jennifer's new life kept her busier than ever and she saw less of her friend. Angel, for her part, spent most of her free time with Neville, and the friends tried to put time aside for each other, not wanting their friendship to dissipate in the hustle and bustle of city life.

Angel tried to set her up on dates with Neville's friends or acquaintances and once, she relented and went on a double date with Neville's older brother, but it didn't feel right.

'I have to go home,' she said after she called Angel into the ladies' room.

'Why?' Angel protested. 'You are getting along so well.'

Jennifer did find Neville's brother interesting, but there was no spark. 'I'm just tired and it's my only evening off this week. And I have a shoot early tomorrow.' They were not lies.

'They are excuses, Jennifer,' Angel said, crossing her arms.

'Yeah, maybe,' Jennifer replied, wishing she did feel something more.

'It's been so long, Jenny.' Angel squeezed her arm and Jennifer felt the tears coming.

'I know that,' she said, angry with herself for still

being affected by a man who'd probably forgotten her existence.

'Okay, I get it,' said Angel and Jennifer knew she didn't but her friend was being kind. She had seen Jennifer's mind float off into the distance on many occasions and she'd come into Jennifer's room at night when the sobbing had gotten too loud and lain beside her, patting her hair.

Jennifer walked back to her apartment, got into bed, and cried into her pillow. She fell asleep cursing ever having met David, and yet waited for him to appear in her dreams which he frequented most nights. She'd wake up with her hands clutching her sheets, trying to hold on to him before the dream vanished and she was forced to face reality. She often thought about where he was, what he was doing, and whether he was happy, hoping he was and at the same time, resenting him for it. She wondered if she would see him again and had never asked her family back home if they had either. There would be no reason for him to go back anyway now that his aunt had relocated. Anyway, she didn't want to know, and she was too proud for them to know that she still cared.

Jennifer had returned home a number times to visit her mother and Elle and was always happy to see them, but as much as she missed them, she longed to get back to her place in the city. She begged off, reminding them she had two jobs to go back to, and they wouldn't wait.

'How is it?' Elle asked. 'You know, modeling.'

'It's fine—fast, busy, and it can be fun sometimes too.'

'Keep your clothes on,' said Judy sternly.

'Oh, Ma,' Jennifer said, embarrassed. 'Of course. I'm already too shy to wear some of the things ...'

'Exactly! I know I can't tell you what to do, but don't show your privates to the world.'

'I won't. I don't know how long it will last anyway, and whether I want it to. It pays the bills.'

'And no drugs, I hope,' Judy continued. 'From what I hear ...' she would go on, cautioning Jennifer about the habits that one could fall into so easily.

And then, before she knew it, it was time for Jennifer to leave. Hugging them goodbye, she felt a stab of guilt and a sliver of sorrow. They were her family and had supported her choices, but she was happy to resume her life as it was. To her, New York City signified independence and everything that didn't remind her of David.

Her modeling jobs were very steady even though she didn't have a manager and she knew that moneywise, she was being ripped off, but she was getting more than enough and she was still enjoying her job at Jang. She had her regular customers, whom she had a lot of fun with. Many propositioned her, but she didn't have much interest in a relationship. She would go for a drink sometimes, but it never led to anything. She thought about her future with a man and figured that time, that healer of all wounds, would get her there, the busyness of her life would keep her going. And if it never happened, well, she had had a love that was great and many people didn't have even that.

On a cool Friday evening in late July, while walking to work, she felt a slight breeze and pulled her scarf around her neck. The tail of the silk scarf wafted to the sky and Jennifer looked upward to yank it back. It was then that she caught sight of the moon.

'David,' she whispered involuntarily and quickly looked away. She felt like she had gone back in time for that split second and for some reason she felt guilty about that.

She stopped suddenly and looked up again. The moon seemed to smile at her, telling her it missed her, and she smiled back. 'David,' she said again, this time with a small smile. She stood still and stared upward at the moon for a few moments. She didn't feel the people who brushed by her, the shouts on the street from the little children who passed by her, nor did she look across the street.

She began to feel good, reinvigorated, hopeful even. This was something she had to face, a thing to overcome, and now, looking up at the circle in the sky, she felt she had. 'I can do this,' she said aloud. 'I can get over this.'

Jennifer strutted the rest of the way to work feeling like she had just won the lottery. She laughed, joked, and even danced with some of the party-goers. She felt like she had a new lease on life, whizzing through the crowd, smiling and chatting.

She had just picked up an order from the bar, three lemon fizzers and a Bud, and was just turning around when she came face to face with him.

Her mouth dropped, a millisecond before her tray of drinks clattered to the floor. But she just stood frozen and stared at him—her David, with the same mop of wavy hair, the same face, the same eyes piercing into hers. She could vaguely feel people moving around her, but all she saw was him.

'Hi, Jennifer,' he said simply, no smile, no expression.

It seemed to break the trance she was in and she quickly bent down to clear up the mess. Joe, her manager, was already bent over on the floor, cleaning the area with a damp cloth along with another waitress.

'Jenny, it's okay, I got it,' he said.

'Sorry, Joe, here let me help.' She took the cloth from him and began to wipe shakily at some of the spillage when Joe caught her hand.

'You okay, kid?' he asked. He glanced up at David, who was looking down at the commotion with the same blank expression as Jennifer. 'He botherin' ya?' Joe asked, nodding at him.

'No, no, I have to, um, no, really, Joe, it's okay. Mind if I take a minute?'

Joe looked at David again and gave him what she thought looked like a snarl. Jennifer would usually have smiled at the man, but not now. 'Yeah, okay, take your time. Sure you're okay?'

But she was gone. Jennifer sprinted to the staff lounge as fast as her heels would let her. She knew that someday this may happen. She had envisioned the many ways it may play out. She would slap him and walk away, or she would fall into his arms. Sometimes, she would kiss him and then slap him. But in her imaginings, she had never frozen, she always had been in control. She leaned against the sink and breathed slowly and began counting backwards from ten. It usually worked, but it wasn't working now. 'Why?' she cried. 'Why?'

She heard a sound at the door and her head

jerked up. David was walking in and then he stopped. They stared at each other for a moment and then they were in each other's arms. They clung together, their mouths hungrily finding each other. Tears streamed down Jennifer's face and David wrapped his arms fiercely around her, so hard it hurt, but she couldn't feel it, not now.

She tore herself away from him and looked straight into his eyes. She stepped back, felt her arm swing backwards and brought it forward, straight into his face, slapping him with all her might. He didn't move, not even to touch the part of his face where a blotch of red began to form. He just gazed at her with intensity. She flew back into his arms and he held her to him.

'Jennifer …' he began.

'I don't care, I don't care!' she said, shaking her head vehemently.

She took hold of his hand and almost ran to the back door, lifting her coat off the rack on her way out. They didn't speak a word as they dashed to her apartment, Jennifer unable to process what was happening. She fumbled with the keys while he kissed her neck, and almost fell into the apartment when Angel, having heard the commotion, opened the door. Angel's mouth fell open, her eyes like saucers.

Jennifer cleared her throat. 'Um, thanks.'

'Hi, Angel,' David said awkwardly.

Angel didn't reply, she just gawked at them, and David looked at Jennifer, who gave Angel a quick nod before dragging him into her room.

They made love with a fury and Jennifer thought for a moment she may die or may even be dead. The joy she experienced was far from anything she could describe or in fact had ever felt before. Afterwards, she tried to stay awake so the dream wouldn't disappear, and leaning her head in her hand, watched him as he slept. She traced the length of his nose down to his chin and followed the trail across his chest. She let her fingers linger on his stomach and he opened his eyes. The moon gazed at them through the curtainless window and when Jennifer saw him turn to it, she did the same, saw it, and smiled.

'That thing!' she said softly.

He slowly pulled her to him and this time, their lovemaking was soft and tender and they took their time exploring and becoming reacquainted with each other's bodies once more. Then she slept, a dreamless sleep for the first time in a long time.

****

The sunlight, which was streaming through the

windows and onto her face, roused her from sleep. The previous night came crashing into her head and she blinked, wondering whether she had dreamt it all. She looked around the room.

David wasn't there. Had he left? Was he ever there?

She threw her head back on the pillow and looked up at the ceiling, fearing the worst. A tear escaped and ran down the side of her face. She lay there, not wanting to get out of bed, and looked at the little alarm clock that sat on her side table: 11.45 in the morning. Did she have a photo shoot? She couldn't remember.

Jennifer sat up, sighed, and reached out for her bathrobe. She shook herself, tried to clear her mind, and went into the bathroom to brush her teeth and wash her face. She needed coffee so badly; it felt like she had a hangover. As she brushed her teeth, she wondered what had happened. Her mind was not making sense, but her body felt glorious and she sat on the edge of the bath, feeling his hands on her. No, it wasn't a dream. She put her hair up as she stepped into the kitchenette and there sat David and Angel, steaming cups of coffee on the table in front of them. They were talking quietly and looked up at Jennifer as she walked in. David smiled, not that dazzling smile of his, but one of pleasure and satisfaction.

She stood frozen and stared at him.

Relief flooded her and feeling her knees trying to betray her, she slowly went to him. Angel had discreetly disappeared and Jennifer sat down awkwardly on the seat Angel had just vacated, trying to smooth out her hair. Between their words of love through the night, they had not spoken much of anything that may have broken the spell. Now they sat opposite one another, with their eyes on each other, both still not wanting to break it.

'Jen …' David started and leaned over to brush a stray hair from her cheek.

Jennifer got out of her seat, walked to him, and straddled him. 'I still don't care,' she whispered. He pulled her close to him and she could feel him beneath her, her own excitement growing. She kissed his neck while he tried to talk to her, not listening to anything he was saying.

But then he stiffened. 'Jen, Jennifer!' He grabbed her by the waist and pulled her off him. She looked up in surprise and a look of hurt crossed her face.

'I have to go away again, Jen,' he said, holding her shoulders. She looked up at him and suddenly a fury began to rise in her and she stepped back.

Jennifer didn't answer him; she didn't ask where he had to go, she didn't want to know. She instinctively looked down at his left hand and saw what she was dreading. It was there. It glinted, mocking her. She pulled away.

'Then get the fuck out!' she shouted.

'I need to explain,' he said, reaching out to her. She backed away.

'I said, get the fuck out.' She pushed at him. She was livid now and shoved him toward the door. Angel was already by her side, carrying David's shoes and coat.

'Jennifer, let me explain!' he cried, his eyes pleading with her. 'I cannot live without you.'

'Well, I certainly survived,' she spat out and slammed the door in his face. She leaned against the closed door and slid to the floor. Angel sat down next to her and held her hand while Jennifer sobbed. Suddenly, Jennifer stood up.

'Fuck him,' she said quietly and with determination. 'Fuck him

# Chapter 7

*David*

David Tremaine, second son of Martha and Luke, loved horses and dogs. It was this that brought together himself and Jack Pardue. Jack came from a long line of horse breeders and was first in line to the family fortune. When David was seven, while ambling home from school, he came upon a lone black horse, saddled and rearing, its strap caught on a wire fence. Although scared, he managed to grab hold of the reins and spoke softly to the horse, calming it. He looked around for the owner and saw a boy, not much older than himself, running toward him. When he reached him, he bent over, placing his hands on his knees, and puffed out illegible words to David. His livery was tightly hugging his stout frame, and in his hands he held a horse whip. David stroked the now composed animal while he waited for its owner to catch his breath and after a couple of minutes, he stood up, his back straight, and stuck out his hand to David.

'Jack,' he said, still puffing.

'David,' replied David, shaking the outstretched hand.

'Thanks, David. Bertie,' he said, shaking his head toward the horse, 'got away from me.'

'He is a real nice horse.' David looked at Bertie, who was now trying to nuzzle his neck.

'No, little bastard ran off, couldn't stop him,' Jack said with a frown. David, not ever having heard a child cuss, looked at him, shocked. Jack laughed. 'C'mon, come up to the house, we can get something to eat. I can thank you for getting this devil back for me.'

David looked unsure and mumbled something about having to go home; his mom would be waiting.

'Just for a little while,' said Jack. His looked pleadingly at David and David relented.

'Okay, but only for a while.'

David and Jack became firm friends and were sometimes mistaken for brothers in the town of Maybury. Although coming from very different backgrounds—David's family were not destitute, but neither were they rich, certainly not anything that could be compared with Jack's family—they found they had much in common and spent all their spare time together. Jack's younger sister, Dell, always tried to join them on their adventures, but they always managed to get away from her and when they returned, found her sulking on the porch steps. They fished, rode horses, and in their teenage years, talked about what they would do when they became men.

Jack would naturally go into the family business, it was expected of him, while David wanted to study. Very early on, following his father's lapse into depression, David decided that he wanted to be a psychologist. David knew that this would be a hard path to follow, but he was extremely bright and his determination surpassed his intelligence. With an aptitude for study, David's mother had always encouraged his education, but had never pushed him so far as to dampen his yearning for knowledge.

As a young child, David had seen his mother work hard to make sure both her sons were well educated. His parents had had a third child, a girl, Lacey, but she had passed away at the age of two from meningitis and David, barely four at the time, had very few memories of her.

David's father, having lost his youngest child, took to drinking and just about held down his job at the local high school. He became more and more disinterested in his family and home and eventually spent most of his time locked up in his study, drinking rum and listening to old music. As much as David and his brother tried to connect with their father, his indifference toward them was evident and they began to rely more on their mother for parental affection and attention.

Martha, for her part, gave all her time and energy to the boys and with her own parents living in Maybury, attention for them was never lacking. They created their own fun, playing on the jetties and in the nearby parks, riding their bicycles, and climbing trees. On the weekends, they rode their bikes to their grandparents' farm, where they took out the horses and even played with some of the very large and noisy farm machinery.

When David met Jack, they began to spend much of their time together, David feeling that Jack, underneath the façade, was a lonely boy in need of a real friend. As young adults, girls naturally became very interesting to both of them and they were certainly very interested in them too. David, more reserved than Jack, usually let Jack take his pick of the girls when they went out, and most girls chose Jack anyway. His demeanor was one of confidence and entitlement and he was indeed a good-looking young man, demanding attention when he entered a room, his black hair styled to perfection, his hooded eyes able to pierce through the thickest veneer. David, for his part, although just as handsome than Jack, with wavy hair and intense gray eyes, tended to fall back and allow Jack to take the lead. David's loyalty to his friend was paramount and they never seemed to be attracted to the same type of girl anyway.

During his late teens, David began to form more than a passing interest in Dell. She had grown to be a lovely young lady; however, she was sick most of the time and David's tender nature always led him to inquire about her and spend time with her, more time than was natural for someone who was just a friend of her brother. At times, he would drop in knowing that Jack wouldn't be there, just so he could have time alone with her, knowing his feelings for her had risen above what they should have been.

Dell had a petite frame and stood more than a head under David. Jet-black hair, cut just below her waist, enveloped her pale face, but her eyes were a striking blue that seemed to penetrate the heart of everyone she met. As fragile as she was physically, mentally she was strong, and knowing that Jack suspected David's and her relationship, she dropped hints to him to prepare him for when they would break the news to their families.

David knew his friend was a shrewd man and that he discerned what was going on between his best friend and his sister, but Jack never discouraged him in any way and David felt that Jack wanted to encourage the friendship and urge it into a relationship. Dell was suffering from epilepsy and Jack knew how hard it would be for her to find a suitor. Besides, he loved David and hoped that the match would provide David as a friend, a brother-in law, as well as a business partner in the future. Jack understood well David's love of horses and knew he would be a great asset to the business.

When David was eighteen, he proposed to Dell.

'I've lost my wingman!' Jack declared, slapping his forehead in mock exasperation, when David told him he was planning to ask his father for her hand in marriage.

'Well,' said David. 'I don't think you ever needed a wingman.'

'No, Flora is nearly done. Anita is looking better and better. She's really filling out those sweaters, if you know what I mean.' He winked.

'You will get caught one day, you know,' David warned.

'So what? I think they like it that way. It makes me a challenge.' He shrugged. 'Today Anita, tomorrow, who knows? I have no commitments to any of them.'

'I'd like to see you when you find the right one,' chuckled David.

'I'm not so sure there is only one,' he said frowning. 'Except for you maybe. You got it bad.' He laughed now.

'Yep, I sure do.' David smiled broadly, thinking about how he was ready to start a life with Dell.

Jack poured two glasses of whiskey, and handing one to David, he raised his high in the air. 'To my friend, my family now.' He hugged David. 'Besides, friends come and go. You will be with me forever. We can do much with the ranch. So much more than Father did …'

'Not so sure that's the path I want,' laughed David, pleased with Jack's reaction, but not wanting to offend his friend.

'We'll see. That's not important now.' Jack punched David affectionately on the shoulder. 'So when are you going to ask the old man?'

'As soon as I possibly can,' he replied. 'I want my future to begin as soon as possible.'

David was very much in love with Dell; they shared many interests and spent their time wandering around the garden and discussing their future. He would finish college and although that would mean a few years, he would not marry her before he could properly support them both. Dell wanted to go to the same university as

David, but her health would not allow it, so she accepted that she would only see him on college breaks and they would write frequently.

In the meantime, she was trying to be patient and spent her time helping out with the farm, although she realized that it was just a token gesture; her body couldn't cope with long days of hard work that ranch work required. But it would pass the time more quickly while she waited for David.

It was in the fall of 1982 when David left Maybury for Boston.

College life was difficult and the study even harder, but David always set time aside to write to Dell and called her in the spare moments that he had. On his breaks, he rushed home to see her and each time, he would find her health had worsened. His own parents had moved to Boston and he found that trying to fit in seeing all of them in his time off left him exhausted. He considered leaving college to work on the ranch with Jack, so he could be closer to Dell, but David had a different plan for his career and although he worried about Dell incessantly, he felt that one day he would make up for his absence and give her a wonderful life.

It was two weeks into his summer break in 1983 when his mother called, asking him to visit with his aunt in Tandaro as she needed help nursing her dying husband. His mother could not leave his father for any amount of time and his father flatly refused to go—his mental health was deteriorating quickly. David, being extremely fond of his aunt, relented. Dell wanted to go with him, but there would be no room and, in any case, he didn't think that he would be away for very long. His uncle was almost comatose and it was only a matter of time before he passed. David would have to help fix up the finances and prepare for his aunt to move and then he could come back. He would return as soon as he could and promised Dell he would write and think about her all the time.

When David boarded the train, he was already missing her.

****

Standing at the bottom of the stairs, making small talk with Judy, David wished he had been more adamant with Aunt Gladys. She had asked David to take out a young lady who was the daughter of a close friend. David, who had not shared his plans of his future with anyone but Dell and Jack, could not find an excuse that was good enough for the old lady. He gave in to make her happy and decided that the date would be short and sweet; emphasis on the short. The poor girl probably didn't get out much, so he would be doing his good deed for the day.

When David turned around to see Jennifer walking down the stairs, he realized that this girl did not need to be set up out of pity and his mouth fell slightly. She sashayed toward him and stuck out her hand. He looked at the outstretched offering, wondering whether to shake it; he instead lifted it gently to his lips and smiled. He wanted to laugh, this was not France!

The evening was not what he had expected. When he dropped Jennifer home that night, he sat in his car in front of her house and tried to gather his thoughts. He was in love with Dell—so he had thought. A guilt crept into his pores and he felt dirty; Dell had not entered his mind that evening—not once. No, he wouldn't see Jennifer again, he decided, he couldn't. It would lead her on and he couldn't do that, not to Jennifer and certainly not to Dell. Perhaps it was better for his own sake as well.

Jennifer was tough, he could see that. She would move on to the next Michael that entered her life. Dell was counting on him. But he had never felt the way he had when he was with Jennifer. From the moment he laid eyes on her, to her temper tantrum in the car, and when she ran out and kissed him … his stomach lurched when he thought of it; no, he had never felt like that, ever. Could he forget it ever happened?

He had to.

Yet, the next morning after spending the night tossing and turning and trying to conjure images of his fiancé in place of Jennifer, he found himself driving to her house. He sat outside, contemplating his actions, and she had run out, had just hopped into his car, leaned over, and kissed him deeply. Right then, he knew that she was the one and they had been inseparable ever since.

'What are you looking at?' she had said sleepily one evening through closed eyes, while David looked down at her, leaning his elbow on the haystack next to her head. He had been watching her as she dozed, not wanting to wake her. He looked at her eyes and the way they were raised slightly at the ends and then at her full pink mouth, which did the same.

'My future,' he replied, knowing it was the truth.

He had to give up Dell. He tried to write it to her, but knew it would be very wrong to break up with her in a letter, so he wrote her letters every few days, trying to sound as he usually would. He would end it when he got back, it was the only way to do it.

David also thought of Jack. His best friend; would he forgive him, had he lost his friendship over a girl? But this was no ordinary girl. He intended to marry her, and as soon as possible. The more time he spent with Jennifer, the surer he was of his future with her. David agonized over his decision and knew that marrying Dell would be even more disloyal to her, because he knew his heart would forever be with Jennifer. He spent many evenings speaking to the moon, knowing its constancy. It would remain; everything else may fall apart, but the moon would be forever. That was what he felt his love for Jennifer would be.

Saying goodbye to Jennifer was hard, the most difficult thing he had done in his short life, but David knew he would be facing an even worse time when breaking the news to Dell … and to Jack.

Arriving in Maybury, he went straight to see Dell. What he saw stunned him. She could barely get off the settee to greet him, but she managed to pull herself up and throw herself in his arms. He held her skeletal figure and buried his face in her hair. David squeezed shut his eyes, trying to make himself love her as much as he loved Jennifer.

'Darling David, I have missed you so, so much. Don't go away again, I will absolutely die,' she cried into his chest.

David held her tight and didn't reply, not trusting his words.

'David!' a voice boomed into the room. David

looked up to see Jack smiling warmly at him. His friend had reached him in three big steps and gave him a warm hug. 'So glad you're home—where you should be.'

'Hey, Jack,' David said, prying himself away from Dell, who still tried to cling to him. 'I've got to get back to school the day after tomorrow, so it won't be for long.' He carefully placed a reluctant Dell back on the settee and walked back to his friend.

'David,' Jack whispered furiously. 'You can't leave her again. You have to stay for a while.'

'Jack, I have to get back to school, my semester starts in less than a week,' David protested. He wished he had been able to tear himself away from Jennifer sooner.

'Come with me.' Jack looked over his shoulder at Dell. 'Will bring him back in a jiffy.'

Dell poked her tongue out at him in response. 'Hurry back, I have so much to tell you,' she called to David.

Moving out of earshot, Jack told David about Dell's decline. 'She is getting bad fast,' he said. 'This is the best she has been, and that's only because she knew you were coming home today. You have to stay, at least for a while, at least until we figure out how to keep you two together. She wasn't lying, she will actually die.'

David remained quiet. His thoughts were whirling in his head. How could he leave Dell like this?

He had to go back to his studies, he had commitments; and he glanced back at Dell, who was gazing at him, while fondling the ring on her left hand.

He had made a commitment to her. She was his commitment, not school; sure, he had wanted to finish quickly, so they could be together sooner and now … all he could see swimming in his brain was Jennifer.

'Dave, buddy, answer me, can you defer for a while?'

'Jack, uh, yeah, I don't know …'

'She needs you, I need you.' Jack's voice was now harsh.

'I need to get back to Dellie; I missed her, you know.' David laughed nervously. Before he had arrived home, he had decided to confide in Jack, but now he wasn't so sure. He had a find a way to make everyone happy. He thought about Jennifer; every minute that had passed after he left, his heart broke a little more.

On his way home, he had continued to make plans for Jennifer and him to be together. He would rent a bigger place near school. He would take her with him. They would be married as soon as possible and he would continue to study, while she worked or even studied herself. They would manage until he finished his studies and then they would be fine. But now …

David had dinner with Jack, Dell, and their

parents. At five minutes to six, he excused himself for a cigarette. Jack's mother insisted he could smoke inside, but David mumbled something about fresh air and quickly headed to the porch. He looked up and saw it. 'Jen,' he said softly. He felt a hand on his shoulder and sprang around.

'Davy, what's up?' Jack fished out a cigarette from David's pack and lit it. 'What's wrong with you?' Blowing out the smoke, he looked up at the moon too. 'You really missing your stars and constellations or whatever it is you're fascinated with up there?'

This was his chance. He should tell him now. He had to.

He took a deep breath. 'Jack, there is something I need to tell you.'

'It's fine, David, you don't have to tell me anything. Whatever happened, it's over now. You're back.' He looked at David's stunned face and laughed. 'Seriously, David, how long have I known you? I know you more than you know yourself. It was a fling. It's over. You're back and you will marry my sister.' David knew that Jack could be domineering, but it was never directed at him and he straightened his shoulders.

'Now wait a minute,' David began.

'No, you wait,' Jack snarled at him, moving so close, David could smell the whiskey on his breath. 'You promised you would marry her. You will. She is not going to last very long. You will not break her heart! Your little fling will not rob my sister of her happiness. Get yourself together … and don't even think about breathing a word of this to Dell. She won't bear it.' He flung his cigarette on the ground, smashed it with his boot, and strode away, leaving David in his wake, staring at his back. He looked up at the moon again in despair.

Back in his own home, a house that was dusty, dark, and empty, he took out the only picture of Jennifer that he had, a snap she had given him of her posing in readiness for prom. She wasn't prom queen, she had said ruefully, but she had come runner-up, so that was something; her mother pushed her to be in the damn running anyway. He let his fingers slide over the glossy paper and felt his heart tighten. He began to write her a letter, one that disclosed everything.

'My darling Jen …'

He couldn't do it. He stared at the page for a long while. He had to hold Dell off. He couldn't lie to her. He did love Dell, but it was Jen he couldn't live without. He would work it out, he had to, he didn't know how, but he knew he had to.

He continued his letter: '… my God, how I miss you …'

David deferred university for a term and stayed

home. Dell was ecstatic that she had him to herself, but she was fragile, and not just her physical state, but her state of mind.

'Are you okay staying here?'

'Of course,' he said, squeezing the little hand that was curled in his. 'I'm with you.'

'I'm getting so thin. Am I even attractive to you anymore?'

David was surprised. She hadn't been so insecure before. 'Dell, you're amazing. Have you looked into a mirror lately? I had to fend off many a chap for your hand.'

'Don't tease,' she said pouting.

'Well, you ask me silly questions, you get silly answers.'

'I just feel like you haven't been here,' she said, her voice small.

'I'm here,' he insisted, knowing exactly what she meant.

'You just seem so far away sometimes.'

David felt the familiar pang of guilt and the ache in his heart that he always did when he thought of Jennifer.

'I don't mean to,' he said kissing the top of her head. 'I'm just planning our future.' He forced a smile. 'And you are as beautiful as ever.'

'At least you're here with me, not alone in that godawful school. I'm so glad you stayed.' She put her arm around his waist and what should have been a squeeze was a light pressing on his back.

David found a job at a real estate firm and spent his evenings with the Pardue family. He tried to spend as little time alone as possible with Dell as every time he touched her or she caressed him, he felt like he was betraying Jennifer.

'Why don't you touch me like you used to?' Dell asked him one evening when they sat together in the gazebo, where they used to sometimes make love.

'I want to but I'm worried that I will hurt you.' He felt sick with himself.

'Stop it, David. I'm strong,' she said, trying to laugh. She pulled out her arm and flexed her little bicep. David leaned forward and kissed her.

Finally, he decided that it would cause Dell a great amount of pain if he were to leave her and as terrible as he felt thinking about it, he knew she would not be around very long. He had to make what was left of her life happy. They told her family of their plans to wed and began planning their wedding. Jennifer would understand, she would forgive him; she would wait, she just had to. He would have to see her; he would have to tell her, and soon.

# CHAPTER 8

'Your little floozy has gone, flown the coop, dumped you,' Jack said to him lazily one day while they were taking an evening ride through the woods on horseback. The sky was still bright, the sun still trying to endure at the end of summer. David tensed, but didn't reply, and Jack looked at him questioningly. 'You don't care?'

'What's to care?' David tried to reply as casually as he could.

After their little chat, the evening David returned to Maybury, not a word was passed between them on the subject of Jennifer. David had not even told him her name. Only once did he feel that he had slipped up.

Jack had unexpectedly dropped in at David's house when he'd been watching a football game on TV and Jack settled in to watch it with him. They spent more time talking than watching the game and at one point, Jack had gone to the kitchen to refill his drink. He had been there a while and David had gone in to see what was keeping him. He bumped into him as he turned into the hallway that led to the kitchen and Jack quickly picked up his glass from the hallway table and pushed David back into the living room. They continued watching the game, but Jack was silent and so was David. He was troubled; he knew what was on that table. Suddenly, Jack gulped down his drink and stood up.

'Must be going, forgot to do that bill for Dad. He needed it sent yesterday. I have to finish it off,' he said stiffly.

'Game's nearly over, stay till the end,' David replied, hoping Jack would insist on leaving. He needed to see what Jack had seen.

'See you tomorrow?' Jack moved to the door quickly and before David could respond, he was gone.

David rushed back to the table. On it sat the picture of Jennifer and a half-written letter to her. A number of other letters from her were piled beneath them. He swore loudly. Jack didn't visit often; David was always at the Pardue house, so he had been careless. Now Jack had seen them.

David wondered how much Jack had read. He looked through what he had written. It wasn't good. His heart was all over the page and he wondered what to do. How would Jack react? He knew he wouldn't take it well at all, but would he tell Dell? He hoped he would, then it would make his life easier. But Dell! It would break her heart. Since he had been back, she relied on him more than ever.

He was nervous when he went to their house the next day, but Jack greeted him at the door with a playful slap on the back. He acted as if nothing had happened. When he went out for a cigarette, which he did at 6:00 p.m. every evening whenever he was at their place, Jack joined him, and he expected Jack to talk about his discovery, hoping that he would. It would make it so much easier, perhaps even give him a chance to vent his feelings, talk it out with someone, and who better than his best friend? But Jack didn't. He acted so normal that David wondered whether he had indeed seen the picture and letters. He let himself believe that he had imagined it and life went on as usual.

Until the day Jack brought her up.

'What's to care?' Jack repeated and laughed. 'Fine, you don't care,' he said, a little laugh in his voice, and dug his heel into his horse's flank.

David followed slowly, his mind in a frenzy, and caught up with Jack who was waiting for him on the ridge of the hill. They continued down the hill slowly, David silent, Jack the same.

'She's gone, left, eloped with someone, I hear.'

Jack clearly wanted more of a reaction from David, who was too wound up to say anything.

But now David turned on him. 'What the hell do you even know about her?' he spat. He could feel his temper rising.

'More than you know, my friend,' Jack said coolly. He chuckled. 'Don't care, huh?'

David felt his heart racing, but tried to keep his cool. He didn't want to hear anything from Jack. He wanted to go home and call Jennifer and was angry that he couldn't. He absurdly cursed Judy for not having a phone. He couldn't speak to her; he wanted to hear her voice, for her to tell him that she was still there, that they would work it out, or even end it with him. He had tried so many times to tell her about Dell, but he couldn't bring himself to do it. He knew he was being a coward. He would have to choose but was hoping he didn't have to. Of course, it would take the death of Dell for that to happen.

But now, what was Jack saying? He had to get home, he had to write her. He had to know if he was telling the truth. He turned his horse around and Jack followed him.

'I'm sorry, David,' he said, more gently now. 'A friend of mine from Tandaro called yesterday. She has gone. Jennifer'—David looked up at the name; so, he had seen the letters—'took off last week, don't know where.' He looked at David again. 'I think it's best she left you alone once and for all.'

David didn't reply; he didn't know what to think. His head was spinning and he was trying to recall the last letter that had arrived about a week ago, which was filled with love and warmth and no hint of anything amiss.

'I understand, David, I really do, but you know it's for the best. You can continue your life here, with Dell, with us. Marry her already. You have to. Rent a place near Boston. Be happy. She loves you; er, Dell, that is. And I know you love her, deep down you know you were meant for her. Make her happy. Make yourself happy,' he said earnestly.

Still David didn't respond. He knew he had to find out for himself.

Arriving at the Pardue ranch, he unsaddled his horse, tied her to the trough, and then left without a word to Jack. Jack called out to him, but David just kept walking.

That evening, he returned to the Pardue house. Jack was out for the evening, and because of his anger toward his friend, which was so unusual, he was thankful. He told Dell he had to go out of town for a couple of days. She was unhappy about it, but trusted that when David had something to do, he had something important to do. She told him to hurry home and he took the next train out of town.

Arriving at the front door of Jennifer's home in Tandaro, David was unsure of what to say or do. He knocked softly and waited. Soon the door was answered by Jennifer's mother.

'Hello, Mrs. Mason,' he said, putting his hand out.

Judy looked at him in shock and mumbled a polite hello.

'Is Jennifer home?' he asked.

'She's gone,' said Judy stiffly.

'May I come in?' Judy shifted slightly and hesitantly. She led him to the settee and gestured for him to sit. David decided to come clean. He needed for Jennifer to know everything. He would come back for her. He spilled the whole story to Judy and she listened, at first cautiously, and then sympathetically. She leaned forward when he was done.

'Marry her,' she said. 'You must go through with your commitment with Dell. Forget Jennifer, at least for a while. It won't be long. It's very sad, but it won't be long.' Judy related to David that Jennifer was not married, but had gone to New York City. She urged him to let her find herself there. 'You're both so young now. Let her grow up a little. She needs to be who she is. If it's meant to be, it will be.'

'But I want to be with Jennifer. She is my life,' David protested. He knew he sounded like a petulant child and he just wanted someone to tell him it was okay to go to her. But in his heart, he knew he had to do the right thing. After talking to Judy for a while, he went home.

****

David and Dell were married two months later, a small ceremony in the Pardue gardens followed by cocktails and hors d'oeuvres with close friends and family. David's parents returned to Maybury for the wedding and returned to Boston the next morning. The marriage took place just before Christmas and David had to be back at college just after the New Year.

He worked hard at his studies and worked some evenings in the college library to make extra money. Although his parents had saved well for his college tuition, he still had to pay a part of it, not to mention the living expenses they incurred, even though the apartment they lived in was owned by Dell's father, who offered it to them for as long as they wanted it. Although David didn't want to live off anyone else, he knew that it was the only way to make Dell happy.

Dell, for her part, was stable. She couldn't work, as her body couldn't cope with too much at a time, so she spent her time writing poetry and keeping house. She grew lonely at times, with not a lot of company in a place she was unfamiliar with.

'I'm with you and that's all that matters,' she said, kissing him, when he asked her after returning home one evening to find her looking out of the window wistfully at passers-by.

Jack visited from time to time, when in town for business; however, lately, his relationship with David was strained and when he was in town, David tried to pick up extra work so he could avoid him. They were not the friends they once were and David regretted that deeply.

David's thoughts of Jennifer were never far from his mind, but he knew that the best thing for both of them right now was to stay away from each other. So, he continued working, studying, and taking care of Dell. He didn't know where Jennifer was and thought it best not to try and find out in case the temptation to contact her won out. And still every evening on the dot of six, he gazed at the moon and whispered his love to her.

It was on a cool February day in 1985 when David came home to find Dell passed out on the sofa, her book fallen to the floor. He darted to her side and pressed his ear to her heart. She was breathing. Quickly dialing 911, he rushed back to her side and cradled her while he waited for the ambulance. She was dead before they arrived. David held her tightly and sobbed, the paramedics trying to pry him off her. He had loved her so dearly and pangs of guilt now shot through him as they took her body away, a hint of a smile on her dead lips. He had never given himself fully to her. She deserved more and he knew it. But deep down, he also knew he had made her happy right to the end and took comfort in that.

The funeral took place in Maybury and Jack and David barely exchanged a word. The only time Jack had spoken to David was at the front of the church, where David stayed after the mourners said their goodbyes and patted and hugged him.

Jack stood beside him for a moment. 'Well, this is what you were waiting for,' he said coldly. 'Good luck, David.' He strode back into the church.

Dell's parents were distraught, although this event was not unexpected, and her mother grieved with David. They asked him to stay on at the apartment, but he gracefully refused and moved into one of the rooms on campus.

****

It was in the summer of '85 when David set out to find Jennifer. He agonized over his decision, feeling guilt for the memory of his recently deceased wife, but he knew he had to see her, just to see if he felt the same as he had after all that time apart. Perhaps it was the memory of her that kept him attached to her, maybe that one idyllic summer was all there was supposed to be. He also worried about her reception to him. He wondered if she was happy, wherever she was, and whatever she was doing. Would his reentry into her life be good for her? Would she even care? It had been nearly two years. She may not be the same person anymore. Maybe she had married …

He started at the thought. He hadn't considered that before. He tried to look her up in the phonebook, but she wasn't listed and he didn't know where else to begin. He thought about asking her mother and decided to go to Tandaro to make inquiries, even if he did end up looking like a dammed lovesick fool.

Fate would have it that he didn't need to make the trip. The day before he left, David was sitting at his local café, scrolling through the morning paper, when her face jumped out at him. He stared at the picture, his heart suddenly threatening to jump out of his chest.

She was a model!

That was unexpected. She certainly had the

looks for it, he knew that, but a model? She had never shown the least bit of interest in things like that and always played down her looks. Maybe he didn't know her as well as he had thought. He analyzed the picture; she looked slightly older and had a mountain of make-up on her face; again, unusual for her.

But she was still his Jennifer. Her eyes, although blurred by the black-and-white print, stared out of the page at him, daring him to find her. She was advertising a nightclub called Jang, in New York City. He thumped the table in elation. This was a start, the start he needed. He knew this was fate and it strengthened his resolve. It meant that he had to go to her, it was too much of a coincidence. Maybe the stars were finally aligning for them. He rolled up the paper and strutted home, a whistle on his lips. He would leave the next day and head straight to her.

David drove to New York, reaching the city within a few hours. He had booked a motel room in advance and settled in, for how long he was unsure. He didn't know what to expect, but he had some time on his hands for the moment. Every time he thought about seeing her, his stomach somersaulted.

How would she react? Would she walk away, would she be nonchalant, and the cruelest thought, would she be with someone else? He tried to prepare himself for the worst-case scenario and wondered how he would be able to face the rest of his life without her, if it came to that. His imagined future with her was what kept him going, that, those letters, and that damned moon.

The first afternoon, he made inquiries about Jang and found that it was quite close to where he was staying. He walked the busy streets that were in the full swing of summer and reached the venue. He was again confronted by her face on the wall beside the entrance. It was a large, full-sized color poster, with Jennifer in a gold lame singlet, with a short black skirt, *much too short*, he thought possessively, fishnet stockings, and red patent leather stilettos. Her hair was teased back and she was stepping out of a car, her head upwardly turned as if inhaling the atmosphere.

*That doesn't look like my Jennifer*, thought David, and tried the entrance. It was locked, so he stood outside, wondering what to do. This place would be able to help him. They may tell him what agency she worked for, perhaps. He surely would get some information from them and right now he would take anything. The sign on the door stated that the place opened at eight. It was only three thirty in the afternoon, so David decided to wander around the city to find out what the big attraction was.

After exploring the city, finding it too busy and

too cliched in equal measure, he headed back to Jang. He understood though, that the way he was feeling right now, his stomach in knots and his mind a blur, he was not going to find anything that would be fascinating to him … except her. There was still an hour before the club opened, so he went to a coffee shop across the road which was bustling with people, to wait. He would approach the first employee that went to the entrance and try to retrieve some information from them.

He was there only twenty minutes when he saw her. She was walking with a man, her arm entwined in his. She was laughing, the sway of her walk so poised, yet so relaxed, and he felt his chest become tight. His heart began to race, but he stayed there and watched as they stopped at the door. She was as magnificent as David remembered and he stared, mesmerized. He hadn't expected to see her there. He went there to inquire about her whereabouts, not find her actually working there. He didn't know what to do; his mind raced and his throat was dry. He wasn't prepared to see her so soon.

He stayed at the café until nine and decided he should go in; this was what he was here for. If it was bad news, it was best he knew, and the sooner the better. He cautiously went to the entrance and stood in the line. The closer he got to the door, the more fearful he became. He could hear the conversations of people around him, people waiting to have fun, boys, men, ladies, and he began to feel awkward. He looked down at his clothes, slacks and loafers with a gray t-shirt—he wasn't really dressed for a nightclub.  He was two couples away from the door when he panicked and bolted. He walked back quickly to his room and sat on the bed, his heart thumping. He put on some soft music and picked up a book. He tried to read, but found he kept reading the same words again and again.

David returned to the café across the road from Jang the next evening and the evening after that and the evening after that one. He watched Jennifer come in to work every night, sometimes alone, other times with the same man he first saw her with. One evening he even stayed until she finished work, so much coffee in him his heart was racing, and watched her leave with the man. He was tempted to follow her but knew that this would be so wrong. What he was doing already didn't feel right, it was bordering on stalkerish. He knew he had to stop; he knew he had to see her or go home. He was also running out of time … and money. He had been there over a week and he had not made a move.

It was on a Friday when he decided that it was all or nothing. He dressed in gray jeans and a black polo top and headed to Jang. He waited outside in his usual place. He watched her as she walked up the street from where she turned the corner. He watched as she reached for the end of her yellow scarf that had flown to the sky. He watched as she stared upward, followed her gaze, and saw the moon.

He knew then.

Entering the club, he hesitated for a moment and stayed near the door. He felt like a coward again and wished that he was anywhere but here. Then he saw Jennifer swirling around the crowd, smiling and laughing with the customers. She was at the bar when he headed to her.

****

'Well, I certainly survived,' she had said and slammed the door in his face. David looked at the blue door with the cracked paint and placed his hand on it. Then he turned around slowly and walked down the stairs. He deserved this. How could he just come back into her life and disrupt what she had made for herself? What right did he have? And what did he have to offer her? She was successful, she was a model, she worked at a place that she clearly loved. He was a broke student, with university bills piling up, and he couldn't provide her with what she deserved, especially after how he had treated her. He had just spent the most wonderful night of his life with her and he would have to live on it until he could give her everything.

He breathed slowly. She still loved him, that was clear, and that had to suffice until he could come back for her. He looked down at his hand, his wedding ring still on his finger. He didn't have the chance to explain about Dell. He couldn't yet, he still felt the loss of Dell deeply and thought that talking about it with Jen, whom he had mentally had an affair with throughout their marriage, would be desecrating the memory of her.

David returned to Boston and threw himself into his studies. If he focused and studied during the summer, he would finish within a year. Then he would come back for her.

# CHAPTER 9

## *Jack*

When Jack saw the letters, he stopped. He had just gone to the kitchen to refill his glass with gin, the only alcohol David had in his house, and on the way to the kitchen, his eyes had come upon them. He didn't think much about it and continued to the kitchen. On his way back, he glanced at the table again and stopped. He began reading the half-finished letter lying on top of a pile. His throat began to tighten and he shifted the letter to look at what was beneath it.

He saw the photograph and his breath caught in his throat. She was the most beautiful thing Jack had ever seen. He held the snap closer to his face to have a clearer look. He then quickly shuffled the envelopes with Jennifer's name and address labeled in neatly curved writing on the back. He mentally took note of the address and began replacing the items. Suddenly, David was upon him and he quickly retrieved his glass and ushered David back into the living room.

He sat down, but couldn't stop thinking of the photograph. He needed to leave. His emotions were awhirl and although he was furious with David, his mind was more on the picture of that beautiful young woman. No wonder David had been smitten, and still was, by the look of things. He suddenly got up, making an excuse to leave, and walked out, frustrated.

On returning home, Jack said a quick hello to his mother and went into the stables. He found his stash and lit a smoke. He inhaled deeply, and hearing a laugh, he jumped and turned around. His father came out from behind one of the hay bales. He was so engrossed in his thoughts, he hadn't checked to see if anyone was about.

'It's fine, boy.' His father chuckled as Jack quickly hid the smoke behind his back. 'Been there, done that. Just don't do too much or you will lose that fine brain of yours.'

Jack breathed, but he still squashed the smoke between his fingers.

'Where you been?' his father asked.

'Just with David, hanging out, you know ...'

'David again. You still think he's good enough for Dellie?'

'He's a good guy, Dad, He loves Dell.' Jack was

not so sure anymore, but he knew that Dell loved David and was determined that they stay together, now more than ever after seeing the photo of Jennifer.

'Well, she seems to love him,' said Frank. 'I don't trust the boy; not of our standard. Has his head in the books too much.' His father sat on a hay bale in front of Jack.

Jack sighed; his father was staying for a talk and all Jack wanted to do was to be alone with his thoughts, which were still a grave mix of anger, frustration, and fascination for that woman in the picture.

Frank continued. 'You make sure you look out for her. She doesn't have very long, we all know that.' He paused, while Jack waited. 'What about you, boy? When are you getting yourself a little woman?'

Jack felt irritated. His father hadn't really cared about his life very much. In fact, his father had not cared about anything that much, apart from his ranch. To Jack, Frank's family were add-ons, appendages to his real love—his business. He treated his kids with nonchalance and his wife …

'Well?'

'I don't know, Dad, got to find the right girl, got to fall in love and all …' He laughed nervously.

'What the hell does love have to do with anything?' his father almost spat out and Jack bowed his head.

'Well …'

'Fuck all that foolish crap. Get yourself a good, strong woman, who will help you do what you need to … to keep this'—he waved his arms about him—'going. This is what matters. This is your legacy.' He got up and moved toward Jack. 'This will be yours. Better start working toward that.' He patted Jack on the shoulder and left the shed.

Jack sat on the same bale of hay that his father had vacated and did look around. Being one of the smaller stables, it housed six horses and Jack began to really think about what it meant to be in charge of all this.

Then he thought of his parents. He knew the story; his mother had told him. Frank only married Cynthia because he had knocked her up and her father had literally held a gun to his head. Jack was a bastard; and his father had always treated him with a certain disdain.

Dell, arriving a year later, was born from make-up sex; yes, his mother had confided all to him one morning when his father had left her physically torn and mentally broken, after one of his drunken tirades. Their marriage was not good; he was aware of what happened between them, had witnessed it on more occasions than he cared to remember. When he was thirteen, he tried to intervene and had felt the solid fist of his father fracture his jaw. The look his father had given him at that moment hurt more. On one occasion, when he was sixteen, he hit his father back and Frank had thrown him across the room and pounced back on his mother.

Cynthia never retaliated and huddled in tears, which seemed to make his father more angry. Previous to that incident, he had talked to his mother about leaving Frank, or at least fighting back.

'Don't think I haven't tried,' she had said tearfully, 'but he is stronger than me. I should never have married him. It's my fault anyway … I can't seem to do anything to make him happy anymore.'

Jack began to resent his mother after this and almost believed that she deserved what she got for being so damned weak. His thoughts turned back to Jennifer. She was not weak, he could tell; her confidence and beauty stood clear. David didn't deserve her.

Jack decided not to confront David. His sister was more important. If he did talk to David about it, it may give him hope that he could go back to Jennifer.

Jennifer.

That was a name, a real woman's name. He had said it out loud on the drive home. 'Jennifer. Jack and Jennifer. Jennifer and Jack. Jennifer. Jennifer Pardue.

Jennifer Pardue.' He was going to have Jennifer. She deserved him, Jack, not David, the poor fool who was obsessed with his studies. Jennifer looked like she needed a real man. He would have her.

For the next few days, Jack couldn't think of much else and decided it was time to go down to Tandaro to see if she had the same effect on him in person.

Parking a few paces from Jennifer's home, Jack lit a cigarette, his usually calm demeanor a little frayed. He looked at the time and if he guessed correctly, it would be time for most people to go to work. He hoped Jennifer worked or else he may be waiting out here for who knows how long! He turned on the radio and hummed absently to Sinatra; Jack preferred the oldies' station with the old crooners, the real men, not the men of today, with their long, bleached hair and make-up, for goodness' sake—he shook his head at the thought of it.

He was tired. He had spent a rough night on the sofa of Teresa, one of his distant cousins who lived a half hour from Tandaro. Granted, they didn't know he was visiting, so were unprepared, but poor cousins always had a way of making room for the richer of the lot at a moment's notice or less. After a quick shower and a promise to keep in touch more regularly, Jack was on his way to see Jennifer early the next morning. Now, he sat awaiting her appearance, trying to quell the anticipation that was rousing his thoughts.

Three cigarettes and a bar of chocolate later, she strolled through the gate. He couldn't see her very clearly, but it was enough to make him shift in his seat. She wore fitted jeans that had been rolled up to just below her calf and black flats. Her blouse was a pale yellow—a color he thought looked like vomit, but made Jennifer look exquisite to him—and had her hair tied up in a high ponytail with yellow ribbons dangling through her mulberry locks. She walked in the opposite direction to where he was parked and he turned on the ignition.

Jack decided to follow her. Visiting the place where she worked, wherever that was, was better than showing up at her front door without reason. He stayed behind her at a reasonable distance, trying not to look too suspicious; people were emerging from their houses preparing for work. He pulled over every little while, ensuring he didn't lose her. He prayed she wouldn't turn around. She didn't.

Fifteen minutes later, she walked into a coffee shop. *So, she's a waitress then?* Well, he had a lot more to offer. As he veered into a car space, she emerged from the coffee shop, carrying a small brown paper bag.

'Oh, okay …' he said to himself and began to

reverse out. Even as he was moving out, he saw her duck into another shop. Would she come out again? He reclaimed his car space and watched the flower store which was already open, buckets of flowers and greenery surrounding the doorway. A sign made from fake red flowers on the window announced *Gateway Florist*.

*Gateway to what?* thought Jack. *This is a little more than a one-horse town.* He waited and watched. He could see part of the window at an angle and every little while, he could see a flash of yellow go past. He decided that she must work there. He needed a cup of coffee desperately and decided to get one first before he met her.

A thought struck him. Would David have mentioned him to her? Maybe he should use another name. Then he smiled; every third person had the name Jack. He thanked his mother softly for giving him a common name. He turned the rearview mirror to face himself and surveyed the reflection. He had been sitting in that car for a long time; his eyes looked a little tired.

He walked over to the coffee shop and ordered a black coffee, then surveying the baked goods, with the sumptuous aromas filling the little room, he ordered a croissant. He asked if they had a bathroom, which they did, and decided to spruce himself up a little while he waited for his order. Looking again in the mirror, he liked what he saw. Black hair, a square jaw, with a perfect set of teeth, and eyes that made most women swoon. Yes, he would win her over.

As he sat sipping his coffee, which, irritatingly, burnt his lip, he began to get nervous. What would he say to her? Would she smile and bat her lashes and make him fall for her spell the same way she, no doubt, had done with David?

David! What was he doing? He loved David. David was his friend. They had grown up together and were almost like brothers. Almost, he reminded himself. Jack finished the croissant and began to read the papers that was strewn on the table; he needed to calm down. The older woman behind the counter called to him.

'Sir, you want another?' she asked, gesturing at the croissants. He looked up and nodded. He needed more time.

****

Back in Maybury, Jack tried not to think about his failed adventure; he balked when he thought of it. He didn't even have the guts to talk to her. He had gone right up to the door and as he began to open it, he heard the tinkling of a bell and came face to face with Jenifer who had opened it from the other side. She looked up at him and laughed.

'Sorry,' she had said and opened the door wider on her side to allow him to enter. She had then flounced past him without a second look. He stood there staring at the back of her and felt his stomach swim. He felt someone tap him on the shoulder, someone asking if he needed help.

*Yes, I need help,* he thought. He mumbled something and strode out. He felt foolish. He got back into his car and banged on the steering wheel angrily. *What an idiot I am, acting this way over a girl, a stupid, dumb girl!* He was frustrated with himself. *And David, how could I do this! Forget her,* he thought vehemently. He turned on the ignition and drove all the way back to Maybury, only stopping on the way once, for a fuel refill and to empty his bladder.

Jack did not forget Jennifer. In fact, he thought about her incessantly. He wanted to know about her, what she was doing, who she was seeing, and he decided that he would keep tabs on her through Teresa. Although Teresa did not know many people in Tandaro, she was resourceful and trustworthy and gave Jack the information he wanted. The more he knew, the more he wanted her. But he knew her heart was with David. He saw that clearly, when she had sashayed past him without a second glance.

Jack would wait; he was patient. It wasn't like he was giving anything up. He still had his girls. He had one in every town wherever business led him. He had hoped that he may forget Jennifer in time, but whenever he was with one of his girls, that laugh of hers floated up to him. It made him angry and excited at the same time. She didn't even know he existed.

In the next year, Jack and David's friendship was strained. Jack didn't want it to be, but he knew that they were both in love with the same woman. He could barely look at David for fear of revealing himself. He had always turned to David as a confidant and friend, but his guilt over his feelings about Jennifer and the fact that he was keeping an eye on her made him keep his distance.

He also felt betrayed by David. Not just for the sake of his sister, but Jennifer was in love with him, which ruined Jack's chances with her. No woman had denied him before and yet, this attracted him to her even more. How could she not have seen him? It was because of David. He knew these thoughts were illogical, but he could not help how he felt. So, Jack and David slowly became estranged and when he went to visit his sister in Boston, although he missed David and wished that they could become close again, he avoided him and found himself resenting him more and more.

When Dell died, he knew nothing would tie

them together again. They were too far apart. He grieved, not just for his sister, but for his friend too. At the funeral, he had wanted to talk to David, to try to find something that would bring them back together, and had approached David when he saw him step out of the church. But as he got closer, his emotions got the best of him and he blurted out something to him—he could never exactly remember the last thing he said to his best friend—and he turned around as quickly as he could before David could respond.

That evening, after the wake, when the house was quiet and all that could be heard were the intermittent cries that came from his mother's room, Jack sat at the dinner table, brandy in hand, and sobbed.

Jack had lost track of Jennifer once she had moved away from home. He knew she was somewhere in New York City, but he didn't know where, and he began to focus on his work more and more. His role in the family business had become larger following the death of his sister, when his father had to relinquish most of the control of the company.

His father's health was declining, cirrhosis of the liver had been diagnosed the previous year, and the prognosis, although allowing him a few more years, had left him in ill health and in an even worse temper. His mother, distraught with grief, needed him more than ever and Jack spent his time between Maybury and New York City, where he began to take control of the company.

****

Jack had begun seeing a woman, a journalist from New York, whom he met at a conference. Her name was Arlene Newell and she too came from a background made of money. They got along well and Jack felt that he had finally made inroads in ridding Jennifer from his mind. He still thought about her, but the attraction he felt to Arlene was strong, stronger than he had felt for any other woman besides Jennifer. He also felt she was of good stock and they would breed well. She was smart and had good business acumen.

Arlene also stood up to Jack and he thought that was a good thing, as most women gave him whatever he wanted and he despised a weak woman; he had lived with two of them for most of his life. He admired the strength that Arlene seemed to possess. Standing at five foot eight, she was attractive, her sharp blue eyes knowingly piercing. He felt that she would be perfect for him. They divided their time between Maybury and Manhattan and he soon began to have hope of forgetting Jennifer entirely, and not four months after first asking her out, he began to think about a future with her.

'Jack,' she said, when he brought her home after dinner and a stroll through Central Park, two months after their first date. 'Why me?'

'Why you, what?' asked Jack, surprised at her frankness.

'You have women throwing themselves at you.'

'You're good for me, Arlene. We're the same kind of people.'

'That's terribly unromantic,' she exclaimed, clutching her chest in indignation.

'I am definitely falling in love with you,' he said and moved to kiss her.

'Well, it's too late for me,' she replied. 'I'm already a lost cause.' She let him kiss her lips and pulled him into her apartment.

At twenty-two, Jack felt he had sown his wild oats and thought Arlene was the one. Why wait? His parents welcomed her, happy to have a girl roaming the hallways of their home again, and he of course charmed her parents and brother, as he knew he would. They had a similar sense of humor and wanted the same things in life, two point five children and two houses, one in Maybury and one in New York. They barely argued over a thing and Jack really felt that this was it. He was excited about life and believed that although he may not be shouting his love from the rooftops as David had been with Dell, he was in love with Arlene. Then he sniffed. David had never been in love with his sister, so all that really meant nothing.

He regretted not having David around anymore. He thought about him often and even picked up the phone to call him a few times, but too much water was under that bridge. He couldn't go back.

It was time to move forward, to ask Arlene to be his bride. Jack needed to buy an engagement ring, one that would be big enough for his future wife, but not too ostentatious. He worried that she wouldn't be happy with it, even though he knew she wouldn't be so crass as to say so, and then would be stuck with something that she hated. *Why were women so difficult?!*

Browsing through a store in New York, he hovered around the engagement rings, unsure of what Arlene would like. Her taste was 'rich but understated,' what she had hinted at when they talked about jewelry. 'Whatever that means,' he said to himself and shook his head as he walked into the glittering store, not knowing where to begin his search. He decided to ask the eager store clerk for help and she excitedly ran into the back room and came out with a number of magazines and brochures. She asked him to take a seat on a plush sofa and peruse the magazines at his leisure. He was not entirely comfortable with this scenario and decided against it; the quicker this process was, the better, so he stood at the counter leafing through the brochures, irritated that this had to be so complicated.

Oh, how he wished he had David with him. David would decide for him, he would calm him, he always had. Pauly, his friend from work, although always ready for a good time, didn't understand him like David had. David had accepted him, no matter what, and had not just put up with his shit, but had also called him on it. He would be perfect to advise him, not just on the ring, but also on his decision.

He shook his head again. No point thinking about that now. He had seen two rings that he felt Arlene would love, but he couldn't decide. Frustrated, he closed the brochure … and stared at it. Jennifer stared back at him, her mouth smiling, her eyes teasing. He picked up the leaflet and peered more closely at it.

'Sir, do you need anything else?' the assistant, a little frustrated by Jack's indecision, was saying. Jack held the paper closer to his face and felt his heart thud loudly. His stomach was churning and he moved to the seat that was offered to him before.

'Sir, sir, are you okay?' the assistant pressed.

Jack waved her away and sat staring at the picture. Jennifer's face took up most of the space on the page and she wore nothing but jewelry, arranged in just the right way to save her modesty. She was even more beautiful than he remembered and she struck his heart just as hard. He looked at the assistant. 'Who is this person? Does she work exclusively for this store?' he asked, pointing to Jennifer.

'Oh, I don't know, she's a model, but I don't know if she works for us,' the assistant stammered.

'Well, find out, dammit!' he barked at her and she quickly scurried into the back room.

He looked at the photo again and ran his fingers over it. His heartbeat was returning to normal and he began to take stock of himself. He got up and left the store, brochure in hand. He headed for Arlene's home where she lived with her parents, just two blocks away, and stopped suddenly.

'What am I doing?' he said out loud. He turned around and headed back to his suite. He was to take Arlene out to dinner, before going to see *42nd Street* straight after that. He had intended to propose at the end of the show on their short walk home.

Jack hailed a cab and went straight back to his suite. Clutching the brochure tightly, he made himself a drink. He sat down on the settee and looked at the page again. The now crumpled face of Jennifer still stared back at him mockingly. Her eyes were as green as emeralds and her lips, full and slightly open, were inviting him. He swore and crushed the brochure, hurling it against the wall. He took out a card from his wallet and dialed a number.

# CHAPTER 10

*Jennifer*

Lounging by the pool in Miami, Jennifer sipped at her cocktail, a yellowy-green concoction with a rainbow umbrella sticking out of the top. She was hungover and Jed had told her that 'the hair of the dog' would make her feel better. Jennifer didn't like alcohol very much, but sweet liqueurs tasted nice, so she lay there sucking on the straw.

She looked about her; there were not very many people around and that satisfied her. She looked at her wrist; damn, she had forgotten her watch. She never went anywhere without a watch, but that stupid new thing was so heavy and bulky, she had to remove it or else it would poke at her all night. It was a gift from Haze, but she missed the simple round-faced, black-banded watch that her mother had given her.

She missed her mother. She needed to call her;

they hadn't spoken for a few weeks. Judy now had a telephone, and had also moved to a bigger place, and they talked often, but lately she had been so busy …

A shadow fell over her and she raised her head, carefully shielding her eyes from the sun with her free hand.

'Hey, baby.' It was Jed.

'Hey, yourself,' she returned, trying to smile, but her head was thumping and it took a great effort to even look up at him. Jed looked down at her and laughed.

'You're awake, good. You need to start getting ready soon.'

'Why, what's the time?' she moaned back. 'My head hurts.'

'I know, Jenny, I know, but we have to get going soon.' He patted her hair and gave her a sympathetic look. 'I'll give you something to help, wait here a minute.' Jed skipped away.

*I'll wait,* she thought, *but take your time.* She liked Jed. Jed was her assistant, hired by the agency, and he had never asked her for anything. Well, he didn't want anything like that from her anyway. She smiled, thinking about some of the conversations they had had. Oh, the scandal! Jed, the tough guy, with the even tougher name; if only they knew!

She let out a laugh and immediately regretted it.

How much had she drunk last night, or was it closer to the early morning? She tried to remember it all but could only recall bits and pieces. It was the wrap party for the Haze campaign. They had spent the entire weekend in the hotel, and Saturday night was the big party, the one where all the big people came to hobnob.

Jennifer was the star of the show. It was her first major advertising campaign and she had spent the last two months shooting magazine covers, brochures, and television advertisements in places all over the States. She had shivered through a photo shoot in North Dakota and had almost burnt her skin in Florida. Luckily, they didn't need her to travel overseas. She had no interest in leaving the US. She wanted to be close to home. Close to David. It had been three months since …

She shook her head, something she did often to remove him from her thoughts. It didn't really work, but she still tried.

Jed returned with a glass of icy water and two little red pills. 'Here,' he said, offering them to her.

'What are they?' she asked and moved her head away.

'It will help you with the headache.'

'Jed, I'm okay, I could use some aspirin.'

'Sweetie, this is better, it will make you feel really great. You will be up and ready in no time,' he insisted.

She took the pills and looked at them. She turned them around in her palm and then threw them on the little table that sat next to her.

'Thanks, Jed, but no, thanks; I have to be able to think. I have to have my wits about me. All those crazies, they will be there again. Owww, it hurts so much.' She moaned again and lay her head back on the pillow.

Jed looked at her thoughtfully and nodded. 'Two aspirin coming right up,' he said and flounced away again.

*Jed*, she thought, *always there*. From the time she had met him; how long had it been? Three months, four? It felt like two years, she had done so much in the last few months. It was getting close to winter again, but here she was, lying in the sun in Florida. Yes, the work was tough, but it did come with perks. Jennifer didn't feel like it was a perk right now. Her head ached, her body more so, and her feet; well, she had lost feeling in them halfway through last night. She scrunched up her toes and felt shooting pains course through them.

'Any chance of a massage before we leave?' she called out to Jed. No reply. She closed her eyes and could feel sleep coming over her. The shadow on her face opened her eyes and she glared at Jed's jaunty face in front of hers. How could he be so alive after last night when she was half dead? She shook her head again.

'Ouch,' she said, wishing she hadn't.

'What's the matter, baby?'

'The aspirin,' she said, just as his hand placed two white pills in her palm. 'Thank you, Jed.' She swallowed the aspirin and downed it with the rest of her cocktail. 'I'd better start getting ready. Maybe another shower, I think.' She eased herself out of the banana lounge and Jed supported her by the elbow.

The hot water scalded her skin, but she was already beginning to feel better. She thought about having to socialize with the throngs of people, most of whom she hadn't met, but there were going to be some familiar faces there too.

Jennifer paused. She thought about the man she had met last night. She tried to remember his face, but he kept running out of her mind. There was something about him that drew her to him. What was his name? She didn't know and she wasn't sure he had even told her. They had chatted at the bar, not really chatted, just acknowledged each other with a smile and a hello, but he dripped with charm.

Jennifer hadn't really been seeing anyone seriously but had gone on dates and had begun to enjoy the company of men. They came in droves and she accepted many invitations, but they didn't go any further than a date or two with the same one. David was always in her head.

'Damn you,' she said out loud.

The day David had left her life, Jennifer had called Petriol Management, who immediately signed her on. She knew her life had to change. She felt she was rotting away, waiting for something that was never going to be. She stayed at Jang for another week and Joe, who was very fond of her and didn't want to let her go, was very gracious. He knew Jennifer was destined for more and he made her promise to visit often. She agreed. He had made her first couple of years in New York so much easier than it could have been.

The moment she was signed to Petriol, the jobs came in scores. Jed, whom she had met on a previous shoot, when she freelanced, took her under his wing and bargained for the best jobs for her. Under his watchful eye, Jennifer was never taken advantage of and she felt herself very lucky as she had heard various horror stories from other models who had not been so fortunate. She had only done two runway shows, but her face was made for photographs. And she preferred the relatively easier atmosphere than the hustle and bustle of the runway.

Jennifer thought of the next jobs that Jed had lined up for her. She couldn't remember what right now, she just knew she had a couple of weeks off after tonight.

*After tonight,* she sighed, *just get through tonight.* She was so tired.

Angel wouldn't come tonight. She had 'a previous engagement,' she had told Jennifer last night, and had left the party early. She missed Angel. She didn't see her very often and it was always for only a few minutes at a time. Jennifer's time was not her own anymore, not if she wanted to become successful. She resented Angel, at times, for being happier than her, for having someone she loved, who loved her back. Jennifer had moved out of their apartment, that beautiful little crap box, that was a symbol of her independence, and Neville had moved in soon after. She had made sure that Angel was not stuck paying the rent by herself, although Angel was earning much more now, working at a boutique hotel. Yes, a lot had happened in the last three months since she banished David from her life.

Jed was calling out to her. The hairstylist would be here soon, so she had better hurry up. She had been in the shower for a long time. She looked at her fingers that resembled raisins and stepped out.

****

Mingling was hard work tonight, but Jennifer smiled her way through it, chatting and laughing with some people she knew and others that she didn't. But she was getting the hang of all this schmoozing; it was part and parcel of the game.

It was when she was talking to the wife of one of her bosses that she looked up and saw him again. He was talking to another man, one of the investors in Haze, who was laughing, a gruff, booming laugh that echoed through the hall, which had caught Jennifer's attention. The man who had made this man laugh was leaning his elbow on a table, a bemused expression on his face.

The man from yesterday! She wracked her brain, searching for a name, trying to remember if he had even introduced himself, but she could only remember his voice, smooth as silk, not what he had said.

Jennifer excused herself from her conversation and walked directly past him, a little tingle in her tummy. He glanced at her as she did and gave her a quick smile, still engaged in the conversation with the laughing man. She went to the bar and asked for a soda. She was determined not to get drunk tonight. Although she never behaved badly when drunk, the thought of the next day was unappealing to her—she was still recovering from last night. She looked around the room while she waited for her drink, taking in the atmosphere.

It was a smaller affair than last night, where the

party was held in the grand ballroom, but she was starting to recognize some of the faces. No one approached her as she stood at the bar, sipping her drink. She was hoping no one would. She wanted to escape early and get a good night's sleep. The room, a penthouse apartment, was dimly lit, and she found herself watching the man. Lulu, another model, just a little older than Jennifer, strolled over to her and began chatting with her.

It was then that she could see, out of the corner of her eye, the man looking at her. She could feel her face reddening and was startled by her reaction. Lulu excused herself and Jennifer decided to go out onto the balcony. As she walked past him, she lightly touched his elbow with hers and swished past.

Jennifer had avoided looking at the moon but had gotten used to it existing in the same universe as her. She didn't speak to it anymore as she used to; there was no point. When she got to the balcony, she gave it a quick glance of defiance, turned around and looked directly at him and curled her lips in welcome. He smiled back.

****

Jack was everything Jennifer could have

dreamed of in a man and more, but he wasn't David. Handsome, charming, with a fantastic physique and a smile to match, one would think he was a playboy, but Jennifer saw a man who was committed, serious, and someone who she could be with for the long haul.

When he had followed her onto the balcony a few minutes after she did, as she had hoped he would, she had been pleasantly surprised by his gallantry. He had held out his hand for hers and she had given it, suddenly picturing David and how he had kissed it when they first met. He held it lightly and kissed it, looking up at her as he did. She was suddenly shy.

'Jack,' he said simply.

'Jennifer,' she said back and opened her mouth to dazzle him with her smile. She was surprised at how much she wanted to impress him. He held on to her hand and she let him.

They had spent most of the evening together on the balcony, except for when Jack had gone in to fetch his jacket for she was getting goosebumps from the chill. It was then that she looked at the moon, mostly cloud-covered, and she dared it to lead her life. She didn't want to go inside; she didn't want to break the spell this man had on her and she already knew that she had on him.

They talked of their jobs and their lives and

Jennifer was intrigued by his lifestyle and the thought of living in the country. David lived in a country town too.

'It sounds so wonderful,' said Jennifer when he described the fields and barns. 'Riding horses for a living!'

'Well, I do love to ride, but it's more than that.'

'Oh, of course,' she said, embarrassed that she sounded like an ignorant woman. 'It just sounds so different from anything I have lived.'

'You must visit me there, then,' he said, curling his lips in amusement.

Jennifer reddened. It was too soon to be talking in that way. 'Have you been married?' She glanced at his left hand and was relieved there was no band or even a tan line. She was irritated with herself. Her conversation was taking an awkward turn; it had been a while since she was actually attracted to another man, and this one, so calm and collected, was playing with her brain.

'I'm not as old as I look,' he joked.

'I didn't mean that,' she said, flushing again. She thought about how to change the subject. 'Tell me about your family.'

'There's my father and mother,' he said and then his eyes took on a sad, faraway look. 'And I had a sister ...'

'Had?'

'She passed away recently. We were very close.' He bent his head and Jennifer saw a man who could show her his vulnerability; his openness was inviting. She moved closer to him at this and took both his hands in hers. She brought them to her lips and kissed them.

Jennifer was feeling things she hadn't felt in a long time, not with another man, and she knew she had to get rid of David from her mind, or risk losing someone who may finally make her happy and erase the memory of David from her mind. Or at least dim it, until it faded away.

At the end of the evening, nearing dawn, in fact, Jennifer opened her eyes to find her head in his lap; she had fallen asleep on a cushioned bench. It was cool, but she had Jack's coat spread over her and she looked up at him. He was gazing down at her and his expression, so intense, so powerful, gave her shivers, except she wasn't sure if it was from excitement or fear. His look was deep, and his brows were furrowed, as if trying to work something out. She raised herself quickly from his lap and looked around. It was quiet. Nothing moved. She looked back at Jack, whose smile was one of amusement.

'What time is it? Where is everyone?' she asked, settling her hair that she could feel was mussed.

'Left, everyone has left. It's only us here, and the barman, packing up, I think. You were sleeping so peacefully, I didn't have the heart to wake you.' He stood up and brushed his creased pants.

'Oh, I'm so sorry.'

'Don't be, I rested too. And the night was so beautiful, I was happy to stay out here.'

Jennifer instinctively looked for the moon, but it was nowhere to be seen, and when she looked back at Jack, he had a small frown that quickly changed to a smile.

'Can I take you home?'

Jennifer put her hands on her hips and looked at him indignantly.

He laughed and held out his hands in a gesture of innocence. 'No, I just meant drive you home, nothing else.'

Jennifer looked sheepish. 'Sorry, there are a lot of nasties that I have had to contend with recently. I'm sorry. Anyway, I'm at this hotel, two floors down. You can walk me home,' she said with a twinkle in her eye.

As the elevator doors closed behind them, Jack moved toward Jennifer and drew her to him. She looked up at him, surprised, but also not so surprised and raised her arms around his neck.

'I want to see you again,' he whispered, pressing so tightly against her, she could feel his chest against her thumping heart.

Jennifer felt her knees give way and allowed him to support her. She looked into his eyes and saw something there that she wasn't sure of. She just knew she wanted to see him again too. She nodded, closed her eyes and leaned in, waiting for his lips to meet hers. He let go of her and moved away to press the button on the elevator.

'Which floor?' he said.

'Er, eighteenth,' she said, again feeling foolish, and faced the front of the lift. Then she began to get irritated. *What the hell was that about?*

Neither of them said a word even when the elevator door opened and he followed her to her room. She pulled out a card and inserted it into the slot. Opening the door, Jennifer stepped inside and turned around. He was right there in front of her, and he pulled her to him, kissing her deeply. She allowed him to and kissed him back, feeling him explore her mouth, tasting the residue of whiskey, mixed with mint. She could feel her knees weaken again and let herself go limp. He held her weight and she began to lead him inside. He frowned.

'Not tonight,' he said. Jennifer just stared at him. He took her hand again and kissed it. 'I must go, and you need your beauty sleep.' He had that twinkling, teasing look on his face again. Jennifer relaxed and moved to close the door. 'Sweet dreams, Jen.' Her face screwed up and she was about to say, 'Don't call me Jen,' but decided that David was not the only one who had claim to that name.

She closed the door and leaned against it. Then she began to cry.

Jennifer called her mother the next day. Everything was moving so quickly, first in her work, and now her attraction to this man she hoped she'd see again. Judy was her stability and she felt a warmth just talking to her.

'Darren finally did it!' Judy blurted when Jennifer asked how her sister was.

'Oh, Mom, that's so wonderful.'

'Oh dear, I wasn't supposed to let the cat out of the bag. She was supposed to tell you herself, but there is going to be a wedding soon and I'm just so excited.' Judy was squealing with joy. 'And they are not planning on making it a long engagement, so you better prepare to get yourself down here.'

'Oh, I can't wait!' Jennifer paused. 'Mother, I know it's too soon, but do you think I could bring someone?'

'You've met someone?' Judy's voice went up another notch.

'Well …' Jennifer hesitated. 'Maybe …'

'Oh, Jennifer!'

'Mom, it's early days,' said Jennifer, thinking it was really only one day since she had met Jack but she couldn't get him out of her mind. 'So I don't know yet.'

'I'm so pleased,' said Judy and Jennifer could picture Judy smiling in satisfaction. She had asked Jennifer about prospects in the last couple of years but didn't push the matter and Jennifer was grateful for that. Now she wished she hadn't jumped the gun. She may never see Jack again.

They talked some more and after she hung up, Jennifer felt a loneliness, for her mother, her sister, and even Tandaro. She decided to call Angel too. Things had been awkward with her friend lately, Jennifer not having enough time to really talk to her, catch up like they used to, and she wished they both had enough time to sit by the river, eating nuts as they used to. Jennifer wished Angel hadn't gone back to New York so soon after the party on Friday; that she'd pushed her to stay for a while. She missed her friend. But there was still the phone and Angel was surprised by the call.

'I saw you two days ago!'

'I know, but it's been so busy, I didn't have time to spend with you. I miss you.'

'Me too,' said Angel.

Jennifer filled her in on Elle's engagement and of

course, Angel would go too, together with Neville.

'And what about you? Angel asked. 'Are you bringing a date? Or will your plus-one be Jed?'

'Well.' Jennifer couldn't stop the smile that was forming on her lips. 'I met someone.'

'Someone? One of your dates?' Angel still tried to set Jennifer up with people she knew, but none of them stuck for more than one outing.

'No.' Jennifer didn't want to talk too soon, but she wanted to talk about Jack and who better to than her best friend? 'I met someone last night.'

'Last night?' Angel groaned. 'Is he going to last more than a night?'

'Oh, Angel,' said Jennifer, slightly irritated, but acknowledging her resistance to any other man. 'I think this is different.'

'Tell me more!' Angel sounded enthused. 'Wait, let me make a coffee and you can tell me all about it.'

Jennifer told her of the handsome stranger who had resisted trying to get into her bed, the chivalrous gentleman, who had kept his hands to himself and treated her like a lady. The man who she wanted desperately to see again.

'Does that mean ...'

Jennifer rolled her eyes. She knew what Angel was thinking. 'He may be the one ... to help me forget.'

'Oh, Jenny,' said Angel. 'I know it's too soon, you only met the man last night, but I haven't heard you so excited about someone that wasn't … you know … him.'

'I am,' said Jennifer, frowning. There was something about Jack she couldn't quite put her finger on, something he was holding back.

'Well, I'm glad. I thought David was the one too, I really did. But I think we both know the stars are never going to align for you. Besides, I want my friend back, the happy, crazy person I used to know.'

'I'm sorry, Angel.' Jennifer knew she had been moping about David for too long and her friend bore the brunt of her moods.

'I'm just glad I have you back. This is great, Jenny. I hope this works out for you.'

It was to be another day before Jennifer heard from Jack. In that time, all manner of scenarios went through her head. Why hadn't he called? Did she not let him know she was interested? Was he just a playboy? She wished she hadn't jumped the gun and told Angel and her mother about him. She went to bed that night, Jack and David both in her head, angry with them and even more furious with herself.

When the phone rang in the morning, Jennifer

was still in bed and lazily picked it up, assuming it was Jed calling to check on her.

'Good morning, Jen.' Jack's voice came through the line and Jennifer sat bolt upright.

'Hello, handsome stranger,' she couldn't help replying.

When Jack arrived to pick her up at seven in the evening, Jennifer had already visited the moon, which was practically non-existent, and she felt it was a sign. But she had been worried about how she was going to feel when she saw Jack again. She was so very attracted to the man, but she thought that perhaps it had been a one-off. The mood, the drinks, not that she had very much anyway, the night sky … She was nervous too. Perhaps he wouldn't be attracted to her anymore either. She took extra care with her make-up and wore a long black skirt with a slit on the side that accentuated her shapely legs, and hoped that he liked more than just the way she looked.

She stared in the mirror and saw the face of David smile at her, an encouraging smile, one that told her to have a life.

'Fuck you!' she said to the image angrily. She worried about how she would really feel at the sight of Jack again with David running around in her brain.

But once she had come down to the foyer, where

he was waiting for her, the hair on her arms stood on end. She watched him walk to her and could see the heads of people turn. He planted a kiss on her cheek and held out his arm for her to link hers into. They glided through the foyer like royalty, every eye on them. They looked like they were born to be together.

Jennifer only had three days left before leaving for New York, where she would be working on a new catalogue for *Harper's*. She was happy that she was returning home, but also felt like she was ending her fairy-tale romance, although Jack assured her he would be in New York in two weeks. It was on the last night that Jennifer invited Jack into her suite. After pouring him a drink, she switched on the radio, turned on the fire, and they sat together on the sofa with Jack humming softly to Nat King Cole.

'I'm going to miss you so much,' she said and buried her head in his chest. Jack didn't answer, he just stroked her hair. She looked up at him and he craned his neck back to look at her properly. She sat up. 'What?' she said.

He put down his glass and faced her. 'I love you,' he said directly. Jennifer didn't reply but moved forward and kissed him. She began unbuttoning his shirt and felt him remove the clip from her hair. Jack was masterful. She had not been intimate with anyone after David and did not have anyone else for comparison, but Jack knew what he was doing. They made love on the carpet and Jennifer was taken by his prowess. Afterward, they lay facing the fire, Jack's arms wrapped around a very contented Jennifer. She heard his breathing become heavier and she let a tear escape.

David. Always there with her. No matter what.

'I love you,' she said softly and felt Jack squeeze her closer.

New York was the same as she had left it. It was home and always felt like home. She stopped to breathe in the air from the cab to her front door and looked at the lights that invaded her living room on most nights— she was home. She was happy to be back, but she missed Jack already. He would be arriving in a couple of weeks, but she was to begin work and would be quite busy, so hopefully time would fly. Her first day back, she took a long bath and then she went to see Angel.

Her friend was now someone's fiancée, and Jennifer was ecstatic. Of course, she would be her maid of honor, but the wedding would need to wait. Neville wanted a traditional affair and they needed to save their money as they wanted all their family and friends to be there. Angel was to be married in New York, which also meant bringing her own family and putting them up for a few nights. Jennifer offered to help, but Angel wouldn't hear of it.

'We want to do this on our own, but I want you right there with me,' she had said.

They had dinner together and Angel could see that her friend was excited about Jennifer's future too, especially one with Jack in it. None of them mentioned David for fear of resurrecting the past.

When Jennifer returned to her apartment, she noticed that the kitchen light was on. She was sure she had turned it off, a habit from her childhood of trying to save on electricity bills. She opened the door slowly and put her key through her fingers, walking cautiously through the hallway. She saw a shadow and backed toward the front door. As she did, she heard Jack call out to her.

'That you, Jen?'

She breathed. How the hell did he get in? But she found herself running to him and as she came around the corner to where the bedroom was, she saw him stand up and threw herself in his arms. It was just this morning that they had seen each other, but they hugged each other so tightly, it could have been forever.

'What are you doing here? How did you get in?' she asked when they finally tore themselves away from each other.

'I couldn't wait,' he said and stepped away from her. Then he dropped to his knees as she stared in bewilderment. 'Marry me.' He drew out of his pant pocket a ring with a solitaire diamond. Jennifer put her hands on her face in astonishment and no words came out.

'Jennifer?' Jack looked uncertain now.

'Jack, I don't know what to say. We haven't known each other for even a week,' she blurted.

'Why wait? I love you, you love me, I heard you last night. I know what I want and I want you.'

'Jack, oh Jack.' She dropped down to her knees and faced him. *Goodbye forever, David.* 'Yes, yes, Jack, I want to marry you.'

He slid the ring on her finger and she hugged him again, tears streaking the back of his light-blue linen shirt

# CHAPTER 11

*David*

When David had found out through Dell's mother that Jack was to be married, he felt happiness and pride. He longed to be reunited with his best friend and was hoping that marriage would mellow his old friend. He wanted to meet the woman who had finally tamed the bull.

Jack would not be returning home for his wedding but was having a small service in New York. David had hoped that Jack had put all the bad feelings behind him and would ask him to be his best man, but as the weeks passed, he wondered whether he would even get an invite.

After David returned from New York, following the best night of his life and the worst morning after, he threw himself into his studies and although he had many young women take an interest in him, he never gave them a second look. His aim was to complete his degree quickly so he could go back to Jennifer a successful man, someone who was worthy of her. He followed her career as much as he could and saw her star rising steadily. Every week he went to the drugstore and bought all the latest women's magazines and would trawl through them looking for photographs of her and each time he saw her face he felt a surge of pride for her success and a stab of guilt for leaving her broken.

He still felt for her as he always had. She still had that same power over him, even if it was just through pictures in magazines. He kept the picture she had given him, always tucked in his wallet, even though she didn't seem to be that young, innocent girl anymore. He took it out of his wallet often and gazed at her smiling face. The moon still waited for him and there wasn't an evening that he didn't go to it and there he would stay speaking to her, waiting for the day that he would reclaim her.

He also knew that she was part of the reason for his estrangement with Jack, that she had come between Dell and himself and that Jack resented him for it. He wished that Jack could have met her; perhaps then he would understand his feelings for her.

He sighed. Jack was his very best friend. He had to make things right. But when time passed and there still didn't arrive an invitation, he became worried and a few days before the wedding, he called Jack's mother.

'Oh, hello, darling David,' Cynthia exclaimed on hearing his voice. David felt another pang of guilt, as he did every time he spoke with her. He should call them more often, but he didn't have the heart to. It had been a nearly a year and Dell's mother's voice trembled whenever he talked to her.

'Cynthia,' he said. 'How are you keeping?'

'Not well,' she said, groaning. 'I'm an old woman now, I have aches and pains … but wait. Are you coming to the wedding?'

'Uh …'

'Didn't you get an invitation yet?'

'I guess not,' said David, his heart heavy. Clearly Jack could not let bygones be just that.

'Well, darling, you must come anyway.'

'I don't think it would be kosher to crash a wedding.'

'Oh, David, he misses you. I can see it. I know he does. He still talks about you. I don't know what happened between the two of you but enough is enough. Please come.'

'I don't think so, Cynthia. I don't want to be there if he doesn't want me there.'

'He does want you there. He has that silly man, Pauly, whom I can see he doesn't really care for. It would be the most wonderful gift if you were there. And it would be the perfect occasion to rekindle your friendship.'

David hesitated.

'For me, David. Please say yes. He has gone and gotten himself the most beautiful bride. He would want you to meet her.' She tittered. 'At least to rub your face in it.'

David laughed. 'Yes, I bet he would,' he said. 'Okay, Cynthia, I'll think about it.'

He hung up the phone after his conversation with Jack's mother and looked at the address. Back to New York City. A quick engagement, Cynthia had said. *Just like Jack*, thought David, and smiled. Cynthia was right. What better way to revive his friendship with Jack?

So, David drove back to New York on a cool Friday in November. He went to the same motel as he had done some months before and felt the same feelings as he had then: fear, apprehension, and longing. He wanted to see Jennifer so desperately and decided it was time. He would try to see her, try to explain everything to her. She still loved him, he knew that, but she had a wonderful career that was on a steady rise; how could he dampen her future with his pathetic studies and not a cent to his name? Maybe she would wait for him, even forgive him … he hoped.

The evening he arrived in New York, he went to her flat, the one they had raced to on that fateful night. *Did she still live there? Probably not,* he thought, *not with what she must earn now,* but he had to start somewhere. He stood at the blue door and knocked, while his heart pounded wildly in his chest. He waited for a while, the butterflies in his stomach struggling to burst through with each passing moment, and knocked again. There was no answer, so after strolling past Jang, which seemed as busy as he remembered, and walking through Central Park, where he sat down to think about what he should do next, David returned to his motel for the night, not having any idea of how to find Jennifer.

The next morning as he suited up for the wedding, he smiled, picturing the look on Jack's face when he saw him there. He envisaged Jack striding over and embracing him, welcoming him back into the fold. David frowned. *What if he didn't? Surely enough time had passed. But had enough time passed for that water to flow under the bridge?* He shrugged and took a breath. If he wasn't happy to see David, well, so be it; he wouldn't know if he didn't try. He had to try.

As he neared the church, winded from his jog, he could see a flash of white emerging from a Rolls-Royce. Several flashbulbs went off at the same time and he could see the bride shielding her face from them, the long veil over her face helping. Two large men and a woman, who looked somewhat familiar, quickly shoved the bride through the church doors and they closed behind them.

*Damn!* he thought. David was not the type of person who was ever late for anything, but his train had been delayed and even though he ran the rest of the way, he didn't make it. He pushed through the throngs of photographers wondering what the fuss was all about, but when he got to the large wooden church doors, he found them locked. He went around to the side of the building and tried the other smaller doors. All locked. *Churches were not meant to be locked,* he thought, irritated, and decided to wait at the front of the church until Jack emerged with his bride. Along with him were another couple who were also late and also trying the doors and David smiled at them and shook his head. They headed to the other side of the garden and sat on a bench.

David stood on the grass beside the driveway and lit a cigarette. He waited and watched the photographers being shooed away by the two large men. They didn't go far and David chuckled. Two cigarettes later, he saw the same two men make their way up the steps of the church, one of them speaking into a walkie-talkie. He watched the photographers close in again, getting ready for their shot. *The vultures,* thought David, and grinned.

The door of the church flew open and the cigarette that dangled from his mouth fell to the ground. He was about ten yards away and could see them clearly on the platform above the stairs as they stopped and gave a quick pose to satisfy the vultures. The same Rolls was parked right in front of the steps and Jack guided his bride to it.

As she bent to get into the car, Jennifer hesitated and glanced up, and suddenly David was gazing into her eyes that widened in shock and disbelief. They were still the most beautiful things David had ever seen, and he stared, his jaw hanging in confusion.

Jack, still behind her, followed her gaze, and now David turned his head to him, his heart trying to deal with the blows that left him weak. He saw Jack wince for a moment and then he pushed Jennifer into the car. He turned back to look at David and shut the door with a bang and walked to the other side. Another glance at David, a small bow of victory, and he disappeared into the car along with the woman David loved.

David continued to stare as the car slowly drove away and disappeared through the crowd of photographers and the wedding attendees. David could see Angel now, getting into another car, and other friends of Jack. When Jack's parents emerged from the church some minutes later, David backed away behind a large oak and allowed himself to drop on a bench beneath it.

He let it sink in. He couldn't comprehend what he had seen. Jennifer … and Jack! He leaned back in shock and stayed there for over an hour. When his pack of cigarettes was finished, the one he had bought just this morning, he finally pulled himself up and walked toward the city in a daze. He kept walking until he was lost, trying to fathom what he had just experienced. There was no pain, but he knew that would come. He had to go back to Boston and the sooner the better. He found himself on a busy street and stepped into the first bar he saw.

# CHAPTER 12

*Jennifer and Jack*

Giving birth was excruciating. She had heard the horror stories but did not expect what followed. Thinking about it later, she wondered which was worse, pushing something the size of a watermelon out of her body, or seeing the pain on David's face on the day of her wedding. At the time, she was at a complete loss as to what he was doing there, but she knew now. What an idiot she had been.

But then she looked at her beautiful baby boy, who although he looked exactly like his father, was anything but; she would make sure of it. She lightly touched the bruise on her arm, fingerprints that scalded her skin, and sighed. Their first anniversary was coming up and so much had happened since then, so much she couldn't wish away, not with this little bundle of love in her arms.

Her mind wandered to David again. She allowed herself to think about him now. There was no betrayal. He loved her and she knew it, but as Angel had once said, their stars were never aligned; they just weren't meant to be. She now also knew about Jack and David's history. He had told her the very night they were married, and in the most spectacular fashion. She shook her head at the thought, a bitter lump forming in her throat as she remembered the hopes she had for their life together.

The day of their wedding had started beautifully; the sun was shining when she tore the curtains to one side and she smiled at the world through the window of her apartment, her last day alone. She soaked in the bath, thinking of Jack and the life they would share together. Jack was a strong man, perfect in every way, and had treated her with nothing but respect and love. The way he gazed at her sent shivers down her spine, and a day without him, while he traveled for work, was spent in misery.

She lay her head on the rolled-up towel and closed her eyes. David's face came to her and she allowed herself to think of him; it was the last time she really could, she reasoned, and she remembered how they had met, the evenings they had spent in the barn, and the others where they had looked up at the moon and loved each other beneath it. She really had thought that he would be the one waiting for her at the altar someday. She felt a tear roll down the side of her face and she propped herself forward, scrunching herself into a ball. She hugged her knees and let herself cry.

It was only a few moments later when Angel barged in. 'What are you still doing in there?' she exclaimed. 'Come on now, we don't have all day.'

Jennifer took a deep breath and hauled herself out of the bath that was already becoming cold. There was still a little to do before the service. The wedding had practically organized itself in the short space of three months and Jennifer didn't really have to do much apart from approve colors, choose her dress, and now, she just had to make herself beautiful for Jack.

Her hair, pinned high on her head, topped with a diamond tiara, accentuated her high forehead and her dress, a fitting, off-the-shoulder, eggshell-white dress that fell in waves around her feet, accentuated her figure.

Angel let out a puff of air when Jennifer walked out of her bedroom, her shoes still in her hands. 'My goodness, Jenny, beautiful people are not meant to make beautiful brides. Jack better appreciate it!'

Jack had gasped in the same way when he saw her at the end of the aisle and Jennifer beamed with joy. She stopped for a moment and took it all in. Flowers, white and yellow, were propped on the end of every pew tied with green and black ribbon. In the front pew, she saw her mother sticking her neck out into the aisle, a smile on her face and a handkerchief wiping her cheeks. Sitting beside her, their necks also craned, were her sister, Elle and her fiancé, Darren. Elle had mockingly berated her for beating her up the aisle, but she knew her sister was pleased. No one thought Jennifer was going to find any man who could replace David.

Angel, her only bridesmaid, wore a yellow satin dress that hugged her figure and she walked ahead of Jennifer, looking back when she had reached the altar, urging her on.

Jennifer looked at Jack again and saw his eyes crease. 'Here Comes the Bride' began to boom from the large organ that sat on the side of the church hall and she began walking toward Jack, slowly at first, and then more confidently, and saw that his eyes were now shining, his mouth wide in a smile. She focused on him and when she arrived at the altar, he offered her his hand. She took it without hesitation.

The service had been short and sweet and Jennifer had not taken her eyes off him throughout the ceremony and he had kept her gaze just as steadily. After she was kissed by Jack, she turned around to see her mother, now openly sobbing, and her sister squeezing

Darren's hand. Angel was hopping from foot to foot in delight. She knew she was going to be happy.

Jack's mother and father were also present and Jack was pleased that his father was able to attend the wedding as he been very unwell lately. Jennifer also realized that someone else was missing from their party; his sister, taken so young, should have been there as well. She smiled at Cynthia who had taken to Jennifer immediately and Jennifer was already fond of the old woman who quite openly referred to her as her daughter.

Jennifer was a little rattled by Frank, whom she overheard warning Jack that Jennifer would be trouble, when she went to the porch to call them in for dinner one evening.

'Just because you don't know what love is, doesn't mean I don't,' Jack had retorted. 'I will have a happy life and a happy family.' His father had shrugged and gulped down his whiskey and Jennifer hurried out of the doorway, feeling like she'd intruded on a private family matter.

She wondered what that was all about, but when the two men came back into the living room, Frank had smiled at Jennifer and wished the couple well. She decided that what went on between father and son was not her business unless Jack chose to divulge it one day. She wasn't going to let anything get in the way of their happiness.

Now, as they walked back down the aisle, their fingers entwined, their faces were shining and all concerns were forgotten. Jennifer had never been so sure of anything, except …

Then, as she was about to step into the car, her spine tingled and instinctively, she turned her head and saw him.

Jack got into the car and turned to her; his face was ugly, he wasn't the person she saw at the altar, and she started. He gripped her hand and squeezed it so hard, she winced. She managed to halt a tear that threatened to fall.

They had driven to the reception in silence and she was happy for it. Seeing David had turned her world upside down again and she couldn't shake the sight of his face from her mind. What was he doing there? She could feel the tears welling again and looked out of the window. The trees rolled by and by all accounts, it was a wonderful day for November, but she didn't see the world around her. She couldn't shake the image of David from her brain.

The reception, held in a little rustic place fashioned like a cottage, set with brass and greenery, was beautiful and intimate, just right for their families and a few friends. Jennifer hadn't wanted a large wedding, even though Jack would have preferred it, but as there wasn't a lot of time to prepare for one, he indulged her preference, as she knew he would.

'This is perfect, Jenny,' said Angel, who sat beside her, surveying the room. Even with the amount of people in attendance, everyone seemed to be having a wonderful time, Pauly, Jack's best man, doing the Chicken Dance with zest, a group of people trying to copy him.

Jennifer nodded. Jack had still not uttered a word to her and she couldn't fathom why, even though she tried to talk to him, and when she reached for his hand, he recoiled, his eyes narrow, his mouth in a grimace. But her guilt overcame her and she excused herself and went to the little room reserved for the bride and groom that led off the main reception room.

She was angry—angry with David! Why did he ruin this for her? Angry with herself—for feeling this way, and angry with fate for ... Why couldn't she feel like this with Jack? He had been wonderful to her, she loved him, but not like ... She heard a knock on the door and Angel called out to her. She opened the door and let her in.

'Are you okay, Jenny?' Angel hovered at the door.

Jennifer sat at the dresser and looked down at

her pearl white shoes. 'David was there,' she said, looking for Angel's reaction through the mirror.

'David? Where?' Angel looked around.

Jennifer smiled. 'Well, he's not here,' she said. 'He was at the church, outside as we were leaving.'

Angel put her hand to her chest. 'Oh, Jenny. I thought this was done. Jenny, you have to forget him …'

'I thought I was done with him,' Jennifer cried. 'I love Jack, I really do. You know me, Angel, I wouldn't ever marry someone for the hell of it …'

There was another knock at the door, cutting her off. Jack poked his head in. 'Are you finished in here? Guests are asking for you.' His face bore a look of worry and irritation and Jennifer nodded, smiling broadly at him. She and Angel rejoined the party, but she couldn't shake the feeling that Jack was not himself. She put it down to the amount of alcohol he had been consuming. She decided it was time to join him; she needed something that would take her mind off David.

Jennifer was beginning to feel a little better when the MC called for the first dance. This song, she had chosen; she had danced to it as a young girl imagining her wedding day—'Could I Have This Dance?' With her head on Jack's shoulder, she closed her eyes and David's face flashed before her eyelids again. Jack tightened his embrace and she clung closer to his neck.

She recognized she probably had had a little too much to drink when she misstepped and Jack, to her surprise, straightened her a little too forcefully. She sipped on white wine for the rest of the evening, which she realized had not been the best idea, as when the car rolled away toward their honeymoon suite, after waving at their guests, she felt nauseous. They had to pull over so she could lean out of the car and she vomited right there on the sidewalk. Jack helped by rubbing her back, which she found irritating, and she wished they could just get back to their hotel to begin their lives as a married couple.

Once there, she felt a little better and Jack insisted on carrying her into the room and even though she giggled at his traditional ideas, she was nevertheless pleased about it.

In the bathroom, she dressed herself in a white-and-pink negligee and gargled furiously. All she could taste was vomit. *Ugh, not the perfect thing for my wedding night,* she thought. She looked at herself in the mirror and she immediately thought of David. She shook her head, trying to free herself of him again. She was not going to let him ruin her life … again.

Coming out into the bedroom, she saw Jack was waiting for her on the side of the bed and he rose when he saw her approach. She hesitated, feeling nervous and a little stupid for feeling that way. They had done this several times already and it was always wonderful. Her stomach turned again and she wished she had thrown up all of what was in her stomach, but the look on Jack's face, a tenderness he had not shown her all evening, spurred her toward him.

Jack placed his hands on her cheeks and moved to kiss her, but worried that her breath still smelled like vomit, she turned her head to one side. Jack dropped his hands and she turned back to him. She saw his face, angry and twisted, and recoiled.

He was suddenly upon her. 'I am not David,' he said and pushed her down on the bed, straddling her. Jennifer saw the menace that pierced through his eyes and a sudden terror beheld her. Before she had time to think about what that meant, he had pushed his mouth on hers, hard, and she felt her shoulders pinned to the bed. She tried to wriggle herself free, but she couldn't, so she opened her mouth and bit his lip.

He stopped, a look of surprise crossing his face for a split second. 'You are *my* wife,' he said between gritted teeth and crushed her mouth with his again. She tasted blood and began to wiggle under him again, but he was so strong, she could barely move. He ripped the strap off her negligee and moved his face to her breasts.

'Jack, stop, what are you doing?' she began and

felt the sting of his hand across her mouth. Stunned, Jennifer lay there, panic engulfing her, unable to help herself. She was trapped beneath him and her best bet was to play along. He loved her and she loved him. Why was he being so violent?

'David!'

Jack suddenly stopped and Jennifer realized she had said his name out loud. Fear began to envelop her again and she remained frozen, looking into his eyes, which glared, venom seeping through them.

'You are mine,' he repeated and began to rip at the silk around her thighs.

'Jack, stop. Jack!' she screamed. She felt him thrust into her, hard and painful. She continued to call out his name and he looked into her eyes as he pushed hard, again and again.

When he had finished, mercifully quickly, he stopped to glance at her body, red raw, with pieces of pink silk flaked over her thighs, and rolled off her. He stormed into the dining room and she could hear the clinking of a glass. He was making himself a drink. Jennifer remained in the bed, stunned, unmoving, trying to work out what exactly had just happened. Then she began to weep.

She realized what this meant—she had just been molested. By her husband. On her wedding night.

A fresh bout of sobs broke from her and she began to count backwards to clear her mind, to assess the situation, to try to figure out what exactly had just happened.

She was married to this man. But she loved him, she really loved him. And what did he know about David? Did he know how she felt about David, even now? How could he? He had mentioned his name, but how did he know who he was? And why would it bother him enough to take it out on her? He had ex-girlfriends too; he had told her about Arlene, but that was in the past, they were each other's present, and future. Now she wasn't so sure.

Jennifer needed to go to the bathroom to clean herself up, she felt sticky, dirty, but she couldn't move; a terror kept her frozen to the bed. Soft music wafted through from the other room and she tried to follow the tune to calm her mind. Jack would probably be there for a while and she had a decision to make. She was scared—no, terrified—but she couldn't stay in this bed, not after what had just happened. She had to leave somehow, even if it meant facing his wrath again. She straightened her torn negligee and turned to the side. She needed a moment more. She wept softly.

She felt a hand on her shoulder and stiffened. A shift behind her; Jack climbed into the bed.

'Jen, baby, I'm sorry, I'm so, so sorry. You know how much I love you,' he whispered, his breath on her neck. She remained unmoving and squeezed her eyes more tightly. 'Jennifer, honey, did you hear me?' His voice trembled and he lightly shook her arm. She stayed frozen, gripping the covers to her chest. She felt him get off the bed, heard his footsteps padding around to her side of the bed. She opened her eyes a slit and found him kneeling on the floor, his face right before her, his eyes watery and bloodshot. He had been crying, that was plain to see, and he reached out and clutched at her white-knuckled fingers.

'Jen, baby, forgive me, please, please, forgive me,' he cried, tears now rolling down his face, which he didn't try to hide. 'I'm sorry, I was just so consumed with jealousy. It will never happen again, I promise, I love you so much, you have no idea just how much and for so long … Jen, Jenny, please, please, forgive me.'

Jennifer reared backwards and narrowed her eyes.

'It won't, I promise, never,' he continued. 'Never, I don't know what happened, I'm sorry, I don't know …' He put his head on his hands that were still attached to hers, and sobbed.

Jennifer's heart broke for him but an odd confusion still remained in her mind. She didn't reply to his soliloquy. She didn't know what to say, how to respond. What was she missing?

As if hearing her thoughts, which she was now fearful he could read, he put his chin on his hands and gazed at her; an expression she couldn't read lay on his face. 'David, I know about David.'

Hearing his name again, she wriggled her fingers out of his grip and sat up, leaning herself against the headboard, while Jack knelt at the edge of the bed, his eyes pleading with her, for what she still didn't know.

A sudden fury gripped her. 'What about David? What do you know about him, and what is there to know?'

Jack told her everything. About his childhood with David, about his sister, about him seeing her at Tandaro, everything. 'I tried when we first met. I really tried to somehow weave it into conversation. I knew you had to know, but I didn't know how.' He wiped at his nose and leaned on his haunches, his head low. 'And I didn't want to remind you of him, remind you that you may still love him.'

Jennifer listened, stunned and angry, but could feel his vulnerability and his love for her. 'You should have told me,' she said quietly, when he had finished.

'I couldn't lose you, I have loved you for so long, I couldn't risk losing you, to anyone,' he replied, looking more desolate than she'd ever seen anyone, not even David this afternoon. 'But now, I wouldn't blame you, not after … tonight.' She saw another tear fall onto his knee.

'Come to bed, Jack.' She sighed and reached out her hand, which he took and held so fiercely, she felt a pang of alarm again. Then he nuzzled his head into her chest with little sobs and she stroked his hair.

The next morning, Jennifer awoke to a bright light streaming into the room and for a moment, she thought it was the day of her wedding all over again. A jolt went through her body when she recalled what had happened the previous night and she felt nauseous. Oddly enough, she had fallen asleep almost immediately after they had both lain down, Jack's hand still clutching hers. Now she turned around and saw no sign of him and felt a sense of relief.

She looked at the clock on her bedside table: 11.30 a.m. Their flight to Niagara Falls didn't depart until 5:00 p.m. and she wondered whether they would be on it, whether there would be a honeymoon anymore. She stared at the ceiling, recollecting what had happened the night before, trying to put the pieces together.

David and Jack. They were friends and he had married Dell out of pity. He had done the right thing. But what had he gone through? He did love her and he was going to come back for her. But what was he doing at the wedding? Was he there for Jack or was he there for her? She thought of his face again, mangled with pain. It seemed to be ingrained in her mind, it was so clear.

*Oh, David! Why didn't you try harder? Why didn't you talk to me about it? I would have understood.* Then she paused. *Would I? Would I have let him go back to her with my blessing?*

Jennifer roused herself out of bed and a stabbing pain ripped through her hip when her foot hit the floor. She stumbled to the bathroom and shed her torn negligee. She regarded herself in the mirror and tears started to well. Her mouth hurt and she leaned forward to inspect more closely small dark spots on the white skin of her shoulder. A bite mark could be discerned; she couldn't remember when that had happened. Her thighs felt sticky and she wearily turned on the shower, letting the water scald her, while she scrubbed the taint from her body.

She thought about David. She loved him and knew that would never change, but she also loved Jack. She was now married to Jack. Jack had raped her. He had hit her, bitten her. Would he do it again?

No, she shook her head. She was sure he wouldn't, not after what he had said last night. He was overcome with jealousy and she could see why—God knows he had reason to be—but she could also see how he felt about her. She felt that way about David. She understood Jack.

Jennifer sighed and stepped out of the shower, wondering what she was supposed to do now. Rolling her hair into a towel and throwing on a bathrobe, she walked out into the bedroom. Jack was sitting on the bed, holding an enormous bunch of red roses. She halted, startled by his presence.

'Sorry you had to wake up alone,' he said, a smile ridden with guilt on his face, and started toward her. 'For you.' He offered her the roses, which she gingerly took. He leaned forward and kissed her lips.

'Jack, thank you, they're beautiful,' she said, smelling them. He took them back from her and placed them on the bedside table with one hand, while the other undid the sash on her bathrobe. She looked up in dread and clutched the robe together.

'It's okay, baby,' he said soothingly, his hands loosening her grip on the sash, and he pulled her gently toward him. She let the bathrobe fall from her shoulders and made love to her husband.

# CHAPTER 13

*David*

In the fall of '86, David graduated. He worked night and day to finish his degree, but once completed, he felt at a loss. He had been trying to keep so busy, that now he didn't know what to do with all this spare time. He wasn't even sure he wanted to be a psychologist anymore, but the thought of more study gave him pause to consider, then he realized he couldn't be a student forever. He had to do something more with his life. He secured a job at a high school in Boston, teaching physics, which meant he would be close to his parents and his brother, Phillip, who has just had his first child. He rented a small apartment in Wayland, fifteen minutes from his parents' home, and began his new career.

He had enjoyed teaching in the beginning, but he soon became restless. He knew he would not stay a teacher and decided to study at night, changing his major to a Master's in Business. He thought about Jack wryly as he put in his application—Jack had wanted him to do just this and he had always resisted, not believing he had the heart for it.

He thought of Jack. He had spoken to his parents a couple of times during the past year and although he didn't inquire about his situation or his new wife, they had volunteered information on Jack and Jennifer, completely oblivious to the events of the past few years. David didn't enlighten them and although they knew that things were still strained between Jack and David, Cynthia always held out hope that they would be close again. And even as his heart ached when they spoke of the newlyweds, he wanted to hear more, to know more. He wished the best for Jennifer and hoped she was happy and when Cynthia called him to relay the news of an impending addition to their family, he congratulated them while his heart wept. Of course he was happy for her; she wasn't the one who had ruined it all. He deserved this, and she deserved the best, even if that did mean his own best friend.

David had thrown away all the clippings and posters of Jennifer; he did that the moment he came back from New York with a broken heart and a new resolve, but he kept the old fading photograph with him always tucked into his wallet. When he walked past magazines with her face on the cover, or billboards, full-sized, life-sized, his heart always skipped a beat, but he smiled, pleased that her star was rising. He still visited the moon, but not as often as he used to—now it just made him sad. The hope was gone. He wondered sometimes if she still did it and hoped that she could still think of him sometimes without animosity.

David also tried to work out how Jack and Jennifer had met. What had happened there? He couldn't think of how they would have met. Pure coincidence? Surely not; it was too *much* of a coincidence. He tried to recall conversations, but nothing Jack had ever said had alluded to Jennifer, except when he had called her a floozy or something like that the day they rode together, when he informed him of her marriage to someone else—which hadn't even been true.

He considered that perhaps Jack had followed him back to Tandaro when David visited Judy, but no, Jack had known about Jennifer before that. It was the reason he went back, to find out the truth. He couldn't put it together, as many combinations of scenarios as he tried, but he did contemplate how he and Jack had steadily grown apart. It wasn't just about Dell. It had to be about Jennifer. Had they been together all this time? Surely not. He had been with Jennifer after Dell had died and she was clearly not with anyone then, not with the way she greeted him.

And Jack, his friend, his very best friend! How could he do that to him? He knew what he had done; it was clear by the look on his face in front of the church and his little nod of triumph. That had hurt. That hurt almost as badly as seeing Jennifer because Jack's betrayal seemed to be deliberate. Jennifer's shock at seeing him was written all over her face. He searched his mind for something, some inkling of the connection, and couldn't work it out and decided that he never would. He had to move on now.

Her name was Ness and David met her at night school. She was also doing her Master's Degree in Business and shared a class with him. Hailing from New York City, Ness, short for Vanessa, came from an affluent family and showed an interest in David almost immediately. She was tall and slim and had the same stately gait Jennifer had. He wondered if their similarities were what had attracted him to her in the first place but was surprised at how quickly he fell for Ness, so much so, that it was less than a month when he brought her to meet his family. She charmed them as he knew she would and he found himself wanting to spend all his time with her. Both were traditional and didn't want to move in together before they were married and they knew that would have to wait, at least until David finished studying, which he now wished he had.

Although he enjoyed teaching, he knew it was short term and got a job as an intern for a brokerage firm in Boston, but he was adamant that he needed to progress further in order to support a wife and he knew he wanted that wife to be Ness.

'I will take you any way I can,' she said when he expressed his plans. 'But you're right, Papa and Ma would love you more if you put a ring on my finger first.'

'That's the plan,' replied David. They were sitting on his porch in the late evening, long after the moon was covered with clouds. Her legs were thrown across his lap and he stroked them absently. 'Don't worry, honey. It won't be long.' He wished he could give her everything she wanted and for a moment, resented Jack for the ease at which he went through his life, not letting anything get in his way. He always had money to back him.

'It doesn't matter anyway,' Ness said with a laugh. 'I'm at your place all the time anyway. Luckily my folks are far away and don't know any different.' She frowned at him. 'Why can't we go to see them? They keep asking about you.'

'I don't know, Ness,' said David. Meeting her family, including her younger sisters, meant going to New York City, where they resided, and David did not ever want to see that place again.

'They are going to think you're a figment of my imagination,' she sulked and David smiled at her.

'We will, soon,' he said, knowing that he would have to face it at some stage if he wanted Ness to be in his life.

Five months into their courtship, there was no choice anymore. David received an official invitation, addressed to him, to the opening of a new gallery that Ness's father had invested in. It was called So-so and displayed two paintings by one of her sisters. Ness thought it was the perfect excuse to go and urged David to attend. Reluctantly, David acquiesced and it was in the spring of '87 that David returned to New York.

# CHAPTER 14

*Jennifer*

Jennifer didn't want to go, but she knew she had to. She needed her career back and it was good PR. Although she had regained her figure after the birth of Jack Jr., the time she had taken away from her career when pregnant had slowed the job offers. There wasn't a lot of work out there for pregnant models. She had done the odd face shoot, but toward the end of her pregnancy, her face was looking swollen and heavy and she also didn't have a lot of energy or inclination for it.

So, she took a hiatus from modeling. And other younger, thinner girls took her place. Jack told her to stay home, to be a housewife and a mother, but Jennifer knew she would be giving up any power she had by doing that. She would have loved to stay home with little Jack and when she began getting some jobs again, she would take him with her, along with his nanny. She couldn't give up her independence, and that meant working, even if it meant giving up time with her baby.

She sometimes wondered if Jack put those bruises on her to hinder her work, but she never let it stop her, always having access to the best make-up and make-up artists to hide it from the camera. She got strange looks on one occasion and when Jed asked her about it, she snapped at him and threatened to fire him. He had nodded, knowing full well that she needed him now more than he needed her. He had simply put his hand on her arm and said, 'I'm here when you need me.'

Jack had not struck Jennifer for more than two months after their wedding night, and after their honeymoon in Niagara Falls, she had convinced herself that it was a one-off, a moment of madness.

The honeymoon had been a mixed bag of love, laughter, and tears and she was still reeling when they arrived home two weeks later. She had started work almost immediately, despite Jack's protest.

'You don't need to work,' he said angrily when she told him that she was needed in Miami the week after they returned. 'It's not like we need money.'

Jennifer laughed. 'It's what I do,' she replied. 'It's my job.'

'But I have a job, a company,' he insisted.

'You didn't mind my modeling when you asked

me to be your wife,' she said, determined not to let him talk her out of it.

'Sure, but you needed to work then,' he retorted.

Jennifer conceded that he was right and thought about what staying at home all day would entail. It may work. She would have time to pursue other hobbies, such as drawing, and she thought she may perhaps join a health club and do some aerobic classes. She knew that this wouldn't fulfill her, but she decided that whatever made Jack happy, she would do. 'I have some contracts I can't get out of …'

'I can get you out of them,' he said, his eyes lighting up.

'No, Jack. A few months' work and we'll see,' she said with determination and saw his eyes narrow.

David's name had not been spoken since their wedding night and Jennifer hoped that was the end of that chapter. She had to focus on her new life. They had moved into Jack's apartment and Jennifer subtly added her own touches to it to make it her home and began to count the days until the end of the next shoot. In the meantime, she accompanied Jack to his business dinners and events and tried to enjoy being his handbag.

It was during one of these business dinners that Jennifer met Arlene. In a hall full of people, who all seemed to know each other, Jennifer had been left at the table while Jack schmoozed around the room. She was quite happy to sit by herself; she detested these events, with their fake flowers and fake people, and wished she could have been friends with some of the wives of Jack's associates. But none had tried to befriend her and she knew what they thought of her—an uptight princess who married beyond her.

Jennifer casually looked around the room and noticed Jack sitting at one of the nearby tables, talking intently with a tall, rather good-looking woman. She had seen Jack schmooze before, but something made her look more closely; this felt different. The woman, wearing a gray velvet, one-shouldered dress, cigarette in hand, was staring intently at Jack, her shoulders inclined toward him, hanging on to every word he said. As Jennifer watched, the woman suddenly leaned closer to him, and whispered something, her lips grazing his ear. She saw Jack chuckle with the familiarity of intimacy and Jennifer, slightly taken aback, continued to observe them, trying to size up the relationship.

She wasn't just anyone, thought Jennifer; Jack seemed to know her well, too well. As if by feeling, the woman turned her head and looked directly at Jennifer. Embarrassed, Jennifer looked away and tapped her fingers nervously on the table. She felt like a voyeur and was irritated she was made to feel that way. A minute later, Jack was by Jennifer's side again. She didn't mention anything about the woman, but took furtive glances at the lady. She noticed Jack do the same and felt a surge of jealousy but tried to quell it by talking about the weather and Jack seemed happy to discuss the unusually cold snap that had come their way of late.

It was during dessert when she felt a light tap on her shoulder and looked up to see the woman whom Jack was with, offer her hand to her.

'Hi, you must be Jennifer. I'm Arlene,' she said, smiling.

Jennifer took the outstretched hand and stood up. 'So nice to meet you, Arlene, I've heard so much about you.'

'Not all good, I'm sure,' Arlene snickered, throwing her head back, and looking at Jack who seemed to be nervous, something that he rarely showed. 'Well, I have to leave, but I didn't want to go without meeting you, Jennifer, the woman who managed to tame the wild man. Good luck and I hope we meet again soon.' She kissed Jennifer on the cheek and turned to Jack. 'Bye, darling, catch up soon,' she said and planted a kiss directly on his lips. She giggled, swung around, and waltzed away. Stunned, Jennifer looked at Jack, her eyebrows raised in question.

'Er, yes, that was, er, Arlene,' he stuttered.

'Yes, I'm quite aware of that,' she said and then she burst out laughing. 'Look at your face! Oh, Jack, I do love you.'

Jack frowned.

On the way home he was quiet, and Jennifer put it down to him being tired, as she was too. These events were tedious, but part of his job description. Once home, he became irritable, and Jennifer decided to go straight to bed. Jack seemed to be in a bad mood and began picking on little things.

'You didn't leave the heater on. It's freezing,' he grumbled.

Jennifer walked to the wall and turned it on. 'It won't take long,' she said and went to the bedroom. 'Come on to bed. You're tired.'

'Don't tell me what I am,' he growled.

Jennifer was a little taken aback at his tone but continued to the room without a word.

'Where are my gloves?' he shouted after her.

*What on earth does he want with his gloves at this time of night?* Jennifer thought, but looked around and found them for him, nevertheless. She placed them on the arm of his chair. Without even looking at them, he poured himself a drink and she said goodnight, hoping his mood would pass soon. The bed was indeed cold without him in it.

It was four in the morning when light flooded the room and Jennifer wrinkled her eyes and turned to see the silhouette of Jack in the doorway of their bedroom.

'It's your fault,' he slurred.

'Jack, it's late, come to bed,' said Jennifer and snuggled back into the blankets. 'And turn off that darned light.'

'You! You and him. I would be happy, but you!' He started toward the bed and Jennifer suddenly felt scared.

'Jack, Jack, baby, come to bed, you're drunk ...'

'I love you, I hate you.' He towered over her and waved his hands about, spilling whiskey on the bed and Jennifer dodged it.

'Don't run from me, you will never leave me, never, you have trapped me,' he said, putting his glass on the side table, and thumped at his chest. Flopping on the bed, he reached out and took her head in both his hands, pressing together hard.

'Jack, stop it, Jack, you're hurting me, stop,' she yelled, breaking free. She rolled over to the other side of the bed and sprang off.

In two strides, he had climbed right over and she tried to duck into the bathroom, but he caught her arm and swung her back onto the bed. She kicked at him, trying to aim for his groin, but he was already straddling her, pinning her down.

He bent close to her face and stared into her frightened eyes. 'You and that pretty face. Showing yourself all over the place. You're a tramp, nothing more, a whore, showing the world what you have. What if you were ugly? I could do that for you.' Jennifer squeezed her eyes shut and prayed for him to stop. She felt his weight lighten and opened her eyes to see a fist come at her. She blacked out.

She had crept away with nothing but her purse in the middle of the night when she came to and found Jack passed out. She headed straight to Jed's.

Jack had tried to call Jed and Angel and every other person that Jennifer knew, but she wouldn't speak to him.

'You can't go back, Jenny,' said Jed, knowing what had happened even though Jennifer wouldn't tell him anything.

'I know,' she sniffed. 'I know I can't.' She laughed mirthlessly. 'Divorced in less than six months. Wait till the tabloids get hold of that.'

'Who cares what they say,' said Jed. 'Besides, you'll be more popular than ever now that you're back on the market.'

Jennifer smiled. Jed always put a good spin on

everything. She was glad she insisted on keeping up with her modeling. Yes, she knew she had to leave him.

It was two days later when she was staying with Jed that Jennifer discovered she was pregnant.

# CHAPTER 15

## *Jack*

He was not in a good mood. He hated these events, but as Jennifer had to go with him to his, he felt obliged to do the same. He had tried to get out of it, but she hadn't been happy about that, insisting he at least show some support for her career. *Her career*, he thought. *If that's what one called flashing themselves around for money.* He could think of another word for it, but he admonished himself. He was being harsh because he was guilted into this thing that he had no interest in whatsoever.

A gallery opening, of all things! He liked art as much as the next person, but to spend a whole evening talking to these new-aged, new-fangled art lovers …

'I have nothing in common with these … these people,' he said, screwing up his face.

'Well, I have nothing in common with the people at your parties,' she retorted.

'They are not parties. It's business. It's necessary.'

'This is business too,' she insisted. 'I need to be seen. I need work …'

'You don't need work. You have everything you want and more.'

'That's not the point.' She crossed her arms and glared at him.

'Oh that's right,' he said with a smirk. 'You want to feel useful. This work makes you feel like you're contributing something …'

'Oh, don't analyze me,' she said and turned away from him. 'Go, don't go, whatever.'

He knew she was angry and he didn't want her to be. 'Okay,' he conceded. 'I'll go for a while, do the rounds, and then I have to go. I have a late business meeting.'

Jennifer turned back to him, her brows furrowed, and he could see she was trying to figure whether he had mentioned it before. He could see she didn't believe him, but she shrugged, and mumbled a thank you.

Jack, in fact, had arranged another appointment but it had nothing to do with business. Arlene would not be happy if he let her down again. She was getting annoying but she threatened to tell Jennifer about them if he didn't see her more often. He had to find a way to break it off with her, and gently.

He did love Jennifer. He had almost lost her that night and if she hadn't found out she was pregnant, he was sure she would not have returned to him. He had been angry and hurt that night and had thought of how happy he may have been with Arlene if he had not met Jennifer. He nearly asked her to marry him. Why, oh why had he stopped into that stupid jewelry store? He shrugged. He would have seen her pictures in other places anyway and who knows what he would have done then? He cursed himself for ever having gone to Tandaro to see her and he cursed David for ever bringing her into his life.

But ultimately, he loved her with every bone in his body and couldn't imagine his life without her. He had been resentful and jealous and the thought of what he may have given up for her broke him. He didn't want to take it out on Jennifer and his heart bled when he did; he just couldn't control his anger and the thought of David in her brain did crazy things to him.

When he started seeing Arlene, not long after that night, she seemed to calm him and his guilt for what he was doing with her, stopped him from unleashing his anger on Jennifer—or at least he managed to stop before he lost control.

'I don't know what I'm doing,' he said to Arlene. 'I can't seem to control my rage when I see her thinking about that man.'

'You don't know that she is, Jack,' replied Arlene, trying to soothe him.

He smiled at her, a sad, wistful smile. 'You are good for me, Arlene,' he said, taking her face in his hands.

'Well, you should have thought about that before marrying your wife,' she said and put her lips on his. 'Come to bed, let's not waste our time talking about her.'

Jack adored Arlene, but she was not Jennifer. He knew he would never leave Jennifer and had decided to let go of Arlene tonight.

****

So-so was an up-and-coming gallery that had lost its original owner through bad management. Nevertheless, of an intimate atmosphere, it had its own charm. Dimly lit in some rooms with soft music creating an alluring atmosphere, and brightly done up in other spaces, with loud and brash music, it catered to varying audiences and tastes.

There were many attendees at the opening of So-so, but not as many as Jack had expected. He thought that perhaps they had arrived too early; it was only five thirty, but he had insisted they be there when it opened.

'You have a meeting tomorrow anyway, so you need your beauty sleep,' he said.

'I guess,' Jennifer had replied and hurried with her make-up; Jack was glad that hadn't come off as too suspicious.

Jack hurried Jennifer into the gallery and immediately spotted Jed. He breathed a sigh of relief. Jed, as irritating as Jack found him, came in handy when Jack needed time on his own and Jed was always happy to take Jennifer off his hands, sometimes to his annoyance.

Jed hugged Jennifer and stood back to admire her outfit.

'Smashing, as usual,' he said and turned to Jack. 'Hi, Jack.' He held out his hand awkwardly. Jack knew the man had never warmed to him, but he didn't care. He liked the effect he had on Jed, often leaving him with a fear in his eyes, especially when he snarled at him on purpose. It gave Jack a little thrill to see the man start.

Jack smirked and mumbled a hello, giving Jed's hand a strong shake. Jed pulled his hand away, shook it and looked back at Jennifer.

'Bailey is already here, come meet him,' said Jed.

'I need a drink first,' said Jennifer. Jack rolled his

eyes. She had been irritable since she left the house, actually before then, when he told her he had to leave early.

Jack guided her to the bar and she ordered a vodka on the rocks. He watched her as she elegantly sipped her drink, understanding the magnetism she had with everyone she met. For a moment he considered staying there with her, especially with all the vultures watching her. He frowned. Should he leave her there? Could she be trusted?

'Hi, I know you.' Jack and Jennifer both turned to see a young girl a couple of years younger than her, her eyes shining. 'You're Jennifer, from Haze!'

'Yes, I am.' Jennifer smiled and held out her hand. The girl ignored it and threw herself into Jennifer's arms instead. Jennifer was bemused and flattered and gently extricated herself from this stranger's embrace.

'I'm Mary,' said the girl. 'My painting is in the other room. You must have a look.' She began to pull at Jennifer's arm.

Jack, also bemused, watched them and decided that this would be just about the right time to excuse himself. He put his hand on Jennifer's arm. 'That's my cue to leave.' He kissed her cheek and she gave him a knowing look, which he ignored. 'See you at home.'

# CHAPTER 16

*Jennifer*

Jennifer followed Mary after downing the rest of her glass of vodka. Her mood needed to shift and she was glad for the alcohol; it took off the edge. At these events where she was obliged to go, Jack always made people feel uncomfortable. He growled at any man that spoke to her and eyed off any that dared to look her way. Even Jed stayed away from her when he was around.

She was already irritable before she left the house, uncomfortable in her outfit, the bruise on her arm popping out below the sleeve of her cardigan. She couldn't remove the thing, below which she wore a strapless yellow dress—Jack had chosen it, he seemed to love the color on her—that was mid-length and hugged her frame. She knew she should have worn the long-sleeved blouse, but she had to make an impression if she was to woo prospective agencies. The make-up she had applied to her arm was starting to rub off already. She didn't have any make-up artists doing her make-up this evening.

Yes, she was glad for the drink and when Jack announced he was leaving, she felt relief. He kissed her cheek lightly and left. In that instant, Jed was by her side.

'What a jerk,' he whispered to Jennifer who looked at him with reproach. 'I'm sorry, I'm sorry,' he said, rolling his eyes.

'Are you coming?' said Mary, still waiting.

Jennifer looked at her watch and followed her. The room was filled with a plethora of colors and Jennifer felt elated. She loved art and with a bit of the vodka beginning to do its work, she felt that she was in for a good night … especially now that Jack had left.

She let Mary lead her by the arm to one of the 'loud' rooms, which had a number of brashly colored paintings on the walls and sculpture that stood on pedestals in the middle of the room. Working their way around to a small corner, Mary stopped.

'This is mine,' said Mary proudly, pointing at an artwork, which took a tiny space on the wall, dwarfed by other, more glaring paintings. It was a white-and-red-splotched acrylic with straight black lines running through it from end to end, without much purpose. 'It represents life and death and see,' Mary said, her face animated, her hands moving along the work, 'the black lines are the scars from life that leads to death.' She looked at Jennifer in anticipation and Jennifer nodded and smiled in approval. She wasn't going to dash the girl's hopes and what did she know about art anyway. It may be a masterpiece, but nothing she would have looked at twice.

'That is, er, nice,' said Jed, cocking his head to look at it from another angle.

'Wow,' cut in Jennifer. 'That must have taken you a long time.'

'Only four days,' said Mary, pleased.

*Yep, that would be about right*, thought Jennifer, and reprimanded herself for her thoughts. They stood by the painting with Mary chattering away about it, the style, the medium, the inspiration, and Jennifer checked her watch again. 'Excuse me, Mary, I need to have a cigarette. Is there somewhere I could go?'

'Sure,' said Mary, 'Follow me.' She led them toward the back of the gallery and stopped at the threshold.

'I'll be back in a minute,' Jennifer said.

Jed crossed his arms and gave her a reproving look. 'Still doing that, are we?' Mary looked at him quizzically.

She let out a quick laugh and told him to go back

in; she would join him soon. She just felt like she needed to do it tonight. She knew by now David would never be with her, but she wanted to feel close to him and to feel like he made her feel again. Mary linked her arm in Jed's and they both headed back toward the room with her painting, Mary chattering away. Jed looked back at Jennifer and raised his eyebrows in mock annoyance. She chuckled and walked outside.

She looked skyward but couldn't see it and she wandered further, passing other attendees, who had come out for a breather. Jennifer lit her cigarette and continued to the far side of the garden, a twisting path by which no one walked or stood. The weather was unusually warm and the trees, hauntingly still, pushed her further away from the gallery doors; she felt a stillness, not just around her but in her heart. She had the sudden urge to cry, but why she didn't understand. It wasn't like this was the first time she had looked at it lately; in fact, Jack had inquired about her staring up at it on a number of occasions, with narrowed eyes. She didn't care what he thought anymore.

She stopped under a large oak and looked around her. No one would see her here and she just wanted to be alone for a moment with David, even if it could only be through the moon. She wondered again if he still looked for it too and right now, she desperately wished he was somewhere in the world doing the same thing as her.

She glanced up again, but it was concealed by hovering clouds and she looked at her watch. It wasn't six yet. She heard footsteps, and seeing a shadow approach, slipped behind a tree that offered her a generous trunk by which she could conceal her presence. Jennifer looked up again, but the size of the branches overhead, although nearly leaf bare in the autumn evening, obscured her view. *Damn*, she thought, and squirmed to peer through them.

'Jen,' she heard his voice call.

She froze. She waited for more. Nothing more came.

She heard another movement and turned her head slowly to the sound. She saw him, his profile, staring up at the moon.

David. Her David!

Her heart began to thwack her chest and she put her hand to her neck. Was she dreaming? Was her imagination getting the better of her? She blinked hard but when she opened her eyes, he was still there, his head still turned to the sky. He hadn't been calling her. He didn't know she was there! She felt her knees weaken and clutched at the trunk to steady herself. She heard the leaves beneath him crunch away; he was leaving! Yet she stood there, still frozen.

'David,' she whispered, a clump in her throat.

The footsteps stopped for just a moment while she held her breath and then they continued away. She let herself slide to the ground behind the tree and felt the familiarity of its comfort. She was shaken and couldn't comprehend what had just happened. Should she have gone to him, alerted him to her presence? Slowly, she began to regain her breath and raised herself from the ground. She tried to look behind her at her dress to see if it was soiled, but she couldn't see it in the darkness. She sighed, realizing that she had probably gotten a wet patch on her bottom. She took a deep breath and turned around.

He was standing right in front of her. They stared at each other, speechless, for a few moments and then she was in his arms. And then he was stroking her hair. And then he was kissing her lips and her neck, his body pressed tightly to hers.

Jennifer pulled him to her, and leaning against the tree, she quickly unbuttoned his trousers. He stepped back and looked at her with uncertainty, but she stared into his eyes with hunger and continued her work. His lips were on hers in an instant, and hitching up her skirt and resting her leg on the tree trunk, she guided him into her. She closed her eyes and felt his mouth on hers. She could taste a saltiness and realized that one or both of them was crying.

Not a word had passed between them the whole time but they didn't need words. Their bodies told them all they needed to know. It would always be like this; for them there were no others and after they felt their bodies shake in pleasure, they still clung on.

Jennifer pulled away first, David unwilling to raise his cheek from hers, but they couldn't stay there forever, as much as she knew they both wanted to. She straightened her dress while David tidied himself.

'Let me go in first,' she said, not looking at him, terrified of how she felt. She dusted herself off, realizing that she must be a mess, and patting her mussed hair, walked back into the gallery. On her way, she glanced up at the sky. The moon was now shining bright, in clear view of the parted clouds.

****

'Jennifer, call for you, that Jed fellow again,' Jack called out from the living room. Jennifer moaned and looked at the clock: 8.30 a.m. *Shit!* She had an appointment at nine. Jack poked his head in the door and tossed the phone on the bed.

'Jed,' she said into it.

'And what happened to you last night, Missy? Am I going to hear the real story today or the same crap I heard last night?' he said in a sing-song voice.

'Shhh,' she said softly. 'I will be there soon, sorry I slept in.' She quickly hung up.

'Jack,' she called out. 'Where's Jacky?'

'Baby's with me,' he called back. That was something at least; the man loved his kid. Well, he completely doted on him. He was a good father. The nanny had been booked for today, but Jack insisted on taking his son to work. Jack didn't believe in 'outsiders' looking after his child, and he really did love the tyke.

Jennifer hopped into the shower and jumped out almost immediately. Coming back into the bedroom, she saw her clothes from the night before draped over the side of the bed. She picked up the dress and looked at it. It wasn't too bad, but did have some smudges on the back of it. She quickly went back into the bathroom and buried it under other clothes that were in the clothes hamper. She hoped Jack hadn't noticed. She never knew these days what would set him off. She felt a shiver of fear run down her spine. If he knew about last night, she would be dead already.

He hadn't been home when she had gotten home the night before and she had been relieved. She'd said goodbye to the nanny and had taken a long shower.

She thought about David and placed her hands on the same places that he had: her neck, her face, her breasts. She touched her lips and could feel his own tender ones on hers and she began to cry. Her tears mingled with the water from the shower and her heart felt like it would explode. It hadn't changed for them. Nothing had changed. It was just stronger, more powerful. For a split second, she wished it had never happened. She hadn't seen him in over a year and the last time she saw him, he was in agony and she was in her wedding dress. But it was all still there.

They had barely said a word to each other. She walked shakily back into the gallery but with her chin high and headed straight to the bathroom. Jed had been waiting by the door and pounced on her.

'What happened to you? Exciting smoke?' he said sarcastically, looking her up and down. She always thought that Jed had some sort of sixth sense; he just seemed to know things.

'Not now, Jed,' she said and pulled away from him, hurrying away.

She leaned on the sink and regarded herself in the mirror. *Not too bad*, she thought, wiping some of the mascara that was smeared near the edges of her eyes. She looked at her dress, which had some small green and gray spots on the buttocks, and shrugged. Well, if anyone decided to ogle her butt, they were certainly not going to admit it to her, but she still removed her cardigan and loosely tied it around her waist. It wasn't a great look, but it would have to do. It also left the bruise on her arm in full view, but it was the lesser of the two evils.

Jennifer leaned on the wall and considered what to do next. Should she leave the gallery? Yes, she had to. But she hadn't been there long. She was supposed to schmooze tonight. It was part of the process of reigniting her flailing career. She needed to do this. She sighed. She needed to be by herself, to think about David, about what just happened. What had she done? She shook her head in anger but realized she was smiling.

David. Oh, David. He was still out there too and she may have to face him again. What would she say? What could she say to him? She put her head in her hands and then made up her mind. She would stay for an hour, away from David, meet the right people, and then go home. This would be something that happened that they need never discuss, an insanity of sorts, never to be repeated. It was just unexpected and caught her in a moment of weakness. But if she were in her right mind, would she do it again? Jennifer didn't let herself answer that question.

Walking out of the bathroom, she was greeted by Mary. 'I missed you,' she said and linked her arm in

Jennifer's. 'Come on. I have so much to show you.'

Glad for the company and the distraction, she followed Mary around the rooms, her head moving around furtively, in search of David. The mellow sounds of the music that played through in one of the rooms helped to lighten Jennifer's heart and she smiled inwardly, thinking of David's hands on her, her leg wrapped around him …

'Oh, hey, Jennifer, this is my sister, Ness, and her boyfriend, or should I say, fiancé'—she giggled—'David.'

Startled, Jennifer turned to see David, and then quickly turned to the woman whose hand he was holding. She was lovely, wide-set brown eyes that widened with pleasure when she beheld Jennifer.

'Good to meet you,' Jennifer said and tried to smile, but knew it came out like a grimace.

'Hey, I know you! You're that model. I've seen your pictures everywhere. So nice to meet you.' She leaned forward and kissed Jennifer on the cheek. 'This is David, my *boyfriend*!' she said and nudged her sister with a laugh. 'My klutz of a boyfriend! Goes out for a smoke and trips on a tree trunk! Just look at him.'

Jennifer looked back at David and held out her hand. He shakily took it and for a second, she was taken back to the night they met. She quickly reclaimed her hand and looked away.

The four of them walked together, commenting on the artwork, Jennifer trying to find something canny to say even though every word in her head was a jumble.

'How are you enjoying the opening?' said Ness, turning to look at one of the sculptures that they had stopped at. She leaned over to Jennifer conspiratorially. 'I don't get some of it, I have to admit, but there are some pretty pieces here. Have you seen Mary's yet?'

'Yes, I saw it earlier, it's lovely, she really has a talent,' said Jennifer with a forced enthusiasm.

'Liar,' Ness leaned over to her and whispered. She laughed and Jennifer smiled. She was really liking this woman as much as she wanted to tear those big brown eyes out. David had not looked at her once and she kept her face firmly in the opposite direction.

Suddenly Jed was by her side, nudging her. 'I have to meet some people,' said Jennifer. 'Business stuff, boring, but necessary. Thank you for the tour.'

Ness hugged Jennifer. 'It's not true what they say about beautiful people. You are absolutely gorgeous, inside and out,' she said.

*Except that I just fucked your fiancé,* thought Jennifer, ruefully. She smiled shakily and mumbled a thank you. She smiled at Mary, nodded at David, whose eyes were creased, and let Jed lead her away.

'And ...' said Jed, leading her to the CEO of

Haze.

'And nothing,' she said. Then, 'That was David.'

Jed stopped and turned her to him. '*The David?!*'

'Keep walking,' she said sternly.

After they wandered about, Jennifer trying to get hold of herself, she told Jed she was leaving and he offered to drive her. As they neared the front door of the gallery, she looked back and saw David looking back at her. She stopped for a moment. Then he smiled. She smiled back shakily.

Now, Jennifer, sitting at the large desk in the Haze building, stared out of the window. She had been kept waiting and was beginning to get impatient. Jed sat beside her, all business-like in his suit and spectacles, his back straight and his chin out, and she couldn't help but have a giggle at him when he arrived to pick her up; he didn't find it very funny.

'We will get this,' he said and patted her arm, just as a secretary walked in announcing that Mr. Jacobs and Mr. Dean, their appointment, would be running late.

Jed relaxed in his seat while Jennifer continued to stare out of the window, her thoughts much too far away from here.

'Want to talk about it, Jenny?' asked Jed.

'I'm fine.' She smiled wanly, turning to Jed, and placed her hand on his. 'Really.' She tried to smile at him without shaking.

'I know where he is right now,' said Jed, mysteriously. 'I also know how to contact him.'

'Who?' Jennifer felt her heart jump; she already knew.

'You know who.'

'Oh, Jed.' She felt tears begin to well. 'Not here, not now; I can't do this. I need this job. Please.'

'I'm sorry, Jenny, sure, okay.' He patted her hand.

Half an hour later, they walked out of the office of Jacobs and Dean, elated. Jennifer had secured a two-year contract, which meant that she could make her own money again, which also meant independence from Jack. She had signed immediately, with a reproving look from Jed, but he knew it was a great deal. They lunched at a café near to her apartment and raised their glasses in triumph.

'Now we talk,' said Jed. 'What happened last night?'

'David happened,' replied Jennifer.

'I know that much.' Jed rolled his eyes and sipped on his green concoction. 'It's okay, Jenny, you don't have to tell me anything. I know seeing him shook

you up. I haven't seen you like that, I don't think, ever.'
He stopped for a moment, sizing her up, and continued.
'Oh, I wasn't kidding, I made some inquiries.' He took a
crumpled paper out of his pocket and handed it to her.
She tried to take it, but he closed his hand over it. She
looked up at him, her hand trembling mid-air. 'You
don't have to. Will it be better if you don't?'

Jennifer felt herself shake and rested her head in
her hands, now letting the tears fall and not caring who
saw her. She told Jed what had happened, not that there
was much to tell, it all happened so quickly. She trusted
Jed, she always had. He already knew about David and
Jack; she had confided in him from the beginning.

Jed raised his eyebrows when she had finished
and then he smiled. 'You should have been with him,
you know that. It's not too late.'

'Yes, yes, it is,' she cried. 'Everything that had
happened … we were not supposed to be together, ever.
And I feel terrible, awful. I have let Jack down …'

'Really, is that how you're putting it?' Jed raised
an eyebrow.

'Jed, please, you know what I mean. I owe him
…'

'Nothing!' said Jed, leaning forward, his eyes
piercing hers in anger.

'Yes, yes, I do. He is the father of my son. He led

me out of my despair. He gives me whatever I want …'

'And more,' muttered Jed.

'And David,' said Jennifer, ignoring Jed's interjection. 'He has his own life, which I know nothing about. A beautiful fiancé …'

'Girlfriend,' put in Jed. Jennifer narrowed her eyes at him.

Jed put the piece of paper on the table between them and she stared at it, her stomach queasy. 'It's there,' he said and his eyes widened with excitement when she reached for it. 'He is not engaged. His girlfriend is Vanessa Martin, and her family are pretty well known—that's how I got the info. They just bought the gallery. She is staying with her parents' and he is staying at a motel downtown. Don't know why because they've been together …'

Jennifer smiled at Jed, not quite sure how to feel and what to do with the paper.

'Are you going to call him?'

'I don't know, Jed. I desperately want to. He makes me feel like there is no life without him. He awakened so much in me … he does every time I see him. I know I can't be with him, but I do want to speak to him. To explain everything.' She paused. 'What if she's there? What if he isn't?'

'Just call.'

# CHAPTER 17

She called. The hotel patched her through to his room.

'David?' she said tentatively. She heard him draw breath. 'Are you alone?'

'Jen ... Jennifer.' She could hear him scrambling. 'Yes, I am. Can I see you?'

She breathed a sigh of relief; he wanted to see her. 'Yes, where?'

'Café, Jersey Street. You know where that is?'

She did. It wasn't far away. 'Fifteen minutes?'

'Yep, oh ... Jen?'

'Yes?' She held her breath.

'Hurry.'

She smiled, her belly in knots, and hung up. Her heart began to thump. She was finally going to talk to him, to get to explain everything ... to see him, just to see him.

She saw him standing outside the door of the café, a rusty old place that was filled with people on their lunch hour. He was wearing faded blue jeans and a gray sweater, and still looked the same, maybe a little older; *well, he was older, but more mature and somewhat more a … a man,* thought Jennifer.

'It's crammed,' he said when she reached him.

'Hi, David.' She couldn't help but smile at him, and held out her hand. He smiled back and lifted it to his lips.

'Hi, my Jen,' he replied and kept hold of her hand. She quickly pulled it back and looked around them.

'Let's find somewhere else,' she said and began walking down the street, which was strewn with brown leaves. It was cool, but she let her hands fall to her side, trying to keep her head straight. David walked beside her, quiet, and she felt his hand brush hers lightly. An awkward silence filled the air, the sound of the city a blur in the background. Jennifer was trying to think of something logical to say to him but she knew she would blurt out something stupid, her brain wasn't working. Then they both spoke at the same time.

'So, Vanessa …'

'How are you …' They laughed and it broke the tension.

'About last night …' said Jennifer. 'I'm sorry about last night. I don't know what happened.' She blushed, trying to extricate the image of the two of them in the garden.

'I'm not sorry, not sorry at all. Guilty, yes, but not sorry.'

They both suddenly stopped walking and turned to each other, and Jennifer wanted to pull him to her again, to feel his arms around her. She looked away, afraid that she just might do it, and spotted a sign a few yards away—*Vacancy*. David had seen it too and he raised his eyebrows in warning.

'At least we can talk in private,' she reasoned and they hurried to the hotel.

David paid for a room and got a key. He led the way, reaching for her hand, and she followed, fear and excitement building in her. When they entered the room, David squeezed her hand and closed the door. Then they were in each other's arms again.

'Talk, we are here to talk,' David said, pulling away, and Jennifer reluctantly let go of him.

The room, which housed a big brass bed and a little settee, was dimly lit and they moved slowly inside. A kitchenette to the left had a kettle on its bench and Jennifer nodded to it.

They sat awkwardly on the settee, sipping at

their coffee, and David began. It was everything Jennifer had already known from Jack, but she listened quietly, angry with him, angry with Jack, and so angry with herself. He also told her about his studies and she was so proud of him.

'I'm nearly done,' he said. 'I was going to come to you as a man of success, something you would be proud of,' he said ruefully.

'I would have had you any way I could. I would have been proud of you no matter what.'

'I couldn't, not after what I had put you through.'

'You made a commitment. You had an obligation to uphold that and I understand, I really do. I just wish you could have told me. Things would have been so different.' Jennifer told him about her own life, her eyes shining when she talked about her son, but didn't enlighten him on the state of her relationship with Jack. It was best he didn't know what he didn't need to know. They talked and laughed and it was like time had not passed at all.

'I have something to show you,' he said and removed her photograph that was tucked deep into his wallet.

'You still have that!' she squealed and reached out to grasp it from him. He leaned back and laughed, waving it at her, and leaning above him to grab it, she found herself on his chest, his face right beneath hers. He gazed into her eyes and she bent down and let her lips touch his. Then she got up, and straightening her dress, stood up.

'This is wrong, David, so wrong.' She began to pick up her handbag.

'I know,' he said, standing beside her. 'At least we got our chance to explain. I feel easier, but somehow it's also so much worse because …'

Jennifer went to the door and opened it. 'Maybe in another life.'

David was behind her and he took her hand, lifted it to his lips, and kissed it. She felt the tears roll down her cheeks and she let them. Then he reached behind her and shut the door.

****

Lying in David's arms, Jennifer never felt so satisfied, so calm, so in love. She stroked his chest. 'Got some new hairs here.'

He chuckled. 'You noticed.'

'And some on your chin too. You really ought to shave,' she said, pulling at the tiny hairs that sat on his chin.

'I hear women love it.' He laughed again and leaned down to kiss her.

'I have to go,' she said and tears sprang to her eyes.

'I know,' he replied and pulled her tighter.

'I don't want to,' she said, pushing herself closer to him, not wanting to be apart from his skin for any amount of time.

'I know that too.'

'I shouldn't have come.'

He didn't answer.

'What do we do, David?'

'Go back to our lives, Jen.'

'How can we, especially after this?'

'We have to. You have a son, you have a …' He couldn't say it.

'I don't love him. Not like I love you.'

'You made a commitment. I don't want you to go back to him, but you have to.'

Jennifer sat up and began to dress, while David walked over to the window. 'I still talk to you, you know,' he said. 'I do it more than I should. That thing in the sky. It keeps you with me. It will always keep you with me.'

'Me too,' she said. She looked at him, the man she loved, and knew she could never be with him, not completely.

****

Even as she turned the key in her apartment door, she heard Jack. It was late. She had spent the whole afternoon with David and they hadn't realized how quickly time had gone by.

'Where have you been?' his voiced boomed.

'With Jed, we had some meetings. I got the contract,' she said, trying to sound light and happy.

'This late?' He appeared at her side and she noticed he didn't acknowledge her. She kissed his cheek and moved to the bedroom where Jacky lay on the bed and he held out his chubby little hands to her. She rushed to him and picked him up and cooed at him as she went back to the kitchen.

'Has he eaten yet?' she asked.

'No, I was about to feed him.'

'I'll do it,' she said quickly and put him on the floor. She needed to do something or else her guilt would expose itself. 'Have you eaten yet?'

'No, I thought we could go out to dinner.' Jack walked to the kitchen and set about helping her get Jacky's food ready.

'I'm not really up to it,' said Jennifer, hoping

they could just stay home. 'Why don't you call Pauly? I can fix myself something.'

Jack bent down behind her and put his arms around her waist. He kissed her neck and she cringed, but she quickly laughed and swerved to the side. 'What's up with you tonight?' she said nervously.

'I want to put my hands all over my sexy wife,' he replied and moved his hands up to her breast. She laughed again and moved to where Jacky lay on the floor and Jack followed, lying in front of her, his chin resting on his knuckles, his adoring eyes piercing through hers. 'I love you Jennifer,' he said earnestly. Jennifer, suddenly afraid of his honesty, reached forward and hugged him.

'Okay, Jack, let's go out; give me a minute, I want to take a quick shower.'

Jack smiled at her. 'Good girl,' he said and patted her bottom as she rose to get ready. 'I'll feed the baby.'

Jacky made little snoring noises as he slept in his stroller at the restaurant, a brightly lit café-style room, with tables so near each other that they could clearly hear the conversations of others. The noise and mood were the perfect antidote for how Jennifer was feeling and it helped to disguise her mix of happiness, satisfaction, and guilt. She told Jack more about her contract and although he didn't seem very pleased, he patted her hand in acquiescence.

He told her about his day and the new acquisition to the firm. They were spreading out and he was opening an office in California.

'How do you feel about moving there for a while?' he asked.

Jennifer was taken aback. 'I just signed a contract for two years, Jack. I will need to be here.'

'But you can do it from anywhere.'

'Not really,' she replied. 'California is a long way from here. I can't travel back and forth at the blink of an eye. There's Jacky to consider. I can't drag him around and I don't want to leave him for any amount of time.'

'Well, you can't have it all,' he said sulkily.

'But New York is my home, my life,' she said, now fearful he was pushing the issue.

'You travel at times here too.'

'But I will be based here. Sure, there's some traveling, but most of my work will be done here …'

'Why does this always have to be about your career?' he growled. 'You don't need the work, I've told you that.'

Jennifer didn't think there was any point in arguing with him. Her career had been a bone of contention since they were married, but she wouldn't give in to what he imagined a wife should be. She lowered her eyes.

'It wouldn't be immediately anyway,' he said in an effort to change the mood. 'We can talk about it when it needs more discussion.' Jennifer wondered how she was going to get out of it then, when it came to it. 'But I want you with me the whole time,' he said.

'We'll see how things pan out,' she said. 'We will work it out.'

'Good girl,' he said and smiled happily and they spent the rest of their dinner talking about Jacky, their work, and other trivial things, trying to keep the conversation light.

They had had a pleasant dessert and Jack had just paid the check, when Jennifer heard someone call her name behind her. She froze.

'Jennifer, hey, Jennifer.' She turned to see Ness heading toward them and a shiver climbed down her back. Jack glanced at Ness, about to plaster a smile on his face, which Jennifer could see changing as she watched him, and fear began to cloak her. She already knew what he had seen. Ness reached their table and leaned down to kiss Jennifer on the cheek.

'Ness, hello, what a coincidence.' Jennifer tried to smile. 'This is my husband, Jack, and little Jacky,' she said, trying to stop the quiver in her voice, gesturing to

Jacky who was still asleep in his pram. 'We were just leaving,' she added quickly.

Ness turned to Jack and held out her hand, but Jack was looking beyond her and she withdrew her hand, the smile on her face turning to one of confusion as she turned to follow his gaze. Jennifer, now a terror attacking her nerves, did the same and she saw David, about to sit down at a table not very far from theirs.

'Oh, that's David, my boyfriend,' Ness explained to Jack and then turned back to Jennifer. 'You know David.' She turned back to Jack. 'We met Jennifer last night at the gallery.'

Jennifer's eyes moved back to Jack, who was turning a deep shade of purple; he looked like he was holding his breath. 'Jack,' she said, reaching her hand to him.

Ness looked confused. 'Do you know David?' she asked Jack.

He seemed to come out of his reverie. 'Yes, a long time ago,' he muttered and stood up. Jennifer had her heart in her mouth and prepared, for what, she didn't know. She looked back to David, who was also standing up now, worry written on his face.

Jack strode over to David's table, his shoulders straight, his mouth set tight. Jennifer knew he wouldn't cause a scene, but she still heard what he said. 'Stay away from my wife, or I will kill you … and her!' With that, he turned on his heel, and grabbing Jennifer by her arm, pulled her to her feet, while Ness looked on in bewilderment. Jennifer grabbed the pram and mumbled a goodbye to Ness.

'Bye, Jennifer, good to see you again,' Ness called out after them.

# CHAPTER 18

Jacky was three when they returned to New York. The past two years had Jennifer picking up odd modeling jobs, which included some television commercials and brochures, but they were not as satisfying or as lucrative as the shoots in New York had been. She had to abandon her contract with Haze, as they had left for Sacramento immediately. Jack would not take no for an answer.

After they had left the restaurant that night, Jack had not said a word and once they reached home, he threw her the house keys and sped off after she had gotten Jacky out of the car. She was terrified, but she didn't know what to do. She had wanted to call Angel but her friend was out of town. She wanted to speak to her mother, but she knew her mother would hop on the next plane to New York with murder on her mind. She called Jed, who had come over immediately and had stayed with her for the night.

'Come with me,' urged Jed. 'There's room, there's always room for you at my place.'

'I can't, Jed. It will make things so much worse.'

'You are not safe here, Jenny,' he insisted.

But Jennifer knew she would have to face whatever came. She had a child to consider now, it wasn't just about her.

The next morning, Jack had still not returned and Jennifer was starting to worry. What if Jack had been to see David? She began to imagine the worst and called David's hotel room. Ness answered and Jennifer quickly hung up. She breathed a sigh of relief; at least he wasn't alone. He would be okay. She paced up and down, fed Jacky and played with him. She decided to take him for a walk to clear her mind; she needed to do something to calm her nerves.

When she returned home an hour later, Jack was still not back. She called his friends, who hadn't seen him and asked her if everything was okay. She assured them everything was fine; that Jack was likely working late and she had probably just forgotten that he told her.

She went to bed worried and woke up the next morning, Jack still nowhere in sight. Now she was really worried. Maybe something had happened to him. She fed the baby and decided she would call to the police; maybe he was in an accident. With the state he was in it was very likely he had done something foolish; he was an erratic driver at the best of times.

While she was feeding Jacky, she heard a knock on the door and dashed to it. 'Jack,' she cried and moved forward to hug him, but he pushed her aside and went straight to the bedroom.

'Forgot my keys,' he mumbled. She followed him, but he was already in the shower. Jennifer went back to the baby and continued to feed him, her heart racing. This was not good. It had been more than a day and his mood had not changed. She was scared.

She was clearing away the dishes when she looked up and saw Jack standing in the doorway of the bedroom. 'We're going to California,' he said simply, moving toward her.

'What do you mean?' she said, trying to digest what he said.

'You heard me. We leave tomorrow.' He threw three tickets on the dining table.

She didn't want to argue right now, knowing what could happen, but she didn't know what else to do. 'Didn't we talk about this already? We were going to see how things went.'

'I changed my mind. We leave tomorrow,' he repeated.

'Jack, I just signed a two-year contract. I can't

leave now,' she protested.

He moved toward her menacingly and Jennifer shrunk back.

'You will,' he said, 'or I will kill you and I will kill him.'

'What the hell are you talking about?' said Jennifer, suddenly furious.

Jack stepped back and began to laugh wildly. 'That got your fire burning, didn't it?' Then he growled—an ugly snarl. 'You know what I've been doing all this time? Finding your precious David. I know everything I need to know and I will strip every bone from his body.' Jack was looking at his hands which were moving slowly, imitating the tearing of flesh. He looked crazed and Jennifer was frightened. He just would do it; he was certainly capable. She stared at him, horrified.

Then he looked up at her and laughed in that wild way again.

****

Life in Sacramento was nice; nice was about the best word for it—and for Jennifer, it was boring. The pace was slower than what she was used to and although the weather was beautiful and there was much to do and see, she felt alone. With all her friends in New York and her family in Tandaro, she spent the days when she wasn't working, which were few and far between, sitting in the spacious backyard watching Jacky while he crawled and played, and even though she loved being with him, she missed adult company. Jack was gone often and in the beginning she was relieved to be rid of his presence, but as one long day stretched into the next, she found herself agitated and lonely and could only annoy Jed and Angel with her frequent phone calls for so long.

When she first told Angel of the move, her friend was unhappy but cheerfully said, 'Telephones exist for a reason. And it will give me an excuse to visit California.' Jennifer had smiled—Angel, always the optimist. Jed was another matter. He stomped and swore and even wanted to confront Jack, as terrified as he was of him. But after Jennifer had calmed him down, promising to be back as soon as possible, he relented and also promised to take a trip to see her.

But a few weeks after the move, it was not enough. She asked her mother to join them in Sacramento for a while and Judy was delighted. She had more time on her hands these days and was excited to have the chance to bond with her grandson.

'Do you think it's a good idea?' Jack narrowed his eyes when she brought up the subject one evening after he had come home much later than she expected him to.

'I'm alone here, Jack,' she said.

'You have Jacky.'

'I also want to work. Ma will help out too. I love being with Jacky, but I can't seem to click with anyone at work. Besides, the jobs that are coming my way are few and I'm only on a shoot for a couple of days at a time.' She sighed. 'I miss my friends …'

'That merry fellow?' said Jack, rolling his eyes.

'Jed is a good friend,' replied Jennifer, her back up already. She changed the subject. 'Anyway, if Ma comes, I'll have someone with me, to help out a bit.'

'The maid is not good?' He now looked concerned.

'No, no,' Jennifer said quickly. 'She's fine, but it's not like she lives here. She has her own life, her own family. Please, Jack, Ma will be happy to stay for a while,' she beseeched him.

'I guess,' he conceded, and Jennifer was relieved. 'Maybe you will be happy to stay home if you have someone to keep you company.'

The smile left Jennifer's face. 'Mother will help out with babysitting too, Jack, while I work.'

'You're a mother, and my wife; you could stay at home.' He was pouting like a child. Every argument led to this. 'Anyway, you're his mother! You should be with him, not your mother.'

'I need to be able to do something,' she pleaded. 'It's not like it's full time, I just need to work; please understand, Jack.'

But there wasn't a lot of work for models in Sacramento and if they had moved to Los Angeles, it may have been different. Jennifer began to worry that by the time she got jobs, she wouldn't have the youth and beauty requirements. She applied for small modeling jobs against Jack's wishes, but she kept reminding him that it was he who wanted to move, not her, and he yielded, more out of guilt than of compassion.

Judy arrived a week later and was set up in the guesthouse, a little bungalow that was built by the side of the main house; she arrived with three suitcases and no return flight. She announced she could stay as long as Jennifer wanted her to and even insisted on getting rid of the maid. 'What am I going to do all day? Get a tan?' She laughed.

Jennifer was grateful for her presence, the fear of Jack's temper subsiding, even though he had not put an aggressive hand on her for a time. The night he told her they were moving, he was in a wretched mood, but it was his cold determination that had scared her more than his usual outbursts because she knew when it finally came, it would be so much worse. Instead, he ordered her to pack their things and he would send for the rest later. Then he had walked out again and she'd not seen him until the evening they left New York.

Since then, he had not touched her at all: not aggressively, tenderly, or in any other way. Jennifer was desperately unhappy and it was only when her mother had arrived that she began to feel better. At first, Judy had also encouraged Jennifer to stay at home, to be a wife, but she also understood her need for independence, something she'd always encouraged.

Jack was more often away than at home and she often wondered whether he saw other women. She thought of Arlene and felt her skin crawl—she was sure he was in contact with her and nothing he did led her to believe it, but his disinterest in Jennifer was out of character; he usually took every opportunity to put his hands on her, but not anymore. She tried not to care, and felt she had no right to question it, especially after her tryst with David, but she did care. Although she hated him, she still loved him too, and she missed him. Things were so strained between them now that her mother had commented on it and Jennifer had dismissed it as everyone being too busy. Jennifer could tell Judy was not convinced.

Two months after Judy's arrival Jennifer asked her mother if she could extend her stay and Judy was thrilled and even Jack seemed pleased as Jennifer's mood had shifted since Judy had been there.

Jennifer thought about David all the time. She visited the moon often now, and although she knew she would never have him again, she still held on to the fact that he had loved her—the whole time.

It was three months after the move when Jack had come home late one night and sat on the edge of the bed while Jennifer slept. He gently shook her awake and when she stirred, he kissed her neck. Even in her haze of sleep, she was taken aback, but when she saw the tenderness in his eyes, she reached out to him. They made love that night and the next morning, Jack was gone again.

The next evening, Jack had come home, and Jennifer had a meal already cooked for them all, hopeful that his love for her the previous night signaled a fresh start for them. Her mother smiled and, Jacky in tow, made a hasty retreat out the back door with a wink, informing them she was keeping him for the night. At dinner, they conversed awkwardly and Jennifer wondered how it had come to this. She wished she knew what was going on in Jack's head, but then, as the whiskey began to work its way through his system, he became more talkative.

'I need to go away again, to Boston,' he said.

Jennifer's ears pricked up. David lived in Boston. He looked at her carefully.

'Oh, why?' she said, trying to sound casual, stirring her soup, trying to calm her mind.

'Some things there that need to be settled … just stuff,' he said and she could feel his eyes still on her.

'How long will you be away?'

'At least a week, depends on other things.'

She decided to change the subject.

'How are things at home? Have you spoken to your mother recently?'

His brow knotted. She thought she had succeeded in turning the conversation, but Jack put down his fork and looked at her. 'We haven't talked about that night.'

'What night?' she said and felt her ears begin to heat.

'That night, you know what I'm talking about,' he said, his words beginning to slur. She could see he was trying to keep his temper in check.

Jennifer put down her spoon and sighed. 'What do you want to talk about, Jack?'

'What happened with him?'

'Nothing, Jack, nothing happened.'

'Why didn't you tell me you saw him?'

'There was nothing to say.'

'Well, I have something to say,' he declared, sitting back in his seat. He waited for her to say something, but she picked up the spoon and ladled her soup onto itself, staring down at it in fascination.

# CHAPTER 19

## *David*

Ness walked back to the table and looked down at David. 'Do you know that man? A nasty piece of work. What did he say to you?'

David was still standing, stunned, watching Jack wrench Jennifer's arm, and moved to follow them. Ness put her hand on his arm.

'Don't, David.'

He looked at her and saw something in her eyes. He pulled out her chair and she sat down. She put her hand on his.

'Is there something I need to know?' she asked, looking at him closely.

He sighed heavily. 'I love you, Ness, so much. But you need and you deserve more than I can give you.'

Ness drew her hand back and David could see tears begin to well in her eyes. How he didn't want to hurt this wonderful woman.

'Is it her?' she asked, turning her eyes from him, and swiping at the fallen tear on the edge of her cheek.

He didn't reply but reached out for her hand. 'I love you …'

'That's not what I asked.'

'I can't do this to you, Ness,' said David and sighed. He realized he may be losing the person who had saved him, but he couldn't hurt her and what he felt for Jennifer would eventually hurt her.

'Is it her?' she asked again and stared straight at him.

'Yes.'

'That is her husband. She's not yours, David,' said Ness, her voice trembling, her façade crumbling. 'Take me home.' She stood up and gathered her handbag and coat.

It was midday when Ness arrived at David's room. She hadn't asked for any explanation, but walked around the room, gathering her things. David was in the bathroom, collecting her items, when the phone rang.

Ness picked it up and the line went dead. David came out. 'Who was that?' he asked, fearful of her answer.

'I'm pretty sure that would have been her,' she said and reached out for her things that were in David's hands.

'Goodbye, David,' she said.

'Ness, Vanessa,' he called after her, knowing it was useless.

At the door, she turned around and walked back to him. 'You're right, I do deserve more,' she said and softly kissed his lips. Then she turned on her heel and walked out of his life.

David left for Boston that evening. Upon returning to his apartment, he looked about and saw an empty life. Remnants of Ness still lingered about him and he sat on his bed, considering his next move. Before he had left for New York, he was happy. He was sure he knew, and had, what he wanted. Now he knew that had never been true.

He lay back and thought about Jennifer. He knew now that she would always be with him in his mind, but knew that she could never be in body. He had to focus on something else … and he squeezed his eyes shut and tried, but her face always came back to him. He succumbed to the vision and fell asleep thinking of her.

David studied. He studied and worked. When he returned to class, Ness was not there. He looked out for her every day, but eventually figured she had left, and when he tried to call her, her phone rang out. When he went to her apartment, she was gone. He felt terrible about it. It was her dream too, to get her degree, and he had stolen that from her. He didn't try to contact her again, knowing it would make things worse for her and him. He had loved her, but it was different, and now, after seeing Jennifer, he knew how different. He ruefully told his family of their split and they were disappointed—they had really liked Ness, the first girl David had brought home after Dell, but his mother trusted David's decision; her son had good sense and even better instinct and she knew he would land on his feet.

David resigned himself to the fact that he would never marry again, but he dated, first with apprehension and then he realized that casual dating was what he needed. He began to think like Jack for a while, Jack when he was a single man, and found that his confidence, and more to the point, false confidence, really worked. The more he worked at it, the easier it became, and he found himself enjoying the dating game, at least for a while. And while he wanted more than just casual dating, he knew the alternative would never work, as whenever he was by himself, the only person he imagined was Jennifer.

Whenever he became attached to a woman or her to him, he knew the time had come to break it off. None of them were Jennifer and try as he might not to, he couldn't help but compare them to her.  And none came close. So, he resigned himself to bachelorhood and came to accept that he needed to make more of his life. Some people would never have what he had with Jennifer and at least, even if just for a moment, he got to feel real love.

A few months after returning to Boston, his mother phoned him.

'David, Jack was over here,' she said with trepidation. He had never told his family about what had happened with Jack and after Dell died, he never spoke of him to them again. His mother had asked, at first often, and then noticing David flinch when his friend's name was mentioned, much more infrequently.

David now flinched again, relieved that his mother couldn't see him. 'Oh?' He tried to sound nonchalant. 'What did he want?'

'He asked where you were. He wanted your address.'

'Did you give it to him?'

'No … I thought …' She hesitated. 'I wasn't sure if you wanted me to. But I can … he left the number of his hotel.'

David was silent trying to work out what that meant. The last he saw of Jack was as he wrenched Jennifer out of the restaurant, thunder in his eyes and murder on his mind.

'David?'

'How was he?' David asked and swallowed hard. 'How are his wife and kid?'

'Oh.' His mother seemed taken aback with the question. 'He spoke of them with great fondness.'

David breathed a sigh of relief. After bidding his mother goodbye, he looked at the number he had written down and wondered whether he should contact Jack. He knew Jack wanted to confront him and wondered how much he knew about them, whether Jennifer had told him about their tryst. If he didn't and Jack was fishing for information, he may put Jennifer in jeopardy. He looked at the paper again, crushed it, and threw it in the wastebasket. He had to leave Jennifer alone to live her life without him.

For nearly two years, David studied, and when he had finished his MBA, he sat down and wondered what to do with it. He had saved all his earnings and decided to travel.

'I was thinking of backpacking,' he said, smiling, already knowing their reaction.

His mother put her hand on her chest. 'Why?' She screwed up her face in disgust.

'Because I want to see my own country, to move around for a while. Nothing is tying me down here.'

'Why don't you go to Europe? Everyone else is. It's all the rage now.' She sounded appalled.

David laughed. 'Maybe one day, but I just want to do something different, Mother.'

'It's dangerous, David. Where will you stay?'

'Everywhere, hopefully.'

'This is completely out of character. Your father will be horrified.'

David shrugged. His father never had much of an opinion on anything; he knew he wouldn't really care. It was his mother's way of trying to talk him out of it. 'The good thing will be that whenever you need me, or miss me'—he reached out and squeezed her hand—'I won't be too far away. I just want to see another world, another life, and maybe I will be more settled when I get back.' He knew he was appealing to his mother's concern for him. She worried about him and his inability to settle down, particularly the absence of a woman in his life.

Moving south, David visited cities, taking in their ambience, learning their histories, meeting locals, and after a few days, sometimes a week, he continued on. He skipped New York, he didn't like the place; it held nothing good for him and memories of Jennifer, whom he was trying to extricate from his mind. Six weeks later he found himself in Atlanta, lonely and tired and considering cutting his adventure short. He decided to stay on for a couple of weeks and then go home.

The more time he spent there, taking in the sights of the city, the more he began to feel an affinity with the place and pondered extending his stay there. The local café he visited every morning welcomed him already, and Doris, his regular waitress, gave him ideas about where to go and what to do and he found himself delaying his travel plans.

David was captivated by the city, from its picturesque cityscape to its history and culture. His mind always harked back to the history lessons in high school, which he further investigated as his interest had been piqued, and being in the same place where so much had happened to alter the culture of America made him feel like a part of it. He was beginning to feel something again, a passion for something, but …

*But what,* he asked himself. *I'm twenty-five years old, alone, no obligations … why not?*

He began to search the classifieds for temporary work and soon found an advertisement in the paper for a kitchen hand at a small restaurant. Although he had a Master's in Business, David didn't scoff at the job as menial as it seemed. In fact, he felt that it would be an easy job to leave when he decided that he wanted to keep moving.

Arriving at the restaurant, Rue George, the sign,

almost hanging on by its hinges, stated, David wondered whether it was the right thing to apply for, *but beggars can't be choosers,* he thought, and walked in.

Bessie, a kindly little lady in her forties, who looked weatherworn and a little too wrinkly, considering the way she spoke, had looked him up and down and asked him about his qualifications.

'Sure, you have a great education,' she said with some derision. 'But can you wash dishes and occasionally serve customers?'

David smiled. 'Well, I've had a few different sorts of jobs, so I'm versatile. I will do my best to learn to wash dishes.'

She looked at him with narrowed eyes and then turned to survey the empty tables waiting to be filled and sighed. 'Okay, you can start tomorrow, 6:00 p.m.'

David's eyes widened in excitement. 'Thank you,' he said, standing up, and began to walk to the door.

'Not so fast,' she called. 'Come on, I'll show you around.'

David was staying at a hotel with shared amenities for backpackers and as a temporary residence, it didn't bother him, but now, having decided to remain in town for a while, he began to look at other options. To stay at a hotel would be impossible. He still had his savings, but he didn't want to touch that, not while he

was here; he needed it for when he continued his travel.
He had dipped into it already as he had stayed longer
than he thought, but he had now secured a job. Sure, a
menial job, with minimum wages, but it would be
enough to rent something small.

He talked to Doris at the café and she told him
she would look out for something for him. Doris, a portly
lady in her fifties, had become quite fond of David, after
serving him breakfast and lunch from the day he arrived,
and when it wasn't busy, she'd sit with him at his table
and chat about any and everything. David, a stickler for
routine, kept coming back, enjoying her company and
chatter, which helped to relieve some of his loneliness.
He spoke to his mother and brother often and he still
kept in touch with some of the friends he had made
through the years, but he needed people, people he could
be with, have fun with, and share his life with. And Doris
had made him feel like one of them, like a local.

He began work at Rue George, named after
Bessie's father, who had passed away some months
earlier. He worked as hard as he could, but it was a job
that didn't require much work and in his spare time,
which was most of his shift, he tried to find something to
do—fix the palings, hammer in unwieldy nails, resettle
the ornaments—so that he felt he was earning his
paycheck. He could already see this restaurant was not

going to last very long, but he was disappointed; Bessie had been good to him, kind and generous, insisting he stay and eat dinner there every night. 'It will go to waste anyway,' she said with a sigh.

It was a week after he started work at Rue George, when he was leaving for the night, that Bessie called out to him.

'Hey, David, where are you staying?'

He turned around. 'Jerry Park,' he said.

He saw her wrinkle her nose. 'Bring your things with you tomorrow. Clear out of there.' She saw him look bewildered. 'Okay, okay, if you really need to see it. Come on back in.'

David followed her through a long corridor which led to the rear entrance of the restaurant, where stood a brown door, which David had never ventured through before, heeding the sign that said No Entry. He hesitated, a frown on his face, and Bessie chuckled.

'I'm not going to attack you,' she said. 'C'mon.'

Behind the door sat a little garden that needed work, a lot of work. Overgrown weeds and brown plants that had been green at some stage in their lives lay limply in pots and in bedraggled garden beds. A narrow walkway made of broken stone tiles led to another brown door and Bessie led him through it. She stood back while David surveyed the room.

'This was Papa's, he would have lived in the restaurant if he could, but this was the next best thing,' she said. 'But you may as well use it.'

David looked at the little living room, which contained a light-brown sofa; a yellow rug sat in the middle of the room with a small ornate marble table on it. There were two tables on each side of the settee with lamps on each and on the left of the rug, an armchair, covered with a green blanket, hiding some sort of damage to the leather. David could see the veins of the breakage in the original covering of the armchair, but it did look comfortable with the indentations of the previous occupant acknowledging his existence.

A kitchenette was attached to the living area, with a toaster and kettle and little red cups sitting upside down on a dish cloth next to it. He wondered whether Bessie had already set it up for him and he moved around to the other rooms. A bedroom, furnished with a double bed and a dressing table, would be the main bedroom, he assumed, as it had a bathroom attached to it. Inside the bathroom he found a shower cubicle and a bath, all fitted into a very small space, and it even contained a vanity which seemed like an afterthought. Stepping into the other bedroom, he found it was much smaller than the first and didn't look like it had enough room for a bed, yet there was one, a little dressing table squeezed by its side.

Walking back outside, Bessie led David to the side of the cottage where a small outhouse, that was in surprisingly good condition compared to the rest of the place, stood, and David wondered whether that actually was an afterthought, a fairly new thought, in fact. It came complete with a washing machine and even a dryer. David was a little suspicious at the newness of the dryer and suspected Bessie had bought it especially for him. Coming back to the garden, Bessie seated herself on the wooden garden bench and leaned her hands on its arm which curved into the ground.

'Papa was simple, he lived for the restaurant.' She looked up at David doubtfully. 'It's fine if it's not good enough. It does need work.'

'No, no, it's great, perfect for me. I really love it!' He frowned. 'But how much?'

Bessie smiled. 'As long as you tend the garden and keep the house clean, I don't want any money. Besides, you can't skip work, I will know whether you are really sick or not.' She winked at him.

'Bessie, I can't let you do this,' he protested.

'It's wasting away anyway, David. It will save you the travel and you will be doing me a favor as well.'

David reached forward to hug her, but remembered himself and took her hands in his. 'Thank you.'

The next day, David packed the small number of items he had with him and moved into the little house at the back of Rue George.

He was home.

****

David enjoyed working at the restaurant and found that he had a keen knack for the business. He spent most of his time working, even when he was not clocked on, even though during business hours, there wasn't much for him to do. One other person worked for Bessie: Lani, a waitress of twenty. A tall, thin girl with light-brown hair and eyes that seemed too large for her face, yet quite an arresting face, she didn't have a lot of ambition and even less interest in her job. She spent most of her time leaning on the counter, reading magazines, and seemed irritated when the little bell atop the door jingled, signaling the arrival of a customer.

But David could see the business was failing miserably. He took note of the issues and tried to do what he could to keep the restaurant afloat. He realized that Bessie did not have much of an idea of how to run the place and had relied on her father as owner and manager, but now that he had passed, she was floundering. Her husband, Tony, a construction worker, was away often and could not devote his time to help the business. Tony liked David immediately and had spent many evenings, after Rue George had closed for the night, having a beer with him.

'I've tried,' Tony said one evening when Bessie was counting the day's earnings. 'But she won't give it up.' He leaned forward, and David felt sorry for this burly man who was trying so hard to make ends meet. 'Maybe you can talk her into it. She respects you. She thinks you're smart and you know more about these things than I do.' He leaned back. 'She's probably right.'

'Wait a little longer,' said David throwing a look at Bessie, whose eyes were creased with worry. 'Give it a little more time.'

Tony followed his gaze. 'I wish I could help here more, but I need to work. Without my income …' He sighed heavily. 'Everything goes on this place.'

David felt compassion for these people who had lived a tough life and had listened on another quiet night at the restaurant, when Tony poured out their story after more than a couple of beers. Tony and Bessie had been married for eighteen years and try as they may, were unable to have children. Bessie had fallen pregnant twice, once when she was twenty-two and once when she was thirty-one, and both times, she had miscarried. Her health had suffered as a result, with doctors telling her that to try again would prove dangerous for her. Although adamant that she would be okay, she kept trying, against Tony's wishes as he worried for her, but when she reached the age of thirty-five, both she and Tony had decided that enough was enough. There had been too much heartache already and they decided to focus on other parts of their life that may bring them happiness.

And happy they were. Bessie doted on the restaurant and Tony continued working in construction, but they also made time to spend with each other, enjoying dance classes and going away on weekend retreats. After Bessie's father had died, she had to focus more of her time on the restaurant, which had been booming until his passing. She realized then how much her father had really done for it and although she learnt from him while working for him, it was the nitty-gritty of things she didn't have a knack for—advertising, bringing in clientele, and managing so much.

Tony continued to work hard, and even harder now that money was tight, and they saw less and less of each other. They began to resent Rue George and had considered selling before Bessie insisted on one last-ditch attempt—Christmas or bust. But now selling up seemed to be their only option.

'I just don't want her hanging on to the hope that this will be what it used to. Bessie's father was a tough old man. He put every waking hour into George and even before he passed, it was starting to go downhill,' Tony said.

'Just wait a little while longer, see how things go,' David asserted, his brain already in motion. This was why he was here. It was fate; his mind immediately went to Jennifer. *Damn fate*, he thought to himself.

He was already thinking about approaching Bessie with a business plan and spent most nights working out what was necessary to turn the business around—a new look, new staff and a new menu, and a good marketing strategy. Everything in the place looked like a relic from the past and if that was the look Bessie was going for, that would have been fine, but it wasn't. David had new hope, and a new focus, which took his mind of Jennifer for more than a few minutes at a time.

Unbeknownst to Bessie and Tony, David had been doing some research in town. In the two months that he had worked at Rue George, he had scoured other restaurants in the city and outer neighborhoods and had picked up ideas and written copious notes. There was no reason for Rue George to go belly-up; it just needed good management. He put together a dossier of his plans and decided to approach Bessie and Tony.

'We can make this place "the place to be" again,' he began, after sitting them both down one evening after the restaurant had closed early again and Lani had left for the night. He paused. Both of them looked at him with blank expressions, waiting for something more. David felt his palms were wet and wiped at his jeans. *Who the hell am I to butt into the lives of these people?* But he knew that both Bessie and Tony had become his family.

David cleared his throat and continued. He opened his folder and showed them his plans, the changes Rue George would need, the advertising, and also the costs.

Bessie and Tony pored excitedly over the pages now scattered over the table and listened in fascination. When he was finished, David sat back, took a deep breath, and waited for he knew not what. They hadn't said much, but he could see the veins popping out of Tony's temples and Bessie's usually creased eyes were wide with excitement.

'David, I don't know; we cannot afford all this,' said Bessie, pointing to the documents. 'We don't have a lot of savings and we were hoping to make at least something from selling the space.'

'Er, yes, I was getting to that,' said David. 'I was hoping to help out. No, no …' he said quickly when he saw Tony sit forward in his seat, ready to protest. 'Not help out, but maybe invest in George.'

'You want to own it? This?' said Bessie, looking around her and throwing up her hands.

'No, no, I'm sorry, this isn't coming out right. I want to put money into it and when it becomes successful, I will take it back, the money, with interest … not a lot of interest, just interest.'

'How much?' said Tony, his eyes narrowing.

'Whatever you want to give me back,' said David.

'What if it doesn't work?' asked Bessie.

'Well, that's a risk I am willing to take. I believe George can be great again,' David insisted. He stood up. 'Both of you need to talk about it. It's just an idea. Let me know when you decide.'

It was at six the next morning when David heard a soft knocking at his door. He hadn't slept; he had been excited and scared and had doubted his plan. What if they declined? Even worse, what if they accepted? Their livelihood was in his hands. He began to worry about his silly ideas. It sounded good … on paper.

David jumped up, knowing that Bessie and Tony had had a similar night. He opened the door and both stood there, their eyes wide in anticipation.

'Not too early, is it?' a sheepish Bessie asked.

David smiled and moved aside to let them in.

'Coffee?' he asked and both nodded.

Before they got to the dining table, Bessie blurted, 'We accept.'

David turned around and both stood there staring at him. Their apprehension was clear, but their faces were shining.

'Wow, okay!' said David. He walked to the fridge and took out a bottle of wine. 'This is not champagne, and it is only six in the morning, but we have something to celebrate,' he said. As he began to pour the wine into three glasses, Bessie came to him. 'Thank you,' she said and hugged him.

It took three months and a bank loan, but Rue George was on its way. Following David's plan, more research in other towns and cities, and hard work, Rue George became the place to be again; in fact, beneath the large sign that hailed its name was inscribed 'the place to eat.' It was simple and inviting.

Lani was retrained against her will—the new Rue George now didn't leave enough time for magazine reading and she resented David for that—and more staff were hired. Through advertising, customers began to trickle in and soon more and more people began filling the dining hall. David realized that they would need another chef and they began to open in the afternoons as well as the evenings. Bessie could not believe what they had made of her precious inheritance. In the next year, they had repaid David and had added interest onto his loan, which they knew he had never wanted in the first place.

All the while David thought of Jennifer. Thinking of her had kept him going. He knew she was with him and felt her spirit pushing him on. He hoped she was okay and hoped that she may find some happiness with Jack and her baby. On the odd occasion, he would see her face in a magazine, usually old magazines that were scattered around doctors' offices, and he'd wince in pain. He had his flings; he even spent a night with Lani after an evening of drinks, regretting it the moment it was over. But she had been fine with it all and the next day had acted as if nothing had happened. David was relieved and made a mental note to avoid work romances.

One morning, David was breakfasting at Doris's when his eyes fell upon a magazine cover, being read by a customer. It was Jennifer. His heart skipped a beat as it always did, but something was different. This looked newer. He squinted his eyes to see the magazine more clearly, two tables away, when the reader of it folded it down. He raised his eyes and saw that the owner of the magazine was looking at him indignantly.

'Sorry,' he called out. 'I was just trying to see if

that was a new *Flow* … for my mother.'

'Yes, it is,' the woman said abruptly and lifted the magazine in front of her face again.

David quickly picked up his wallet, paid for his breakfast, and headed for the nearest newsstand. There it was, there *she* was. He bought a copy, sat himself down on a park bench, and began to turn the pages. He stopped his trembling hands at a four-page spread, Jennifer's sparkling eyes beckoning to him. After poring over the pictures, his mouth dry and his stomach in knots, he leaned back and breathed hard.

He looked at the cover again. It was a brand-new copy. He had looked before, but she hadn't been in any magazines for more than two years. He contemplated that, but he was more concerned about his reaction to it. He hadn't seen Jennifer for more than three years and his feelings had not diminished, not a bit. As he wandered back home, he attempted to ditch the magazine in the nearest waste-bin, but couldn't, so he rolled it up and took it home.

That evening David asked for a quick break at 6:00 p.m. and went into the garden. He sat on the bench and gazed at the moon that was mostly covered with clouds.

'I miss you still.' He looked up forlornly. 'But I'm happy here and I think I may stay for a while. I wish you could see me here, be with me here, meet my new family.' He found his eyes moist and took a deep breath. 'I'm so proud of you and what you've done. I hope you are happy with your husband and your son. I know it's terrible, but I wish it was our son. I also hope that you think of me sometimes too and know that I always loved you … and I still do.' He blew a kiss to the moon and sighing, stood up to go back into the restaurant. Bessie stood at the door, her arms crossed against her chest, a frown on her face. Embarrassed, David smiled shakily and apologized for taking too long and moved to go inside.

'I'm sorry, David,' she said.

'You heard me?'

'Yes, I'm sorry. I just heard a little, but it explains a lot.' David looked at his shoes uncomfortably. 'I knew there was something, but I didn't want to intrude. I thought you were … you know …' she said. 'Not that there's anything wrong with that,' she quickly added.

'We should go in,' said David.

'No, let's chat,' said Bessie, gently guiding him back to the bench. He went reluctantly, but thought it would be good for him to finally have someone to talk to about it all. So, he did, and Bessie listened without interruption. He ended his story in tears and Bessie held his hand the whole time he talked of Jennifer.

'You have to let her go, David,' she said, when he had finished.

'I can't ever; believe me, I've tried,' said David, putting his head in his hands. 'Wait here for a minute,' he said and went into his cottage. He came out with the magazine and showed it to Bessie. She let out a low whistle.

'Well, she is certainly something to look at,' she said, 'but she's broken your heart, David; you must at least try to move on.'

'Well, thanks to you guys, I have been able to keep busy and apart from Jen, I'm really enjoying being here. So much for a quick stop in Atlanta!' said David.

'Are you planning on leaving soon?' asked Bessie slowly.

'I love it here right now, Bessie, but I want more,' said David, looking back at the moon. 'I love what we did with the place, but I feel that now it's well underway, I don't know what to do with myself ...'

'Do it again!' Bessie jumped in.

David looked at her, wondering if she had already guessed at his intentions.

'Tony and I were talking; well, we have been for the past few weeks. We were thinking of opening another restaurant.'

David's eyes widened. 'Really?' he said incredulously. He had seen how hard they had worked to come this far and this wasn't at all what he'd expected. He had been considering leaving, now that they had built Rue George into something worthy of Bessie's father.

'We were looking at a place on Darcy Street. It's closer to the city center.'

'You've already done your research?'

'Well, we were hoping you would do most of it again, like you did last time,' she said guiltily and paused. 'Tony and I wanted to talk to you about it together, but … well, here we are, so I may as well put it to you. We want you to come into it with us, as partners. You pretty much built back George and you didn't take anything for it, even put your own savings at risk. We were thinking that with this one, we could go halves. Straight down the line.'

'It's your brand name, Bess, I can't take that, it wouldn't be fair.'

'Not fair is you not already having a part of this George. You really don't understand how grateful we are, do you?' She looked around at the now beautifully sculptured garden, which David nursed in his spare time. 'Even this place looks like the Garden of Eden,' she said and laughed.

David chuckled. 'We should go back in, Bessie, Lani is probably having puppies and kittens in there without us,' said David, standing up. 'We can discuss this again with Tony.' He looked at her with love. 'Thank you … for everything.'

Bessie stood up and hugged David tightly to her. 'You are family to us, David, you must know that by now. And go put that thing away,' she said, gesturing to the magazine.

He looked down at it and nodded. When he got to the door, he heard Bessie call his name. He turned around.

'Thank you, David,' she said and went inside.

****

Within three months, work had begun on a dilapidated space that was once a restaurant. Tony and Bessie, and David had split the costs, with the help of another bank loan, and had put all their efforts into the building of Rue George II—The Other Place to Be. The original Rue George had become so popular that customers had to book well in advance for a table. Bessie had taken over it completely and sought David's advice on all aspects of the business, learning as she did. David and Tony, on his days off, worked on Rue II, as they called it. It offered fine dining, but they also tried to keep it from being too ostentatious and pretentious. Two chefs were hired, already tried out in Rue I, and waiters were trained for two weeks prior. David wanted perfection.

On opening night, four months after beginning the new venture, Rue II was fully booked. Customers, old and new, flowed in and left with compliments to the management. David was relieved but knew it would take more than opening night. He had been confident, but also nervous.

He had also invited his family for the grand opening and his parents and his brother came with his family. David was delighted and they left the restaurant with smiles and congratulations. His brother, Daniel, had two children and a lovely wife whom he and his family adored and David looked at them wistfully while they interacted, Daniel's young son, Jesse, pulling on the pigtails of his older sister, while she shooed him as if shooing a horsefly, and Daniel and his wife talked and laughed with each other and the rest of the family easily, while also giving each other looks that showed their affection for one another.

*How I want that,* thought David, *but I won't ever have it, not without Jennifer.* David's mother was so proud of him, and told anyone who cared, and even those who didn't, that she was his mother. His father sat and smiled and shook David's hand at the end of their evening. It was enough.

Opening night also brought something else to David, in the shape of a woman. He had seen her walk past the restaurant with a child of about six while in the process of its building and she always stopped and inquired about its progress. Her name was Elizabeth and she was in her late twenties, and as David found out later, a divorcee. That night, she had dined at Rue II with an older woman who David presumed was her mother and both had given David more than a passing glance. He stopped at her table to ask her how everything was and David was introduced to the older woman, who in fact, was her mother. On their way out, David escorted them to the door and she thanked him for the meal and service and put her hand on his. Her mother had raised her eyebrows at this and had then smiled.

The next afternoon, Elizabeth was at the restaurant again. David was quite taken with her and decided to take a chance and ask for her number. She gladly gave it and he quickly asked if she was free the next Thursday evening, the night he was free. She accepted.

Three months later, he asked her to be his wife. She accepted again.

# CHAPTER 20

## *Jack*

Jack had looked for David. He wanted to know where he was and more importantly, what had happened between him and Jennifer. He was sure something had transpired between them, but was too proud to confront Jennifer about it, hoping that she would come out with it herself. As time passed, he began to think that perhaps nothing happened at all, but in his heart, he knew them. He knew them both well.

He had seen David's feelings for her, back on that day on their horses. He had seen it with her on their wedding day when she had looked at him from the bridal car. He had seen it in the way she looked out of the window in the evening and when she called his name softly in her sleep.

He had to find David. He needed to know what happened, even if he had to kill it out of him. He had tried to get information from David's family in Boston, had visited with them and although they welcomed him warmly, they wouldn't give him David's whereabouts, knowing that something was not right. He wished he could have been more convincing, but knew their loyalty was to their son. So, Jack stayed in Boston for two days and returned to California.

The night he had confronted Jennifer about 'that night,' he had beaten her to almost a pulp. He couldn't stop himself; the rage had built up so much because she just wouldn't tell him what he needed to hear. He had in fact already been to Boston, but was hoping that Jennifer could give him some idea of where David was.

At the table, he had told her about his own dalliances, had rubbed her nose in it, the women he had been with, 'Yes,' he had said, 'including Arlene.'

He stopped to look at her and she turned her face away from him. She didn't say anything and he couldn't quite read her expression but she didn't looked surprised. How he wanted to hurt her, like she was killing him. He made love to her last night, for the first time since they had left New York, but afterwards he had felt shame and a sense of betrayal. Now she sat here in front of him, still that innocent look on her face, not giving away anything, even after what he had just disclosed about his own deceit.

'Look at me,' he yelled, leaning over the table, his nose brushing her hair.

Jennifer didn't reply but stood up and began to pack away the plates of barely touched food. This enraged Jack even more and he wrenched her arm, the plate she was holding clattering to the floor and breaking into a hundred pieces. She looked at him.

'Please stop now, Jack,' she said without emotion and started for the kitchen. Almost without realizing what he was doing, his hand was clutching her hair and he had pulled her to the floor. He was on top of her in an instant, holding her in place, and she looked up at him, her teeth clenched, hatred in her eyes.

'Get away from me,' she screamed into his face.

'That's it, that's the Jen I know. Is that what you did with him?' He moved his face forward to put his mouth on hers, but by leaning forward, he had become lighter and not on guard and she pushed her hips forward with all her might, rolling out deftly from under him.

He got to his knees and she darted to the other side of the table, and finding a bread knife on it, picked it up and brandished it at him. He leaned back in his haunches and laughed.

'Bring it, Jen. Try to. I dare you!' he snarled.

She placed the knife back on the table and stood

there, hopping from one foot to the other uncertainly.

'Jack …'

'Where's your precious David now?' he said, becoming somber, almost sad, his shoulders slumping.

At the sound of his name, Jennifer lifted her eyes to his with revulsion. 'Don't you utter his name. You are not fit to speak his name!' She regretted it before it had even left her mouth.

Jack was upon her almost before she had finished the sentence.

If her mother had not heard the commotion and had broken her way in through the glass door, she would have been dead, Jennifer considered later. By that time, Jennifer had given up fighting back and was lying unconscious on the floor, the white rug beneath her streaked red. Jack was in a trance; it was as if his hands had a mind of their own and he hit and hit, smashing David from her brain. It was the force of Judy's body thrown against him, pushing him off Jennifer that seemed to bring him back to reality.

Judy was screaming, but had quickly regained her composure and leaned her head on Jennifer's chest to see if she was still alive. Once she had confirmed this, she looked at Jack, who was leaning against the wall and looking at his hands, and yelled at him to call the ambulance. Jack didn't move; he seemed to be in another sort of trance right now, so Judy, quickly looking around, located the phone and called 911. As she was led out in the stretcher, Jack saw his wife open her eyes to look at her son, who was standing beside her mother and looking up at her, terror in his eyes.

He tried to see her, but Judy wouldn't let him anywhere near Jennifer and he wandered around the house trying to find a way to make it right. He would do anything to make it right. He couldn't not have her by his side and he would give his right arm to take back what he'd done.

'Time,' he said and stopped pacing. 'She will need some time. To think, to miss me.' He gave Judy, who wouldn't look at him, a set of keys after she insisted, and left for New York, relieved that Jennifer was not pressing charges. He did wonder if she would still be there when he came home and hoped she at least loved him enough to forgive him.

In New York, Jack set his focus on work. Arlene had been over to his apartment the moment she knew he was back in town, but Jack was not in the mood to deal with her. He had asked her to leave and she had threatened to tell Jennifer about them.

'Go ahead,' he said wryly. 'I've already done that.' Arlene's face registered astonishment and she had picked up her things and walked out, slamming the door behind her. Jack did not even have the energy to smile at that.

His acquisitions were increasing with his business growing at a steady rate, but Jack was unhappy. All he wanted was for Jennifer to be happy … and want him. He thought about David. He thought about his own relentless quest for answers and tortured himself over what he had done to his wife. But he wanted to win her back and needed to figure out how he could. She had stayed with him, well, at his home in California, thousands of miles away from him and he longed to be with her, but he knew he had to give her time and space.

He had really tried to be patient, to not care about David, to trust her, but he just couldn't help himself. Just looking at her still drove him crazy and just the thought of her with David had driven him insane.

Jack decided now that he would try to ignore David's existence, realizing that the more he pushed Jennifer against David, the more she would react and would keep him with her. He had called home every day in the month he was in New York, but Judy had refused to let him speak to Jennifer, but she would let him talk quickly to Jacky, who now sounded timid and sad. It broke Jack's heart and he always got off the phone with tears in his eyes, but he knew that he had done it—he had made his little boy scared of him. He vowed to make it up to him, to both of them.

Arriving back in Sacramento, Jack went straight home. Judy was home with Jacky, but Jennifer was not. He was somewhat relieved, but Judy was cold, only looking up when he came in and then went about doing her chores, while Jack unpacked his suitcase. Jack didn't try to explain himself; he knew by now that Jennifer would have spoken to her mother about everything, and what was there to explain? Judy had seen it for herself. Still, he did care about what the old lady thought of him and hoped he could somehow make it up to her too.

But it was his son that he was most worried about. He wasn't sure of how much he had seen or understood and hoped that he was young enough for his memory to have cleared; he was relieved when Jacky ran to greet him with a hug when he arrived.

When Jennifer returned home that evening, she stood in the doorway, her back straight. She wore a long green skirt and gray stilettos. A yellow cardigan covered her arms and a large pair of sunglasses covered her face. She looked at Jack, who was sitting at the dining table with a cluster of loose-leaf papers in front of him, and he turned to look at her. She still managed to take his breath away.

She raised her glasses; she wasn't wearing any make-up, and Jack was relieved that no remnants of his tirade remained on her face. She walked over to the table and looked down at it.

'Divorce papers?' she said lightly and walked away.

Jack sighed. 'Jennifer, Jen …'

'Don't call me Jen.' She spun around sharply. Then she turned and walked through the back door toward the guest house, where Judy had coaxed Jacky to.

Jack sat there feeling stupid, but he could already feel his temper rising. He knew he had to control himself; this was the point when he knew he had to regulate his emotions. So, he let her leave, and put his head into his hands. This wasn't going to be easy. He hadn't known what to expect when he returned, so he wasn't really surprised with anything that happened, but his heart was sad. He knew he had lost her. He went to the bar to pour himself a drink and heard the back door open and shut. Jennifer came into view and walked to the table. She sat down.

'Make mine a double,' she said. Jack poured two bourbons and gave her one. He then sat down at the table with her, waiting for her to speak. She downed the bourbon in one gulp and shook her head with its sting. Then she looked defiantly at Jack.

'David came to New York. We fucked. We met the next day. We fucked again. Then he left town,' she said, staring straight into his eyes, waiting for his reaction.

He clenched his jaw and fisted his palms. He knew she was testing him, and he didn't reply. He looked into his glass, finished it in one swig, and got up to refill it, trying to ignore the swirling of grief in his stomach. He was right and for once, wished he wasn't. Jennifer lifted her own glass and he took it from her. He came back to the table with both glasses filled to the brim and sat down at the table across from her.

'Clearly we are gonna need these,' he said.

She picked up her glass and held it in the air. They clinked them together. 'Where to now, Jack?' said Jennifer, wearily.

'All I know is I love you, Jennifer,' said Jack. 'I want you with me forever. You're my wife.'

Jennifer laughed, a laugh that turned into a sneer. 'Yes, that's about right, Jack. Husbands do this to their wives. That's what real husbands do.'

'Real wives don't go around fucking their ex-boyfriends either,' he retorted.

'Like you hadn't gone around screwing all of New York's finest,' she yelled back, standing up.

Jack looked up at her. 'I didn't love them,' he said quietly and stood up. He began to walk away and turned around. 'Figure out what you want, Jennifer and

let me know,' he said quietly and he walked out of the
front door.

# CHAPTER 21

*Jennifer and Jack*

Jennifer sat on the back step and leaned on the railing of the patio. It was a quiet evening; Judy had taken Jacky to visit one of the friends she'd made at the fair last summer and Jennifer thought it amusing that her mother had more friends in this place than she did. She lifted her eyes to the stars and wished the moon could come out tonight, but the clouds had gathered, and she felt desolate. Jack was away again and although there was always a sense of relief when he left, she still missed him.

The last couple of years he had been on his best behavior even though their conversations remained stilted and uncomfortable. But since then, he had given her what she wanted, didn't complain whenever she got a gig, and had not brought up David's name.

'Okay, Jack,' she'd said when he came home that

evening and sunk into the bed, his head in his hands. 'Let's try again. Let's give this a chance.' And he had dropped his head into her chest and she stroked his hair while he sobbed.

Everything was on the table now, there was nothing to hide anymore, and Jennifer knew she could never be with David again; the odds against them were too high. She could love Jack again; she did once and she knew there was a part of him which was good and a part of him that would love her forever.

Jack had promised fidelity and Jennifer had done the same and their lives resumed in a more detached manner. They were intimate, but it was not love and they were both acutely aware of it. They had their jobs and Jacky and the brief conversations they had were focused on their son. Judy, although giving Jack the cold shoulder for a long time, accepted Jennifer's decision and had forgiven Jack, but she insisted on remaining with them.

But Jennifer missed New York and her friends there, even though Elle, Jed, and Angel had made exactly one visit each. She knew Jack wouldn't approve of her going to New York for any period of time and thought it best not to antagonize him. She spoke to Jed often and he always asked her when she would be returning home; she never had an answer for him and

Jed would huff and puff and tell her to leave the bastard.

She spoke to Angel often and kept the conversation around Angel's life, avoiding any references to Jack and their lives; there was no point in lying to her friend about a happiness that had long been missing. Angel was doing well in the hotel industry, managing one of New York's largest hotels, and was ecstatically in love with Neville and her son, Charles, her voice taking on a dreamy tone when she talked about them, and Jennifer felt a sliver of envy and a plethora of joy for her friend.

Angel had made the trip to Sacramento once, but she had left her husband and son at home, so she only stayed for three days, missing them so terribly, she cut her trip short. But Jennifer was so glad to see her, and they spent all their time at home reminiscing about their childhood and their hungry years in New York, two girls really, when they adventured to the big city, and couldn't believe how far they'd come in just a few years.

When Jack left for Maybury to check on his mother a few hours after Angel's arrival, Jennifer breathed a sigh of relief and Angel didn't miss it.

'Are you two okay?'

Jennifer nodded wearily and then smiled widely; she wasn't going to harp on about the state of her marriage when there was precious little time to be spent with her best friend.

But when they sat on the porch in the evening, sipping on wine after Jacky had gone to bed, Angel looked into the sky.

'Have you seen him?'

'Who?' Jennifer knew who Angel was talking about.

'Come on, Jenny.'

'No, not for a while,' replied Jennifer, feeling the same stone that lodged in her throat every time she thought of him, emerging now.

'Which means you have seen him?' asked Angel.

'I can't talk about him, Angel, I think about him too much already.' Jennifer swallowed the urge to let it all out to Angel and shook her head, smiling broadly. 'So, what are we going to do tomorrow?'

Angel lifted her glass. 'More of this … lots to catch up on.'

When Angel left, Jennifer felt lonelier than ever. She couldn't tell her friend that he was always with her, always in her mind, in her heart, and that she found herself in her backyard most evenings, gazing at the moon and thinking of him. More than once, she had caught Jack observing at her through the window, a contemplative look on his face, and he'd quickly close the curtain when he realized he was discovered. She was glad he never asked her about it. She knew it was wrong to think about David so much, but she couldn't help herself and convinced herself that there was no harm in doing it anymore.

She wondered what he was doing with his life and hoped that he was happy. She thought about him with Ness and felt a jealousy surge within her, but she quelled it; he wasn't hers. She wished she could see him again and was also glad that there wasn't a choice; who knows what might happen again? She needed to make her own life without him in it.

Jennifer was more homesick than ever after Angel left but tried to make the most of her life where it was. Jack had been the perfect husband for the last couple of years, but she felt very alone and he had noticed it.

'What do you think about returning home?' he asked one evening when they were sitting on the front porch after dinner.

Jennifer narrowed her eyes at him, her heart skipping a beat, and saw that he was serious.

He chortled at her incredulity and had put his hand on hers. 'I mean it,' he said. 'I know you're not happy here and I want you to be happy.' Then he looked into the distance and said more softly, 'That's what I've always wanted.'

Jennifer squeezed his hand. 'Why the change of

heart?'

'No change of heart,' he said and shrugged. 'I can conduct my business from New York as well as from here, now that the ranch is set up and the business is running smoothly.'

'Oh, Jack!' she squealed and jumped into his lap.

'And I know you want to get back to work, not like here, but properly, like you were there. Every time I'm back there, I have people asking after you,' he said, rolling his eyes. 'And Jed … don't get me started on Jed! The man is obsessed with you.' He held her tightly and pulled her back, smiling at the exultation in her eyes. 'At least I know how I can make you happy again.' Jennifer put her head on his shoulder and knew she could love him again.

When Jennifer broke the news to Judy, whom she hoped would return to New York with them, Judy had told them that it was best for her to go back to Tandaro, now that she was satisfied that Jack had indeed changed. Jennifer was disappointed but she knew that her mother needed to have her own life; she had another daughter and other grandkids to spoil too.

'And,' Judy had said, 'Tandaro is not far; I can be there in a couple of hours. Your friends are right there too. Not like here, where you're so far away from everything.' Jennifer knew then that her mother had stayed all that time just to protect her.

It was a cool November day in 1990 when Jennifer returned to New York. Her thoughts immediately fell to David and for the first time, was anxious about her decision to return. Then she sighed; it wasn't as if she hadn't thought about him anyway.

The first thing she did was go to Petriol, her old agency, and Shane, new in management, took one look at her and signed her on the spot. Jed, still at Petriol, begged to be assigned to Jennifer, got his wish, and she began her first assignment the week after she arrived. Jennifer felt full of hope and began to look forward to living her life again, this time with purpose.

She invited Angel and her family for dinner two nights after they returned and they resumed their friendship easily, Jennifer excited to have her closest confidantes back. She was already missing her mother and was glad to keep busy.

Her first modeling job, for *Hush* magazine, was tough. The pace was so much quicker than she had remembered and Jennifer was relearning the ways of working with an agency. She nevertheless got through the three-day shoot and was sent on another assignment very soon after. She was happy with the way things worked as she also had time to spend with her son.

Three months into her contract, Jennifer was

asked to do a runway show. She did have the choice to refuse and discussed it with Jack. He said she could do whatever made her happy and that he would be in the front row to support her. Jed was ecstatic and she was put into the line-up for the *Hush* Spring Collection. It wasn't a big event and Jennifer was relieved. She wasn't sure if this was her thing, but wanted to give it a shot to see how it went.

She found it was crazy and exhausting, and even though the models had rehearsed a number of times, she felt uncomfortable with the process. Nevertheless, she persevered and took on the runway jobs she was offered, but she also continued her photoshoots. She didn't want to leave New York, and the agency tried to accommodate her, but she had to acquiesce at times and found herself in Rome, the Netherlands, and Australia, all in the space of three weeks. She had come home exhausted and missing Jacky, and to some extent, Jack, as well. She vowed never to leave them for that amount of time again and resisted the offers to leave the country.

Jack was happy and so was Jennifer. She was back on top of the world.

# CHAPTER 22

*1998*

*David*

David had made a name for himself in the restaurant business, perfecting Rue II and successfully setting up two other restaurants in the next two years. He handed over ownership of Rue II to Bessie and Tony after asking them if they wished to continue with the business as a franchise. They had insisted that they had enough on their hands with two restaurants and David relinquished control, setting them up with an efficient manager. He promised to check in with them often and they asked him if he himself needed their help with his own ventures. He assured them he would if he did, but David was becoming more confident and felt like he was putting to good use the degree he had worked so hard for.

The first restaurant of his own was also in Atlanta, but not close enough to Rues I and II to be a threat to Bessie and Tony. He called it Moon and turned it into a lucrative enterprise almost immediately. He knew by now he had found something he was good at, and that he actually enjoyed doing, and decided to continue, relishing the entire process, raising a place from the bare bones to a polished product. But the moment he completed Moon, he was itching to do another.

Elizabeth had been perfect. With a young son, David had been hesitant, but he took to the boy immediately. They had been married within a year of their meeting, their wedding taking place in a small garden filled with white daisies and large yellow sunflowers. An afternoon buffet was served under a large pergola that sheltered less than fifty guests, which included David and Elizabeth's families, as well as Tony, Bessie, and the few people David knew in Atlanta.

Bessie approached him while he sat watching Elizabeth dance with her son. He had been smiling and Bessie whispered in his ear. 'You are a lucky man, David, but she is too, remember that.'

David had looked at Bessie quizzically and she had pinched his cheek.

'If you can't be with the one you love, love …'

'... the one you're with,' David finished for her.

David moved into Elizabeth's home as her son was settled where he was and so was she. David didn't protest and although he missed the little cottage behind Rue George, he knew it was quite impossible for the three of them to live there. He did visit often to tend to the garden, which he now loved, and made it an excuse to see Bessie and Tony, although he knew he never needed any excuse.

Elizabeth, although at first interested in David's ventures, wanted her own career to progress. A grade-school teacher, she had not wanted to move too far away from Atlanta and she couldn't follow David on his business; her son and her career kept her where she was. They had been happy for three years, but had slowly grown apart; David was traveling often and Elizabeth, trying to get back into the swing of things at her job, was working hard, and they barely saw each other.

David, realizing that his heart was only half committed, let the marriage dissolve and moved out. By then, he was already working on the third Moon. His second was also in Atlanta and he called it Atlanta Moon. The third, in a city on the outskirts of South Carolina, he called Carolina Moon and all had gone well, but the last one had taken more time than he anticipated, which didn't help the situation at home, and

David gave up on his marriage; he thought later, probably too easily.

By the time David was thirty, he had been married for a second time, divorced, owned four restaurants called Moon, and was working his way toward Washington, planting his restaurants along the way. He was making a name for himself in the business world and he was working hard but enjoying himself, so he decided to continue until he stopped having fun.

David still kept track of Jennifer's modeling activities, and with the rise of the internet, he was able to see more of her, sometimes his heart in his throat while the page slowly loaded. He felt like a stalker at times, but he just needed to see her, to remind himself that he loved and could be loved. He didn't attempt any other long-term relationships and reverted to casual dating. There just wasn't any point anymore; he had tried and failed.

His fifth restaurant was set up further away into Richmond and he was working toward Baltimore and Philadelphia, but he had decided to bypass New York, even though he knew that this would be the most lucrative move. He had planned to take them all the way to Boston and then, he thought, he may stop to consider his next move, perhaps take a holiday, finally go to Europe. David was not greedy; he was wealthy enough, but his drive and his love of the business kept him going.

It also helped fill the void of loneliness and keeping busy doing something that he loved was a blessing.

By 1998, David had moved to Baltimore. He felt like a gypsy sometimes, but his roots were now in Atlanta and he made excuses often to go there. It was on the opening night of Baltimore's Moon that David wondered whether he was done with the restaurant building. He was thirty-three and felt as though he should be slowing down. *But what do I do?* he thought. He was still enjoying himself and couldn't imagine himself idle.

It was on the same opening night that he came face to face with Jack. Jack had come in for dinner with two other men. It looked like a business dinner and David had spied him as soon as he had walked in and his heart raced as he searched for Jennifer, angry with his disappointment when he discovered she was not there too. He wondered how to approach Jack and whether he should at all, but decided that he wasn't going to hide from him. He was more worried about how much Jack knew and didn't want to put Jennifer in jeopardy. So, once the waiter had seated the party at a prominent table, David walked over to them.

'Hello, Jack,' he said and put out his hand.

Jack looked up and his face didn't register surprise; he clearly knew who the owner of this establishment was. 'Hello, David,' he replied, shaking the outstretched hand. Jack introduced his companions, who were indeed business associates.

'Well, I hope you all enjoy your meal, which is served with my compliments,' said David with a slight bow and continued around the room. He was shaken, but somewhat relieved that he had finally seen Jack after that night all those years ago, and he wondered why Jack was here. He kept his eye on him all evening, irritated by the distraction, when he usually greeted and chatted with diners, and when he saw Jack stand up to leave, he extracted himself from an over-chatty client and walked to the door, which Jack seemed to hover next to.

'I hope you had a good time?' David asked, half expecting Jack to spit in his face.

'Can you meet me after you finish here?' Jack asked, unsurely.

David was taken aback with the request, but even more so with Jack's uncertain composure.

'I can't tonight,' he said regretfully. 'It's opening night and it will be a late one.' He saw Jack's face fall and quickly added, 'Will you still be in town tomorrow? I can do tomorrow.'

Jack smiled and nodded, and David gave him the address of a nearby bar. He went home lost in thought, wondering why Jack wanted to see him. He worried about Jennifer. Was she okay? By all accounts, her career was still going strong, even into her thirties, and he managed to smile at the thought; he was so proud of her.

They met at a bar in the center of the city the next evening, both making small talk, tentatively at first, discussing business and staying well off the topic of Jennifer. Both were becoming relaxed with bourbon dissolving their nerves. Jack told David about his son, who was now eleven years old, which led them to talking about their own childhood and the pranks they played and the fun they had had. David updated Jack on his own family and Jack told him about the death of his father, which meant that his mother resided in the big old house all by herself with just the housekeeper for company. She had refused to leave as it was her home, where her husband and daughter, Dell, lived.

The mention of Dell sobered David and he thought about how long ago that was and how young they had been. They had been talking and laughing just as they used to so long ago and it didn't feel unnatural, so much so, that they forgot themselves and it was only when Jack discussed going back to New York to his family that there was an awkward silence.

'How did we get here, Jack?'

'We fucked up, David. Both of us fucked up,' said Jack, swirling the remaining bourbon and gulping down the last sip.

'And what now?'

'I go back to my life and you go back to yours, and "never the twain shall meet",' said Jack and David nodded.

'Too much water … and all that …' said David sadly and Jack nodded.

On their way out of the bar, they shook hands. 'For what it's worth, I have missed you,' said Jack. 'You were like my brother.'

'Me too,' said David and they both hugged quickly and then turned around and walked in different directions.

# CHAPTER 23

*Jennifer and Jack*

Jack had returned from Baltimore feeling relieved after his meeting with David, but also disturbed. He wanted to discuss Jennifer with David, to talk about their life together; he wished he could confide in him, the only real friend he ever had. 'Well, I'm the one who wrecked that,' he said to himself with regret, but he had enjoyed the evening with David; it felt so… right.

But now he was back in New York, his old fears began to resurface and his suspicions were aroused. He wondered whether they had been in contact, especially these days when it was so much easier for them to speak or even see each other, even living in different parts of the country, but he didn't get that feeling from either of them. When something had happened between them, he had known immediately that something wasn't right, so he decided to trust his intuition. *Yes*, he thought, *David is not a threat anymore.*

He hesitated at the front door, a nagging doubt in his brain, and turned the key in the lock.

Jennifer was used to Jack going away on business trips, so when he arrived back from Baltimore, she greeted him with a bourbon, sat beside him at the dining table, and asked about his trip.

'Same ol',' he said. Her face was shining and she had a little smile that was about to burst through her lips. He couldn't tell her about his meeting with David; he himself was not sure why he went to see him. Bringing up his name may reignite lingering embers and though he was almost sure they hadn't been in contact, why tempt fate? 'Business is business. Happy to be home,' he said and pulled at her chin. 'Are you okay?'

'Yes, I'm fine,' she replied. 'So, I had my last show for *Hush* and I was wondering how you felt about me taking a few months off, maybe a year or so even.'

Jack looked at her in surprise. 'Whatever you want to do is fine,' he replied. 'Why the sudden change of heart?'

'Well, Jacky is going away to school soon, so I thought I may need to prepare his things and spend some time with him before he leaves and ...' Jennifer paused and her brows creased.

'And ...?'

'Well, it's hard to model with a baby bump.' She looked for his reaction with trepidation.

It took a moment for it to sink in and she saw the curl on his lip straighten.

'Jack? So, what do you think?' Jennifer's forehead crinkled and her shoulders slumped. But Jack was on his feet, lifting her in his arms and spinning her around so hard, her breath left her. She laughed, trying to stop the twirling, which was making her stomach turn. 'Jack, put me down this minute,' she demanded.

'I will not,' he said, but stopped spinning and held her face to his. 'Right now, I'm the happiest man alive,' he said and the tears that welled in his eyes confirmed it. He leaned down and kissed her and it was the first time in a long time that she thought maybe he did really still love her.

Jennifer and Jack had both tried their best to be happy since their return to New York, but they knew that it was a strained, if uneventful marriage. Jack had not struck her since the fight in California that almost took her life and she felt that part of him was gone; he had control of his temper. She also realized that although he was still extremely jealous with no reason, there had never been any provocation; the only man she would leave him for was out of their lives as far as he was concerned.

*We can be happy*, she thought, *as long as David is out of the picture and he can keep his hands off me*, and both had focused on Jacky and their work. Their marriage was working, as unhappy as it sometimes was, and now there was going to be another baby. Jennifer's modeling was at an end; she knew it was a matter of time, she had pushed the extent of her time as it was.

A baby at the conclusion of her career would be the perfect end. She would still get guest spots on television shows, from which she could promote the new beauty line she had begun with Jed as her partner. 'My idea', he reminded her often, 'but it wouldn't be anything without your name.' She was happy for him to brag; she credited him for most of her career, his street-smarts and his financial prowess keeping her relevant in the fickle world of modeling.

'Moondance,' she said when he bit the end of his pencil, contemplating a name for their company.

'That's a bit ...' He stared at her wryly. 'Really, Jennifer? Really?'

'Well, that's what I want it to be.'

'Won't it stir the pot with your husband?'

Jennifer smiled. 'Jack doesn't know about our thing,' she said.

'Won't it stir the pot with you?' He raised his brows in question.

'Nope,' she replied, shaking her head. 'Just something I've thought about for a long time.'

'Yes, since you were eighteen,' said Jed, rolling his eyes. 'Fine,' he said sulkily, and then he smiled. 'Actually, I really like it.'

Moondance was past its infancy and with the advent of the internet, she was able to work from home, Jack happy that she actually chose to remain there.

At the end of May, Jennifer, three months pregnant, together with Jack, took Jacky away to school. He would come home for term and semester breaks, but having to leave him for more than two months at a time broke her heart.

'It will be good for him,' Jack insisted. 'It will turn him into a man, not a little mama's boy.'

Jennifer didn't have the energy to be wound up by his comment, she was so saddened by her son going away. But he held his head high and smiled through his watery eyes when she kissed him goodbye.

'We agreed for a year's trial,' said Jack on the three-hour ride home. She had blubbered with her head to the window for most of the way; Jack didn't know how to console her and he took her hand.

'I didn't agree,' she couldn't help saying and felt Jack take his hand back from hers.

She spent the next two days huddled in bed,

missing her son, wondering how he was coping, whether he would be bullied, whether he would make friends. He was a personable young man, she reasoned; he made friends wherever he went, but the thought of not seeing him every day, hearing about his day, while he proudly displayed his artworks or his report cards, gnawed at her soul. On the third day, she tore herself out of bed and convinced herself that there was work to be done; she couldn't let Jed down. Besides, being busy had always been the perfect antidote to her woes and she threw herself into the company.

She didn't see a lot of Jack, dinners together rare and nights together even more so. Without Jacky to keep them together, to talk about and talk to, they found they had not a lot in common anymore. It wasn't as if they didn't make an effort; they made date nights but found that they sat at the table at a restaurant, gulped down their food, and came home early. They would then both yawn and go to bed, usually without touching each other and more often, not at the same time. On occasion, Jack went out afterwards to have late-night drinks with his friends and Jennifer worried about where he was going but didn't want to rock the boat, so she never asked him about it. Besides, she didn't feel that she had any right to, since she thought about David at every moment; in her heart she had cheated so much more than Jack ever could. She sought the moon often still and even more often now that she was more alone than ever.

Angel and Jed were constant companions, but both had their own lives, Angel with three children of her own and Jed with his own partner, a lovely young man, Kevin, and there was many an evening spent in joy and laughter; it helped to keep her mind from roaming even if for a little while.

But David lived in her heart. When she first looked him up on the internet, her jaw dropped and her heart twisted. And when she saw him standing in front of a restaurant, the proud owner of Moon, she let a tear fall, as she ran her fingers over the screen. She thought of how they were when they were together and realized that intermittent encounters were all they really had. Was the thought of him, the memory, more powerful than the reality? No, she knew what she felt when she was in his arms. But would it have worked for them if they had given it a fighting chance? She nodded, still staring at his smile, the uncomfortable pose, the same cock of his head … Just his name was enough to heighten her senses and send shivers down her spine. Once, when she and Jack had been introduced to an associate, who introduced himself as David, both had had palpable reactions: Jack, a stiffening of his body and a tightening of his voice and her, a hard thud in her chest and a weakening in her knees. *Yes*, she thought, *David will always be with me.*

****

It was on a rainy August evening when Jennifer was working with Jed on their marketing promotions that she felt the pain, a shooting in her belly. She stopped for a minute and held her stomach and it was gone.

'Gas?' asked Jed with a giggle and Jennifer laughed.

'I'm fine,' she said and they continued working. A few minutes later it came harder and longer. 'Jed, I think you need to call the ambulance,' she said suddenly, looking down at the chair on she was sitting, a little patch of red on its white upholstery. 'And Jack.'

Jennifer was being seen to when Jack arrived at the hospital, his forehead sweating, his body shaking in fear. 'Why can't I see her?' He banged his fists on the counter of the nurses' station, frightening the little man who jumped up and went in search of the doctor.

'Come on, Jack,' said Jed, leading him to a seat, but Jack shrugged him off and paced up and down the corridor. Jed just walked helplessly by his side, trying to keep up with his large strides.

Jack bolted to a doctor who had come out of the swinging doors and nodded at Jed.

'I'm her husband,' he said.

'I'm so sorry,' the doctor began.

'She'd dead,' Jack blurted.

'No, no,' said the doctor, putting his hand on Jack's shoulder, 'but the baby didn't survive.'

Jack stared at him, his face slowly twisting, then shrugged the doctor's hand off him, turned around, and strode away.

'Jack,' called Jed after him and then turned to the doctor. 'Is she going to be okay?'

When Jed walked into the room, Jennifer was staring out of the window and Jed approached her tentatively.

'Jennifer,' he said putting his hand on her own. She didn't move. 'I'm so sorry, Jenny.'

Without turning her head, Jennifer asked, 'Where's Jack?'

'He, um, he had to leave,' said Jed. Jennifer didn't reply but continued to look out the window. After a minute she turned her hand around in Jed's and squeezed.

'Thank you, Jed.'

'The doc says you will need some care and time,' said Jed. 'The emotional impact can sometimes take longer than the physical. He gave some information on some local support groups ...' Jed held out some flyers which Jennifer took from him and placed on the side table. She knew Jed was trying to distract her from the absence of her husband.

Jed stayed with Jennifer until she was allowed to go home two days later. Angel had been to visit her and had told Jed to go home for a little while to get some sleep 'and a shower!' she declared, sniffing him and turning up her nose.

Jennifer didn't ask about Jack the first day, but when he hadn't come to see her, she began to worry and asked Jed to check on him, a favor he passed on to Angel.

'He's okay, Jennifer,' said Angel. 'He's just really busy at work.' Jennifer could see Angel tremble slightly and knew she was angry with Jack. 'Hey, I was talking to Nev,' she said, her eyes lighting up. 'We were thinking that maybe you could spend a few days with us; you know it's been a while since we caught up.'

'You don't have to feel sorry for me, Angel,' said Jennifer wryly. 'I'm fine. I've been fine by myself for a long time.' She sighed at the confusion on Angel's face.

'But you and Jack …'

'We're fine,' said Jennifer, knowing she would be. She always landed on her feet.

'Seriously!' Jed chimed in, after sitting through the conversation next to the window, fuming. 'Leave the bastard.'

Jennifer snickered. That she had heard so many times from Jed, but the astonishment on Angel's face sobered her. 'I just want to go home,' she said.

She did want just to go home. She also wanted to see her son and regretted that he was so far away. It would still be a month before he returned for his break and she decided she was going to visit him as soon as she was able, even if Jack got angry about it. But when she asked the doctor how long it would be before she was recovered, he had dashed her hopes; she wouldn't be up to travel for at least four to six weeks. Jacky would be home and gone again before then. She knew then she had to convince Jack to let him stay in New York and enroll him into a local school.

Upon returning home, Jennifer found herself alone and Jed offered to stay with her until Jack got back, but she refused to be babysat.

'But you need help, Jenny,' he insisted. 'Kev is fine with it. I already told him.'

'Don't be silly, Jed,' Jennifer replied. 'I have the phone, I have neighbors, I have you down the road if I need anything.' Jed didn't look convinced but Jennifer gently guided him out the door.

'But I do want to get back to work as quickly as possible. So I need my beauty sleep.' She closed the door and leaned against it, wishing she had relented and let him stay with her. But Jack wouldn't like that.

She hobbled to the bedroom and called Jacky's school and talked to her son, tears streaming down her face when he happily discussed his studies with her.

'How's Gerald?' she asked. Gerald was a friend that Jacky made when he first got there.

'He's okay. I don't talk to him anymore.' Her son's voice dropped, and her heart bled for him. Children were so fickle. 'I miss my old friends, Mom. But I made another friend, Melissa.'

'Tell me about Melissa.'

She hung up the phone after an hour and it was then that she broke down.

****

Jack returned home two days later and in that time Jennifer resisted the urge to call him. She was angry, but for the most part, she realized she didn't care anymore: not about where he was or what he had been doing.

He walked in, planted a kiss on her forehead. 'Are you okay?' he asked casually as if she had just been recovering from a bad headache.

She nodded. 'Are you hungry?' She shuffled off

the sofa, heading for the kitchen.

'No, I'm going to take a shower,' he said and went into the bedroom.

Half an hour later, wondering what was taking him so long, she wandered into the bedroom to find him asleep in bed, or at least pretending to be. The next morning, their listless marriage resumed.

When Jacky came home for his term break, Jack's habit of going out didn't subside and Jennifer found him dismissive and irritated with his son. She broached the subject of Jacky staying at home, but Jack flatly refused and insisted on sticking to see how it went for at least a year. She didn't want to fight in front of her son, so she let it go for now. Jacky didn't seem to mind the school and that satisfied her for now.

It was the week after he left when she brought it up again. Jack had retired to the study after dinner and Jennifer took a deep breath; she couldn't keep putting it off. She knocked at the door and pushed it open. Jack looked up at her from his book in question.

'Jack, I really think we should bring Jacky home. Don't you miss him?'

Jack looked up at her, his face registering irritation and indignance. 'Didn't we discuss this already?'

'Yes, but I thought that now he's gone again, I

miss him more than ever. Don't you? I also feel that he misses his friends here, as much as he says he's okay.'

Jack sat back in his chair and regarded her with contempt. 'You really are a selfish woman, aren't you? First you are happy to get rid of him …'

'Jack, I never—!'

'Not finished.' He held up his hand at her. 'Then you lose our baby because your ridiculous idea of work is more important to you than anything else. And now you think you're lonely, so you want to use our son to cure your loneliness. No, he stays, at least for a few years.' His eyes returned to the book in his hand.

Jennifer stepped backward, her hand on her chest. She could feel her blood begin to boil. 'Jack! You said a trial year! What do you mean?'

Jack looked down at the floor, his hands clenching again and again. 'Just go away, Jennifer, I have things to do.'

'You bastard! I don't need you. I will get him out. I will get out too, leave this sham marriage,' she said, turning on her heel and walking out of the door.

Before she reached the kitchen, he was on her. He pinned her to the floor, his fist pummeling her face, her head, and she saw again the fury, the blind rage. She scratched and bit anything that came close to her mouth, and suddenly there was a sharp pain in her groin; he was inside her, pushing hard. Jennifer passed out.

She woke up in the dark, lying on the floor with every part of her body burning. She couldn't lift herself off the floor and dragged herself to the bedroom where she managed to crawl into bed and sobbed through the night. When the first signs of morning appeared, she tried to move and found her body unwilling. She waited for a couple of hours, thinking about what to do, and called Jed, who was there in fifteen minutes. Having his own key, he let himself him and almost dropped the coffee he had picked up on the way at the sight of her. He rushed to her side and Jennifer saw the fury in his eyes.

'I will kill him, the bastard! Jenny, why are you still with this man?'

'Not now, Jed, I just need some help getting into the bath. Can you stay for a couple of hours?'

'I'm not leaving you alone! You are coming with me …'

'Jed, the bath,' said Jennifer, trying to get out of the bed.

Jed helped Jennifer bathe and she could see he found it hard to look at the damage done to her body. 'Does anything feel broken? Should we take you to emergency?'

'I think I'm okay, Jed; my head hurts and, well,

everything else should fade.'

'He's still doing this. I just knew it!' Jed's eyes widened.

Jennifer smiled ruefully. 'Not for a long time. I didn't think he would again, but here we are.'

'You have to run, Jenny, you have to go away from him. You can report this, you know,' he said rubbing the dried blood from her breasts and shoulders. He suddenly turned around. 'What if he comes back?'

'I know, Jack; he won't come back for a while, at least a few days, I would think.'

'What are you going to do, until then?'

'I wanted to go to see Jacky at school first, then …' Jennifer paused.

Jed sat back on the stool. 'Then you are going to look for David,' he finished for her.

Looking at him, Jennifer saw a smile of approval. 'I don't know where he is. I know he has a new restaurant in Baltimore …'

'Jack will kill you, for real this time!'

'Does it look like I give a shit right now?' said Jennifer, pointing to the reddish-brown water in the bathtub.

'You have a son, what if …?'

'That's the one thing I can count on: Jack loves his kid, he would never hurt him over me.' Jennifer leaned forward. 'He won't know where I am. I just want to see him, to see if he's okay. He's probably happy with someone else right now, maybe even married …'

'Actually, no. He's not married, not anymore anyway. He opened his last restaurant in Baltimore, yes, and I can even find out where he lives,' said Jed triumphantly. 'But you have to get better first, you can't go anywhere like this.'

'Jack could come home before that happens,' argued Jennifer.

'At least a few days then …'

It was five days later when Jennifer arrived on the doorstep of David's home in Baltimore. She hadn't called him because she didn't want him to change her mind and when she got there, she began to second guess her decision. Jed had packed a few things for her and put her into a taxi for the four-hour ride.

Jack had sent Jennifer a text message saying he would be out of town for a while. *Perfect*, Jennifer thought, *he won't hunt for me immediately*. She decided not to see her son before going to Baltimore, not in the state she was in; she didn't want to upset the child who probably already felt helpless and alone.

Jennifer knocked on the door of the house, an old-fashioned, two-story townhouse, with a wide porch on which sat two armchairs. There was no answer and

Jennifer wondered if she had the right place. She decided to wait for a while; she had had a long drive and her body was still aching. What a sight she must be.

'What if he doesn't love me with the way I look right now? What if I scare him away?'

Jed had smirked. 'He loves you, it won't affect anything, and if it does, well, you have killed two birds with one stone. Fuck them both!'

So here she was, about to test David's love. Jennifer smiled sardonically; the fact was, if he rejected her, she felt like she would die. She placed herself in one of the armchairs and fell asleep.

She felt her arm being shaken lightly and opened her eyes to see David's peering back, a look of shock and concern on his face.

'Jen, Jen, are you okay?' He was on his haunches, and he put his hand on the side of her face. She leaned into it.

'Hi, David. Is this a bad time?'

'Are you okay? What happened? Were you in an accident? Jen, what's wrong?' The words kept tumbling out of his mouth.

Jennifer managed to sit up and took his hands in hers. 'Can we go inside? Are you alone? If it's a bad time, I can go …'

'No, no, nothing like that, yes, no, wait here a

minute.' He walked to the front door and opened it. He walked back to Jennifer and lifted her in his arms. As he took her over the threshold, she smiled sadly.

Putting her on the sofa, he knelt in front of her. 'Can I kiss you?' he asked. Jennifer leaned forward and kissed his mouth and with the touch felt such a torrent of sensations—physical pain on her bruised mouth, love, and relief. She leaned back and gazed at his face, the one she had thought about every waking day.

He squeezed her hands and rested on his heels. 'Did he do this?' he asked.

Jennifer didn't answer and David slowly nodded. He bowed his head and mumbled something to himself, Jennifer couldn't decipher what, and placed his head in her lap. She ran her fingers through his hair, the knot in her throat loosening. She felt like she was home.

# CHAPTER 24

*Jack*

Jack was angry.

He had made the reservation for seven and it was an hour's drive to the restaurant. It was nearly six now; Arlene was late. He was pacing the kitchen with a whiskey in hand and slammed it down on the table, feeling a rage he didn't need to keep in check here. He checked his watch again.

'Inconsiderate bitch!' he muttered, realizing it was best to call the restaurant and cancel but he really wanted to go out. He had been staying at Arlene's ranch in Denver for three weeks and was going stir crazy. He wanted to go home, but couldn't, not yet. It was too soon, she needed time. He had sent Jennifer a message saying that he was needed for work and would be away for a while, no ETA.

His chest hurt when he thought about what he

had done to her. He took a deep breath and paced, trying to quell the waves of guilt that attacked. He had promised her he'd never do it again and had kept to his word for a long time, managing to calm his temper when he felt it rise.

But this time, he lost it. Jack leaned his hands on the edge of the bar, his fingers turning white when he thought of what she'd done. She had killed his child. He was hurt and angry and couldn't help himself. She deserved it this time, he tried to convince himself, but he still needed to give her time to get over what had happened. He also needed space from the situation, space from her. He should have left earlier, when he felt it brewing, when there was still time. He knew; the signs were there.

Arlene was there too. She always had been there. She forgave Jack for telling Jennifer about them a long time ago and accepted that even if she only saw him from time to time, it was all she was going to get from Jack and she was willing to have him any way she could. He called her as soon as he left the house and she had invited him to stay with her for a while.

'This is the best place for you right now,' she said, averting her eyes from the scratches on his face when he walked through the front door, instead planting her lips on his tenderly. Jack relaxed and let the events of the past few hours escape his mind.

But three weeks being stuck in the middle of nowhere had put him in a foul mood, even though there was a lot to do. In a sprawling patch of land, so vast one could not see its end, Arlene owned her own stables, and Jack went out to the horses and rode with Arlene across the grassy lands, and a lot of the time, without her. He was able to conduct business from her large home atop a hill, from where he could see nothing but blue skies and the tops of trees. It was a slice of serenity but he was beginning to feel on edge.

Arlene stayed with him for the most part, even though she was due back in New York a week after he arrived, but she nevertheless compromised and instead visited a branch of her company that was more than thirty miles from her home. She asked Jack to accompany her on a number of occasions as there was plenty of room for him to work there, but he always refused, knowing word about him being there would get back to Jennifer and he didn't need any more ammunition against his marriage. Although he had told Jennifer of his affair with Arlene, she was still a sore point and he avoided bringing up her name at home.

He bided his time at Arlene's place while he tried to come up with a plan and wondered what a decent time was to stay away from her and how long she may need to get over this last indiscretion.

He loved Jennifer and although their marriage was a 'sham,' as she had called it, he still needed her to be there. And there was Jacky to think about; there was no way that he was letting go of his son. These days, the women almost always got sole custody and he wouldn't give up Jacky, wouldn't be the dad who only got to see his son every second weekend. He didn't stop to consider the fact that with Jacky away at school for most of the year, he barely saw him now. He smiled when he thought of the boy, his grip loosening on the bar. He did miss him and also wanted him to be home, but the best education would turn Jacky into a better man, a more successful person, so he had to sacrifice time with him for the boy's future. He frowned.

The sound of gravel crunching turned his head and he gritted his teeth as he checked his watch. 'Too late,' he growled and loosened his tie. Arlene walked in with a load of shopping bags and dumped them on the floor.

'Hello, darling.' She walked to him and kissed his cheek. She craned her neck backwards, regarding his attire. 'Why are you … oh, shit! I forgot. Oh, I'm sorry,' she said and then looked up at him and began pulling at his tie. 'We can stay home, eat in, and you know, do other things that could be so much more fun.' She smiled wickedly.

Jack glared at her and wrenched his tie from her hands. 'I wanted to go out for a change. I'm stuck in this damned house, a million miles away from civilization. I just wanted to see other people for a change.' He walked back to the bar and poured himself a drink.

'I'm here,' said Arlene and pouted.

Jack shrugged and gulped down his drink.

'What the fuck do you want, Jack?' He could hear the annoyance in her voice and it turned him on. 'I didn't ask you to come here, but you came, and I let you stay. I have a life too, you know, I can't babysit you the whole time. I have work, I have a job.'

'Let me stay?' said Jack, slamming his glass on the kitchen top, and strode toward her. 'You let me stay?' he repeated. 'You little tramp, it was your fucking dream come true, to have me here all to yourself.'

Arlene began to back away, her eyes scared. 'Go home then.' Her voice quivered. 'You're a useless piece of shit anyway. No wonder she doesn't love you.'

Jack got to Arlene in three strides and pinned her against the wall, his hand against her chest. He curled his brow, staring straight into her eyes, and he saw her flinch.

She stuck out her chin, her own eyes daring him. 'Is this what you did to her? That's right, this makes you a man, a real man. Remember, I'm not Jennifer. I will have your head on a platter if you touch one hair on my head.' Arlene's eyes were locked with Jack's, although her bottom lip trembled slightly.

Jack loosened his grip on her and he strolled back to the bar.

'Get the fuck out of my house,' spat Arlene.

'I'm gone, baby,' he declared, gulping down what was left of his drink. *Probably best*, he thought, as he gathered his clothes from the bedroom and shoved them into his suitcase. He collected his briefcase and his work items and headed for the open door which Arlene was waiting by, her hands on her hips, her mouth pursed. Without glancing at her he stepped onto the porch and heard the door slam so hard, the figurine that sat on the windowsill fell and broke into a hundred little pieces. Jack smiled; it was one of her favorites.

Boarding the first flight to New York, Jack was at a loss as to what to do when he arrived and now he was nervous. Was it too soon to face her? Maybe he'd left it too long? How long was it the last time, in California? He couldn't remember; it had been so long ago …

He sighed. Well, he was here, he had to face it some time or another. He looked at his watch. It was late, she'd probably be asleep. Good, it would give him time to think about what he needed to do, depending on her reaction to him. He would have to grovel; he could do that.

Turning the key in the lock of their home, Jack was faced with silence and darkness. He turned on the lamp and looked at the place where he had left her, unconscious and battered. It was spotless. He swallowed the lump in his throat. He was dying for a drink but he didn't want to wake her and went to Jacky's room and lay on the bed, wondering how he had made such a mess of things.

He could feel his temper flaring again. It wasn't him who had made the mess. It was her! Jennifer's obsession with David … A thought struck him and he tried to brush it aside, but it niggled at his brain and overwhelmed every part of him that told him to let it go. He got out of bed and crept to their bedroom. The light from the streetlamp hit his bed, his empty bed. He turned on the light and his heart almost stopped. Where was she?

Sitting at the dining table, nursing a bourbon, Jack deliberated his next move. How long she had been gone, he didn't know; he himself had been away for over three weeks. He looked at the time and then at his cell phone. It was one thirty—the middle of the night. He couldn't call her friends, it was too late, and how was he to explain not knowing where his wife was?

Where could she be? He tried to call her cell, but heard it ringing in the bedroom, still connected to the power point. So, she had left without her phone; she never liked that thing anyway. He searched the house for any clue to where she may be, but couldn't find anything obvious.

Where could she be? David's name kept popping into Jack's head, but he tried to ignore it. He then considered that she may have gone to see Jacky. She had said that she had missed him. Yes, that's it! Jack went to his own bed and tried to sleep but couldn't get David out of his mind and by the time he rose from the bed again, after a night of no sleep, he was livid.

After hanging up from Jacky's school the next morning, Jack's ears were beginning to burn. Jacky had spoken to his mother a few times in the last few weeks, so she was fine. He was not concerned about Jennifer's welfare anymore; he knew she had left him. He searched the house again, this time for a note or anything that may help find her, but nothing.

Finally, although he despised having to do it, he called Angel, who said she had no idea where Jennifer was, but Jack knew she knew something. She was off-handish and unconcerned about her friend's disappearance, which disturbed Jack even more. When he tried to call Jed, his call remained unanswered. He sent him a text message asking him to call him back, but that went unanswered too.

Jack paced the house all morning trying to persuade himself that Jennifer wasn't with David, but he knew. He felt it deep down. He sat down at the dining table with a bottle of whiskey and tried to work out what he was going to do. He would get her back, of that he was sure, but how?

It was late in the evening when he fell asleep at the table in a drunken stupor. Early the next morning, he dragged himself into the shower, put on a clean set of clothes, and went to work.

# CHAPTER 25

*Jennifer and David*

The days became weeks and Jennifer had never been happier. Fearful that Jack may find her at David's home, Jennifer wanted to stay at a hotel. David did one better. He took her back to Atlanta, to his home behind Rue George, introducing her to Bessie and Tony, who immediately welcomed her into their lives. David stayed with her every day, nursing her back to health with love and food.

Rue George was just as popular as when he had left it and Bessie brought delicious fresh food to the cottage every day. David took time off work: 'I'm the boss,' he had said with a laugh, when she asked him when he needed to return to work.

Jennifer kept in touch with Jed and Angel, but told them that it was better that they didn't know where she was. It would be safer for her, and them. She spoke to Jacky often and called her mother a few times. At first, she hadn't told Judy the whole story, fearing her mother's disappointment and anger, but her mother guessed almost immediately. She begged Jennifer to come home, back to Tandaro, but Jennifer knew Jack would find out that she was there, so Judy relented.

Jennifer spent some of her days helping in the restaurant, doing minor things to keep herself busy, and the rest of her time with David, playing games, making love, and they spent their evenings in the garden, talking under the moon.

This was the life Jennifer wanted and she would give anything to stay like this forever, but she knew it had to end. She had a son to go home to when he returned for his school break. She calculated that she had more than two months with David before then. David didn't want her to ever go back, but knew he would have to let her go before he could get her back. They would work it out, they tried to reassure each other, both not as sure as they would have liked.

David was seething when Jennifer told him about Jack. He had wanted to go to New York and confront him, but they both knew how dangerous it would be, especially for her, and he stayed with her, vowing to make her happy for as much time as they had.

David told Jennifer about Jack's visit to him, one

evening while they watched television on the sofa, and her eyes became enormous.

'You didn't kill each other?'

'No, Miss Vain, we didn't talk about you at all,' he said, laughing, and pulled at her chin. Then he became serious. 'I saw in him my friend again, that sweet, playful kid I grew up with. He always had something ruthless about him, but I thought it was more about business. I never suspected … Oh, Jen, never, ever did I think …'

'How could you, David?'

'I saw him push you out of the restaurant that time, but I never thought he would hurt you. I just thought he wanted you away from me. How could I not see it? All I saw was you.'

'I married him; it should have been you, but I jumped too soon. And now, here we are,' said Jennifer. 'And can we not talk about him anymore?' She took his hand and led him outside. She pointed to the sky. The moon was just coming out from behind a large gray cloud. 'That thing, that beautiful thing in the sky. I have always relied on it. And I hated it at times, but it always kept me with you. And no matter what happens after this, I will keep returning to it. It gave me hope and here I am, with you.' Jennifer leaned upwards and kissed David.

****

It was just over three weeks since Jennifer had come to David when she received a call from Jed.

'He's back,' was the first thing he said when David passed her the phone.

Jennifer felt her heart pause.

'Jenny, you there?' asked Jed.

'I'm here, Jed. How do you know? Did you speak to him?'

'No, I didn't answer, but Angel called me and he called her too, asking where you were.'

'What did she say?'

'She said she didn't know where you were. She wasn't lying, but I think he knew something was up. What are you going to do, Jenny?' Jed sounded scared.

'If he contacts you, just tell him you don't know where I am. You won't be lying either.' Jennifer looked at David, who was pacing beside her, his eyes narrow, his mouth set in a straight line.

Jed talked for a few more minutes, telling her how he was getting some of the paperwork organized for Moondance while she was away.

'I'm sorry I'm not there to do it with you.'

'Don't worry, there's plenty to do when you get

back … by the way, are you coming back?'

Jennifer sighed. 'I have to, I just need some more time. I was hoping for at least another few weeks. I will have to be back before Jacky returns from school.'

'You take all the time you want. You deserve this. By the way, Jenny …'

'Yes, Jed?'

'Are you happy, there, with him, with David?'

Jennifer looked up at David again and smiled. 'More than I could have ever imagined,' she said.

****

Two days later David told Jennifer that he had to go on an overnight business trip.

'Not going to see one of your lovers, are you?' she teased.

'You got me,' he said and rolled his eyes. 'I have one in every city. They miss me and they want to strangle the woman who has kept me all to herself this last month.'

'Well, tell them they can wait for you … forever.'

David took a flight to New York and took a taxi straight to Jack and Jennifer's home. He had a peek at her driver's license, noting the address, and now found himself on their doorstep. He rang the doorbell a couple of times and finally, Jack answered, his shocked face slowly shifting to rage.

'What the …' he began, but before he could complete the sentence, David's fist came straight at his mouth. Jack fell backwards, but regained his balance quickly and came back swinging at David. David dodged and punched his stomach with full force, winding him, but he persevered, trying to pin David down. David dodged him deftly and soon had Jack trapped beneath him on the hallway floor.

'Is this what it feels like, you coward?' David growled as he looked at the manic face glowering at him. He took his weight off. 'You're not worth it, you pig.'

As he stood up, he felt Jack rise from beneath him and he felt a sting in his crotch. He buckled and saw Jack's fist about to collide with his head. He swerved to the side, pulling Jack's legs from under him, and Jack came crashing to the floor again. He stood up and allowed Jack to stand too. They looked at each other, both fight ready.

'Take a shot, you deserve to,' said David, pointing to his own chin.

Jack punched David with all his might and David staggered backwards but regained his balance quickly and pounced on Jack. They fought and David found himself on top of Jack again. This time, he looked him square in the face and threw a volley of punches at it. He couldn't see straight; his rage had engulfed him, and he suddenly stopped.

This was what Jack had done to Jennifer; he had lost control, just like Jack. He was no better. He stood up while Jack lay on the floor, his face swollen, but he was conscious. He looked at David drowsily.

'Touch her again, I will finish you,' said David and walked out.

Returning to Atlanta, David knew he would have to tell Jennifer about what he'd done. He couldn't hide it; his chin was bruised and his cheekbone was swelling. On the way home, he had wondered whether he had done the right thing, but he knew Jack would continue to abuse Jennifer if she went back, and he knew she would go back. She had to and no matter the plans they made, they both knew they were nothing but dreams. They would have to embrace the time they had right now and hopefully he would be more cautious of hurting her.

When he got home, early the next morning, Jennifer was still in bed and he slid under the covers. She stirred and pulled his arms around her.

'You're back early,' she murmured.

'Missed you,' he said snuggling into her.

'All go well?'

'Fine, for now; go to sleep, Jen, we can talk in the morning.'

Jennifer turned on the nightlamp and turned around. 'David!' she said, sitting up. 'My gosh, look at you. You need something for that thing on your face …' She stopped. 'You went to see him?'

David nodded.

Jennifer jumped off the bed and brought some ice from the freezer wrapped in a tea towel. She put it on his face and waited for him to speak. David looked up at her sheepishly.

'He looks worse,' he said with a grin.

'Oh, David, how can you joke about it? What did he say?'

'I'm sorry, and actually, he didn't say much at all. Neither did I really.' Jennifer moved close to David and put her head on his shoulder.

'I love you,' she said simply.

The weeks raced by and Jennifer and David's time was almost over. By this time, they had agreed that she had to leave Jack. She would ask for a divorce and give him whatever he wanted. She just wanted their son and she knew she would have a fight on her hands, so how long she would need was the question. David wanted to go back with Jennifer to New York, but she insisted that it would make things worse. She had to deal with the fallout and she had already spoken to her mother about coming home with her; Jack wouldn't dare do anything in front of Judy. Hopefully, it would go smoothly and she could move out as soon as possible; she knew it was not going to be that easy.

The night before she left Atlanta, Jennifer and David sat under the moon and talked, laughed, and tried not to cry, then they spent the night awake in each other's arms, holding on for dear life, hoping it wouldn't have to be their last.

The morning was somber, and they stiffly packed Jennifer's things, unable to say anything to each other without breaking apart. They rode to the airport in silence, only holding each other's hand, and when they got to the terminal, Jennifer put her luggage through and walked back to David. She kissed him lightly on the lips, put on a smile, and said, 'See you soon.'

'See you, Jen,' David replied and watched her disappear into the boarding area without looking back. David kept watching and then walked over to the window. He stayed there until he saw her flight take off, then he turned around, put on his sunglasses, and went home.

# CHAPTER 26

*Jennifer and Jack*

Judy was waiting at the airport in New York for Jennifer's plane to arrive. Jennifer saw her mother from a distance and ran to her, throwing herself in her arms. They chatted all the way back to the house, with Jennifer filling Judy in on whatever she could in the short ride they had back. She promised to tell her everything when they had the chance, but they needed to be in the right frame of mind when they first encountered Jack. Judy was fearful, as was Jennifer, but as they were together, they felt safe. It would be a few more days before Jacky came home, so they had time to sort things out and make a plan for Jennifer to leave him.

By the time they reached the apartment, Jennifer's nerves were raw and a pang of fear hit her when she walked through the front door, but Judy's reassuring arm on hers calmed her. It was still early in the afternoon, so she had counted on Jack still being at work, which would give her time to settle. He wasn't home and she felt a flood of relief; he wasn't aware of when she would return, but she was still wary. She looked around, noticing that the apartment was spotless. He must have gotten the maid to visit more often, she thought—the guilt began to rise in her and she tried to quell it.

They unpacked their things quietly and Judy sat down at the table while Jennifer went to turn on the kettle. It was then that she noticed the dossier on the kitchen top. It had her name on it, typed neatly in large letters, so she opened it and her knees gave way. Right on top was a picture of her with David—in Atlanta! There was nothing compromising about it, they were just sitting in a park, hand in hand, but something about the fact that it existed terrified her. There were some other photographs of them as well, in the restaurant, taken through the glass, even photos of them kissing in the private garden outside the cottage, and how he got those, she would never know. She took the dossier over to Judy and together, they looked through it, Jennifer's hands shaking as she moved the papers from one side of the folder to the other. Pictures and other documents, including copies of the deeds to David's restaurants, were there. There was another picture—one of Jack, his face and body bruised and swollen—with details of the 'attack' by David, and a police report.

'What is this?' Judy exclaimed.

Jennifer just sat there, open-mouthed. 'Looks like blackmail,' she said putting her head in her hands. Judy put her hand on her daughter's head.

'We'll beat the bastard!' she cried.

'I don't think so, Mother. He's way too smart. I can't beat him like this.' She stopped and looked down at the documents and pictures again. 'But I will beat him, my own way.'

Jennifer sat down with her mother and related the details of everything that had happened, and Judy felt partly responsible for sending David away the evening he had come to visit her, so long ago. Together they discussed the situation and both knew Jennifer had lost. The contents of the dossier were incriminating and threatening to both Jennifer and David. Jack knew they had been together and had pictures to prove it. He would not let her go, not with Jacky. He would paint her as a philandering wife, unfit to be a mother. The pictures of his own injuries would prove that the man she was with was violent to her own husband and not fit to be around his son. The copies of the deeds showed that Jack had the power to ruin David. It was a threat, to her and to him. Jack had planned it all nicely; he would never let her go.

She called David and told him about everything she had found, leaving out the discovery of the copies of the deeds. David was incensed and wanted to come to her immediately, but she knew she had to deal with this herself. She asked him not to call her. She would be in touch with him soon. Wishing him goodnight, she went to bed in tears.

She recalled the afternoon after David had left her for a day in Atlanta and gone to New York, when she and Bessie were having a nightcap in the backyard after the restaurant had shut. Although much later than six in the evening, she was leaning on a cushion on the patio couch, looking at the moon and missing him already. Bessie noticed and had chuckled. Jennifer looked at Bessie in question.

'Yeah, he did that a lot too.'

Jennifer smiled and then snickered too.

Then Bessie became serious. 'I hope you both know what you're doing,' she said and sipped her drink, a green concoction that was especially made for her by the new bartender: 'Midori and something special,' he had said.

Surprised, Jennifer sat up and waited for her to continue.

'He has been here for a long time, and I've never

seen him so happy, the way he is since you came.'

'I feel the same, Bessie. I can't think of living without him, not now, not ever really, but there wasn't much of a choice, you know.'

'But you got yourself married—to his friend, no less,' said Bessie.

Jennifer was annoyed. 'In case you missed it, he went off and got married first!'

'Oh, Jennifer, I'm sorry.' Bessie moved closer to Jennifer and took her hand. 'You both belong together, but are you making plans that may not materialize?'

'We are living in a dream right now, Bessie,' said Jennifer, softening. 'And we both want to keep the dream, at least for now, even if that means making plans. And I intend to come back to him. After this, how could I not?'

'Your lives so far have already told you that maybe you're better off apart.'

Jennifer sprang back. 'No!' she exclaimed, 'I can't think that a universe would allow us to feel this for each other and yet never be together; how could that be?'

'Again, I'm sorry, Jennifer, but I just worry for David.' She paused. 'And for you. I knew him before you came and I see how he is now and I don't know what he will be like if you don't come back.'

'That's not an option, Bessie. I will be back for him and with him and I will never leave him when I have him.'

'I hope so,' said Bessie, her eyes doubtful. 'For you, for him, for all of us.'

'I promise Bessie,' Jennifer had said and hugged her tightly.

She had broken that promise now and she lay in bed wondering what to do and yearning for David, who should have been lying right beside her.

Jack didn't come home that evening and Jennifer spent the evening and all night pondering her dilemma. He had won. She would never be with David, she would never be happy, but she at least could be safe.

The next morning, with barely any sleep, she got out of bed and went to Judy.

'Mother, after Jacky gets home, I need you to go home too,' she told her.

Judy was aghast. 'I can't leave you with that man; no, I won't do it!'

'I can't live in fear of him forever, Mother. I have decided to get a gun.' And before her mother could protest, she put her hands on her Judy's. 'I have to learn how to defend myself. And I will. I don't want you to worry about me all my life. I will be fine.'

'What about David?' Judy asked.

Jennifer's eyes filled with tears. 'That is over now. It was never supposed to be. I see that now. I think I saw that all along. I need to focus on what I do have— my son. He's the most important thing right now. So, I need you to leave. When Jacky gets back, if you want to spend a couple of days with him, that would be great, but I need to work this all out, by myself.' Jennifer saw her mother's eyes begin to fill and she hugged her. 'You can come any time after that.'

'It's not that …'

'I know, Mother, I know … I will be okay, I promise you, I will be okay.'

It was then that there was the sound of a key turning in the lock of the front door. They both heard it, paused, and looked at each other.

'Let me deal with him, Mother, please.' Jennifer shot a warning look at Judy, who grimaced, but nodded.

Jack walked in the door with his briefcase and glanced at them still sitting at the dining table. He didn't look surprised.

'Back, I see?' His eyes scanned the room and stopped at the dossier that was lying open on the kitchen top. He looked back at the two of them and walked to Judy, bent down and kissed her cheek, which she shied away from. 'Hello, Judy, nice to see you.' Then he leaned over to Jennifer, first pausing to look into her eyes, and kissed her on her lips. 'Welcome back, honey,' he said simply.

Jennifer pulled back and went to the kettle. 'Tea or coffee?'

'Nothing, thank you. I just have to shower and I'm heading back out,' he said and walked into the bedroom.

Judy and Jennifer looked at each other in bewilderment and Jennifer began to make breakfast. She made some for all of them and waited for Jack to reappear. When he did, he was fully dressed, and kissing them both in the same manner that he had when he walked in, he strolled over to where the dossier lay, picked it up, and walked out. Judy and Jennifer both looked at each other again.

'That was odd,' said Judy.

'Wasn't it!' replied Jennifer, and for the next four days, until the day Jacky came home, it went that way every morning.

In the meantime, Jennifer got busy. She set up her studio room again, calling Jed to tell him that she was ready to go ahead with the business. Jed, who had been working on minor things while she was gone, was overjoyed and had come to her place the same day with all the plans he had made. She spoke to Angel and they set a time to catch up. Yes, she decided, she was going to have a life. It may not be one with David, but it would at least make her as happy as she could be without him.

Jennifer also enrolled in self-defense classes. She knew he would try to hurt her again, but she would be fighting back, properly, from now on. And whether or not Jack knew, she didn't care, but she did stop short of buying a gun. Her mother had talked her out of that.

The day before Jacky came home, Jennifer called David.

'I'm sorry,' she said, trying not to cry. She prepared herself for this.

'Are you coming back to me?' She could hear his own voice filled with trepidation.

'I can't do that. There is too much to lose. We made plans that were never going to happen, David. We were lost in our own world, a beautiful world, but a temporary one.'

'Are you safe, Jen?'

'I'm safe. I know what I need to do.' She bit her lip to keep from crying.

'Will you call me? Can I call you?'

She didn't expect that. 'I don't know. Maybe not for a while. It's going to be too hard.'

'Jen ... Jennifer ...'

'Goodbye, David.'

She hung up before he could reply and burst into

tears and stood up with a new resolve.

Jacky came home on a Friday afternoon, a week before Christmas and Jennifer was wild with excitement. She hadn't seen him in so long and so much had happened in between that it felt like forever. Judy left three days later after showering Jacky with hugs, kisses, and gifts, and Jack began to spend more time at home, even coming into their bed late at night, something he hadn't done since she had been back. They didn't talk a lot, except when with Jacky, and it was perfunctory and stilted, but she knew that once Christmas was over, she would have to broach the subject of keeping Jacky at home—she remembered what had happened the last time she had.

But she didn't have to. Jack brought it up when Jacky was tucked into bed on Christmas evening and Jennifer had poured herself a glass of wine. Coming out of his son's room after kissing him goodnight, he leaned on the doorway and gazed at her with uncertainty. She glanced up and raised her eyebrows at him.

'I was thinking …'

Jennifer looked down at her glass of wine, swirling it.

'I was thinking that we should enroll Jacky at Xavier High for next semester.'

Jennifer's eyes turned back to him, a light in

them, 'Oh, Jack! Really?'

'Wait, I have made inquiries, but I don't know if he will be able to go there until the start of the next school year … and that's more than six months away.'

Jennifer jumped off the chair and went to him. 'We can try. I've loved having him home and I can tell you have too. And he seems to be so happy to be back.'

Jack walked into the kitchen and Jennifer followed. 'Yeah, I see that. It makes you happy too.'

Jennifer wanted to embrace him but stopped herself.

'Okay, we can try,' he said, and looked back at her, his face resigned. 'And you will stay here too. No more running off.'

So that was it. He was worried that if Jacky were to go away again, that she may do the same. She knew he had ulterior motives, but if that was what made him want to keep her son at home with her, well, that was fine. She had already given up David, but he didn't know that. She did wonder what he did know. He hadn't discussed the dossier with her, but her seeing it was enough of a threat and he knew that.

'No. I'm not going anywhere,' she said and turned to walk away. At the door, she turned around again. 'Thank you, Jack,' she said.

He looked at her and said, 'I still love you,

Jennifer.'

She turned and walked out of the room.

****

Jacky was accepted into Xavier and although their listless marriage resumed, Jennifer was happy that her son was home and her business with Jed was beginning to take off. With the internet, their opportunities had multiplied and they had to employ several workers and eventually opened a store. It began as a small shop with a warehouse attached where they kept their stock, and slowly it began to grow, with make-up and accessories as well as a small photography studio. Moondance was beginning to make a name for them. Jennifer knew that she was too old to model for the company, but Jed had insisted that a silhouette of her face should be its logo.

In a year and a half, she had three shops, boutique stores, intimate and unique, but she was a success and she was enjoying it, more than she initially thought she would. Jed felt that he was born for this business and was a great asset and partner. They had always worked well together and now as a team, their business was beginning to thrive.

Jennifer messaged and emailed David a few

times a month, but their contact was superficial, with most of their exchanges relating to business and how they were doing. They steered away from anything that would break them and make them look for each other again.

She saw him once when she was fixing the window dressing in her shop. She was kneeling and intuitively looked up through the glass. He was sitting in his car across the road, his eyes on her, and her breath caught. She stood up slowly and raised her hand in a wave. He waved back and smiled. The he turned on the ignition and she watched him drive away, a tear sliding down her face, her heart in her mouth. She smiled. He still loved her.

Things with Jack had not changed all that much but his attacks were not as vicious and as calculated as they could have been. For one, Jacky was home and he tried not to touch her when his son was around. The other thing was that she fought back, and did it well. For a few months after they had resumed their marriage, Jack had not touched Jennifer, but they began talking a little more and the familiar routines began to emerge. He still hurt her in different ways: a push, a twist of the arm, and once when he had twisted her hair in his hand and had her face close to his, yelling into it, she had raised her knee with all her might into his groin. He had fallen back in pain and surprise and had then sneered at her.

'Is this what you've been learning?' he said, but backed away, nonetheless.

They made love every few weeks and Jennifer would endure it for the sake of peace. She knew that he had other women and used sex as a form of control, but as long as he used protection and didn't bother her too much, it was worth it to have the other parts of her life in order and even flourishing.

One evening, she received a message from David, just letting her know he was building a new restaurant in Florida. She smiled and replied that he was going to take over the whole of the US soon, and closed her phone.

'Who was that?' Jack said suspiciously. He was sitting on the sofa with Jennifer watching a show, a rare occasion.

'That was David,' she said. She was not going to hide it from him.

She saw his eyes go dark and he lunged at her, trying to snatch the phone from her hand. He got hold of her wrist instead and began to twist.

'Stop it, now!' she said and shook herself away from him. He grabbed at her again and she stood her ground. 'You remember the last time you touched me like that?'

'You've been messaging him?' Jack backed away.

'C'mon, Jack, as if you didn't know. I know you check my phone and email. I have nothing to hide.'

'Why are you talking to him?'

'Because I want to, because nothing you say will make me stop. I don't see him. I haven't seen him since …'

Jack looked at her with sorrow and sat down again. He looked defeated. 'I have tried. I've tried so hard to make you happy. What more do you want from me?'

'Jack …' She didn't know what to say to him anymore.

Jennifer moved closer and sat beside him. She took his hand in hers and they sat in silence.

Jacky, a teenager by now, was becoming aware that his parents were unhappy and had caught Jack being rough with his mother on a number of occasions. At first, Jack was so mortified that his son had seen him that he stayed away from home for a few days. Jennifer spoke to Jacky about it and made excuses for his father. But Jacky was a smart child and began to resent his father, especially when he had seen his mother being slapped after they had gotten home late one evening. Jennifer had punched Jack back and only noticed Jacky was in the room when he yelled for them to stop. They had frozen in horror.

It hadn't stopped happening though and Jacky got used to coming across it on the odd occasion. He had tried to prevent it and had jumped in to help, but they always stopped when he came in. He tried to talk to his mother about it, but she would always make excuses or tell him she was dealing with it.

It was just the way their life was now.

# CHAPTER 27

*2006*

Jennifer sat with Jack in the pew, with Lucas in his pram. She looked at Jacky on the steps of the altar, watching as his bride-to-be walked down the aisle. His face was shining, but she worried for him. At twenty, he was just a baby himself, but she also recognized the expression on his face. She had felt it too once, and her mind was cast back for a moment to her own wedding day, but the memory was not one of walking down the aisle or a celebration of love as it should have been; it was of the moment she had seen David outside the church.

Jennifer thought about Jack. Not much had changed where Jack was concerned, but she was dealing with whatever came her way. Jack, in a moment of weakness, had told her of his own father's abuse toward his family, when he tried to justify his own behavior, and

Jennifer had tried to understand that it had impacted on him and what he did to her. She had asked him to seek therapy, but he absolutely refused, deeming therapy a crux for weak-minded people. Then he flatly blamed his moods on Jennifer and David's dalliance.

Jennifer quickly regained her focus and concentrated on her son and his bride, while Jack held her hand, squeezing it from time to time. It was irritating, but she let him. Today was special.

Eliza and Jacky had been together just over a year, but they already had Lucas, just three months earlier, and decided that they wanted to be married. They insisted they would have anyway, even if it wasn't for Lucas being born. Jack had protested; he had scoffed at their meeting at a bar and had ranted about 'the type of women one meets at bars,' and Jennifer reminded him in whispered tones that that was better than how they themselves had met. Jack had still been reluctant, but Jacky had talked to his mother about it and she had seen how much he loved Eliza. She understood well enough and spoke to Jack about it. Jack had no choice but to accept the nuptials and ignoring the wishes of the bride and groom, turned it into the event of the decade, a lavish affair with half of New York's elite as guests. For the sake of peace and relieved that he accepted their plans, they had relented and let Jack invite whomever he wanted.

At the reception, Jennifer spent most of her evening talking with Jed and his partner, and Angel and her family. Jennifer had been excited to see her friend, whom she rarely caught up with anymore, and they spent most of the evening talking and catching up with their lives. Jennifer's own family, including Judy, Elle, and her children, were also present and she was pleased her family were with her. She thought about her life at this moment; a little over forty, she had it all. A business that was booming, friends, loyal friends, and a wonderful son, who was about to begin a life of his own with a beautiful bride.

'Treat her with love,' she said as she tucked the rose in his lapel. 'Give her the world. And love her forever.'

'I do, Ma,' said Jacky, his large brown eyes shining.

'And if you love her, don't let her go.'

'Like Dad?'

Jennifer flushed. 'No, not like Dad.'

Jacky frowned. 'Like David?'

'What do you know about David?' she said, surprised.

'It's okay, Ma, I know you, that's all.'

'I'm happy that my son is going to be happy,'

she said and kissed his cheek.

'And you?'

'Well, this is not my day, is it?'

Jennifer looked about her and seeing the happy couple stealing kisses, while guests clinked their cutlery to their glasses, thought about David again. Even after all these years, she missed him. His restaurant chain had taken off, covering most of the East Coast and some of the West. She had felt so proud of him each time he created another Moon and always wished him the best. She didn't communicate with him much anymore, just on those occasions that warranted it. She felt so far from him now, but what was the point of speaking to him? It only made her heart ache more, so she tried to do it less and focused on being productive. She didn't know much about his love life, except what she read in the papers and on the internet. On occasion, she would see pictures of him with a lady on his arm and Jennifer found herself seething with jealousy, knowing well that she had no right. She had not seen him since that day through the curtains at her store and she still missed him so much it hurt.

Now, she looked at her son and his wife leave the reception for their honeymoon and tears streamed down her face; she wished so much for him and knew he had followed his heart, unlike her, who had been too cowardly to follow her own. She walked back into the room with the crowd and went to the pram that Lucas lay asleep in. His maternal grandmother, Lorraine, more than ten years older than Jennifer, was sitting with him and Jennifer sat down next to her and held her hand. Together they watched their grandchild and smiled.

****

*2016*

It was early on a Saturday morning in April when Jennifer got the call. She had been awake and jumped to answer the phone. It was time. She threw on her clothes and headed out the door. Jack wasn't home, so she drove to the hospital by herself, calling Jed on the way. As she got to the ward, she heard her name and Jed rushed to her.

'How is he?' asked Jed.

'It's time soon,' she replied.

Jed went to hug her, but she pulled away.

'I can't, Jed, not now. I need to be strong.'

Jed nodded and squeezed her hand instead. 'You go in,' he said. 'I will be right here. Should I call Angel?'

'You call her, let her know, she will want to

come for the funeral. I wish she were here but tell her it's best if she wasn't right now. She will understand. Oh, and call my mother too, please.'

Jennifer walked into the room.

The last ten years had been good to her, in business, but in her marriage, not so much. Jack had become more violent once Jacky had moved out and she had to deal with his moods on a regular basis now. She tried to leave him but she couldn't, worried about how the people she cared about would be affected. He had threatened to kill David so much so that she stopped talking to David altogether. It had calmed Jack for a while, but his rages didn't stop.

She hadn't seen Angel for over four years, but kept up with her life through Jacky, who saw her often. Now there wouldn't be that connection anymore either. She doted on her grandson, who spent many weekends and holidays with her, and they holidayed with Eliza's family often. Jack was never present for these gatherings and saw less and less of his son as the years went by. Jacky was working in a bank and was happy and Jack had resented him not wanting to join his father's company. Many arguments ensued and Jennifer suspected that it may have been the reason Jacky had wanted to get married—to leave the house, even if it meant leaving his mother alone with Jack.

Jack and Jennifer had moved and were living on the outskirts of the city. It suited their lifestyle as she was less recognized, or at least less noticed, and it was close to Jacky, Eliza, and Lucas. Having a large garden, the house was smaller and less cluttered. It also housed a bungalow, where Judy stayed from time to time. Jack's own mother had passed away some years ago and Jennifer lamented her loss. She had become close to the woman, who she now understood only too well.

The main reason for their move was to be near Jacky. After a near fatal accident, he had been diagnosed with epilepsy. Jack had taken it very badly, already having lost his sister to the disease, and his way of dealing with it was avoidance. He stayed away from home more often, citing work commitments in the city as his reasons. He knew the prognosis was not good, and it wasn't. Jennifer, on the other hand, began to stay at home more, doing whatever she could to help the family and spend as much time with her son as she could; she knew how precious that time was now.

In moments alone, she would crumble and curse the universe and there were times she would find herself lying passed out on the bedroom floor. She put it down to stress and ignored it, trying to retain an atmosphere of normalcy for the sake of her family. In the days leading to Jacky's death, she found herself coughing up blood, and wondered whether she had been smoking too much, but she knew it was a matter of time and she focused on being there for her family in whatever way she could, rather than worrying about herself.

Jacky had been taken to the hospital a number of times and each time, Jennifer rushed to be with him, ready for the worst. It was one of these times, when Jennifer had gone home to have a quick nap, that she got the call.

********

Now, standing in the setting sun, alone, except for Jack, who waited at the car, Jennifer stared at the coffin, already rolled into the earth. She couldn't cry, it wouldn't happen. She sat on the dry ground and picked at a stem of a wildflower.

'Shall we go?' asked Jack, coming up beside her.

'I don't want to. I want to stay here.'

Jack stepped back and waited again. He watched her, worried. The sun went down and she still didn't move. He suddenly saw her body heave and convulse and went to her. He sat beside her and held her while she wept. Then he picked her up in his arms and carried her back to the car. She cried all the way home, refusing to go to the wake, and had lain in bed for the next two weeks, refusing to eat.

Family had come to visit and Eliza brought Lucas to see her, but even though she loved seeing her grandchild who reminded her so much of her son, she still couldn't get herself out of bed. When she finally did, her life seemed worthless and she dragged herself around the house every day, waking at midday and going back to bed at seven in the evening. She took to drinking often and even Jack became worried about her state of mind.

It was one evening when he returned home from work that he found her passed out on the floor. At first, he thought she had drunk too much again, but his instincts told him that it was something else. He checked her pulse and found it weak. He shook her unconscious body and called 911. That was the day Jack knew he was going to lose her, and not to David this time.

# CHAPTER 28

*2017*

## *David*

David had been talking to the concierge when he saw her. She was standing at the elevator with a young boy, her grandson, he presumed, and suddenly she was looking at him.

'Sir, sir!' The concierge was pulling at his arm and David turned to look at him. When he looked back, she was gone. His heart beat fast and he looked around for any sign of Jack. It had been a long time since she had seen him and he didn't know whether she had recognized him.

But he had recognized Jennifer. She was still the same beautiful woman and although it had been so long, his response to her had not changed. He wondered if she was attending the gala and began to consider whether he should go. It may put her in danger, but Cherie had been looking forward to this night for weeks. At that moment, Cherie came up behind him.

'All good with the room?' she asked.

'Yes,' he said, driven out of his reverie. 'All checked in.' She linked her arm in his and they proceeded to the elevator.

David had been with Cherie for three months and Cherie, ten years his junior, was beginning to become attached. He knew this was not going to work as all the others hadn't, but he was sick of being alone. He needed company and by now, knew he and Jennifer were never going to be, so although he made no promises, he still enjoyed her company. She was full of life, always cheerful, and had no baggage; well, apart from a hovering mother, who Cherie couldn't be without for more than a few days at a time. She even insisted on bringing her here.

And now, when he was thinking about getting serious, fate had intercepted … again.

When Jennifer had lost her son, he had gone to New York. He needed to see her, to see how she was and if he could be there for her in some way. He went to the cemetery and watched as she crouched on the ground until Jack picked her up and David knew she was going to be okay. He left without her knowing he was there. He also left there knowing that Jack loved her too. He would take care of her; she didn't need him anymore.

And now he had seen her and knew that nothing had changed, not for him, anyway. It had been more than fifteen years since they had spent those magical three months together and it had stayed with him; they were memories he kept returning to in times of desolation. He never found that feeling again, no matter how many women he met and dated or how successful he was in business or any other part of his life.

In the ballroom, he listened to Cherie chatter on while his eyes never left the door and his heart began to race when he saw her walk in, Jack behind her. Cherie was so enamored with the pomp and glamor of the evening, star spotting celebrities, and had even pointed out Jennifer, talking excitedly about how much she adored her and her products, claiming to have used them, even tonight. Inwardly, he had smiled; he had always felt so proud of her success as it was just that—her success. She had done it for herself, not taken it from Jack.

He watched her walk to the ladies' room and a moment later Cherie excused herself too, her mother following closely behind.

David nodded and went to the bar and Cherie smiled and gestured for him to get her a drink too. He nodded and looked back to Jennifer's table to where she was heading now, Jack behind her. He sipped at the drink in his hand and suddenly, she was walking toward him, defiance on her face. He gaped at her in alarm and his heart began to thump.

'Take me away, quickly,' she said.

Without a thought, David reached out for her hand and they both dashed out of the golden-framed doors without looking back.

Jack had watched in fascination and fury as they ran out with their fingers entwined. He looked around the room to see if they had made a spectacle of themselves and saw that no one had really noticed, apart from a couple of women who were also watching in horror and fascination. He got up, excused himself from the table, and walked in the opposite direction.

In the garden, he lit a cigarette and contemplated his next move. Then he raised his head, looked at the moon, and said, 'I give up.'

****

# Epilogue

Sitting in the pew, David felt a hand on his shoulder and looked up. Jack nodded down at him and he shifted to let him through. Jack sat beside him and they both waited for the service to begin. Looking around the church, David spied the people that Jennifer loved: her mother, sister, grandson, Jed and Angel, and, as much as she had despised him, Jack.

At the wake, David sat on the garden bench under the moon and lit a cigarette. He thought about the last three years, the happiest of his life … and hers. They moved back to Atlanta and Jennifer had not looked back. Jed took care of the business and David and Jennifer took care of each other, living in the dream that they always envisioned. She had chosen not to live in fear of Jack and would deal with him when it was necessary. David assured her that Jack couldn't harm him and if he did, David didn't care; the only thing that mattered was being with Jennifer and making her happy. He got to do that for those three years and by the time she passed away in David's arms on a cold November evening under a full moon, he felt that he had finally lived the life he was meant to.

Gazing at the moon, he heard Jack approach and David offered him a cigarette. Lighting it, Jack sat on the bench beside him. He followed David's gaze.

'What was it about that thing you both were obsessed with?'

David gave a short laugh but didn't answer.

They both sat in silence and shortly, Jack rose and walked back to the house. Then he turned back, walked to David, and putting his hand on his shoulder, squeezed. David put his own on Jack's and then Jack went back inside.

David looked back up at the moon, which had a twinkle in its eye tonight.

*The End.*

# ACKNOWLEDGEMENTS

Emerald: My eldest, my mini-me, who has been my social media manager and the first person to read my story and who has encouraged me throughout.

Alexis: My shadow, who put up with my ramblings throughout the process and talked through ideas with me.

Dean: My motivator who has kept pushing me to write and who has somewhat reluctantly read all my boring work for my Master's.

Mum: Always encouraging, but not too scared of telling me the truth.

My proofreaders: Marisa, Natalie, and Laura, who gave me some truly valuable feedback, and Dawn, who so very patiently helped me with my designs.

And to the rest of my family and friends, who didn't think that I couldn't do this and if they did think so, they kept it to themselves.

And of course, John, who has put up with my incessant chatter and who has always had faith in me, encouraging and humoring my sometimes silly endeavors.

And to you dear readers, thank you for taking a chance on this unknown.

# ABOUT THE AUTHOR

Rita H Rowe has a passion for words, encouraged by a mother who spent most of her spare time with her head buried in a book. Of course she was going to become dazzled by the words of Enid Blyton, Louisa May Alcott and later on, the likes of Sidney Sheldon and even the early works of Harold Robbins. Her tastes are diverse, and she can go straight from Margaret Mitchell and Alexandre Dumas to Liane Moriarty and Jeffrey Archer in the blink of an eye.

It was finding her own style that was problematic. Trying to create stories in the same vein as her gurus was not fulfilling and in 2019, she embarked on a Masters in Writing. She discovered her passion and established her style; so keen was she to get going, that by the end of the year, she had published her first novel, Never The Moon.

Most of Rowe's work deals with the human condition, particularly from a woman's point of view, which at times draws on her own experiences and that of others, with their permission of course.

Rowe lives with her family and teaches secondary school English and Art in Melbourne.

Find out more about Rita H Rowe

Website: https://www.ritahrowe.com/

Facebook: https://www.facebook.com/ritahrowe/

Instagram: https://www.instagram.com/ritahrowe_writes/

# OTHER NOVELS BY RITA H ROWE

## She Remembered

Her beauty is a curse. Her memories a void.

Elena cannot remember. All she has are fragments of a past life that feel foreign to her, only glimpsed in fleeting moments through violent nightmares.

Struggling to put her life together and find acceptance, she takes comfort in Luke, a charming boy who seems to like her as much as she likes him. But nothing has ever come easily to Elena—and when she wakes up between blood-soaked sheets next to the body of a man recently stabbed, what little stability she had comes crashing down around her.

With no one to help her and nowhere to go, Elena has to salvage the broken pieces of her life all on her own. If only she could remember …

# The Bad Seed

Love, betrayal and murder.

He's the new kid in town, complete with a sordid past and a tarnished family name, doomed to fail even before he begins. Jenna is the only person who sees beyond Joey's past and they fall deeply in love.

But there are already forces determined to separate the pair by any means necessary. Tommy, the thug, who is hell-bent on breaking Joey by brute force, Jenna's mother, whose connection with Joey cannot be ignored, and Joey's own past, the strongest weapon against them.

Only Tim, the local police officer, shows any compassion to the plight of Joey and Jenna, but is Tim all he seems? And what role will he play in their fate?

Can young love survive in a town filled with discrimination?

Can Joey and Jenna get out before they fall apart, or is it already too late?

# Becoming Ruthless

When all the men she knows are liars, maybe it's time to become one too.

Ruth is young, excited about life and not looking for love. Yet love finds her, and Ruth is thrilled. But she is left devastated when she finds out that her the man she loves has deceived her. Still hopeful, she embarks on another relationship only to find herself in the same predicament.

Ruth becomes disenchanted with love and decides that if she can't beat them, she may as well join them and begins a journey that will change her very being and endanger her life.

Can Ruth find herself before it's too late? Or will she become what she has always despised—a loathsome liar?